FOLDED CORNERS

THE KNOCKNASHEE STORY - BOOK 5

JEAN GRAINGER

Copyright © 2025 by Gold Harp Media

All rights reserved.

No part of this book may be reproduced in any form or by any electronic or mechanical means, including information storage and retrieval systems, without written permission from the author, except for the use of brief quotations in a book review.

NO AI TRAINING: Without in any way limiting the author's or publisher's exclusive rights under copyright, any use of this publication to train generative artificial intelligence (AI) technologies to generate text is expressly prohibited. The author reserves all rights to licence uses of this work for for generative AI training and development of machine learning language models.

To my loyal readers, who have stuck with Grace and Richard this long.

CHAPTER 1

LONDON, ENGLAND

AUGUST 1942

Richard suppressed a smile. Jacob could be very funny when he was furious, unintentionally of course, and Kirky had a way of winding him up that no other person had.

They were sitting in their apartment on a sunny Saturday morning. Richard had arrived back from Ireland three days ago. To his frustration and admittedly a bit of relief, he'd discovered Pippa had gone to Manchester. The munitions factory she worked at had another one up north, and the management had asked her to go up and train new recruits in a bullet-making process they'd recently adopted. She was an expert, it seemed.

He'd considered writing to her, but that was not a decent way to break off an engagement, and there was no way he could go up there right now.

Sarah read the telegram out loud again. 'Come to NYC. Be here by August 20. You're getting award. K.' She grinned. 'He's a piece of work, huh?'

'I wonder what award?' Richard mused. It was exciting, even if Kirky's telegram was short on detail and even shorter on praise or congratulations.

'I think it's the Bustemer Award. I heard that anyway,' Jacob said.

'No way?' Richard almost spurted his coffee. 'The Bustemer? Are you serious?'

'That's what I heard from some of the guys from the AP. The piece we did on the Fall of Singapore was syndicated so often, apparently FDR even read it and called it important work in making the American people understand how critical our response is.'

'No kidding?' Richard couldn't believe it. Such

recognition was much sought-after by far more seasoned newspapermen than he or Jacob, so to win, if it *was* the Bustemer, was amazing.

'No, but Kirky couldn't even say well done, or tell us what award. He couldn't stand for us to feel even a tiny bit proud of ourselves.' Jacob was still furious, scowling and pacing up and down.

'It's just his way, you know what he's like. Not worth getting your knickers in a twist, as Pippa would say.' Sarah laughed as she made another big pot of coffee, which was in fact not coffee at all but roasted chicory and so disgusting he couldn't stand it.

'Sarah's right, Jacob. He was smirking as he sent it, you know he was. He's determined to not let us get too full of ourselves.' It didn't bother Richard as much that Kirky never praised them or gave them any credit, though a small bit of recognition would have been nice.

'We got the tickets sent to the UP office, only three unfortunately,' Sarah said. 'Ernie handed them to me as I was leaving. Not that Pippa could have come anyway with her work, but it would have been nice to show her New York City.' She sounded a bit disappointed that her friend wasn't to be included in the trip, but getting passage was extremely difficult. All non-essential travel was curtailed, but their press passes allowed them to move around far more than the civilian population. 'I suppose I should consider myself lucky to be included, considering it's you two getting the award.'

'Yeah, it's a pity about Pippa,' Richard heard himself say, and cringed inwardly at the lie. He was relieved. He would have to speak to her before he left, though. 'And as for you, you know Kirky has a soft spot for you. When do we sail?'

'Here's the thing, we need to go the day after tomorrow.' Sarah showed him the tickets. Sure enough, their passage was booked on a troop ship leaving Southampton in two days' time.

'But Pippa won't be back before we go, will she?'

Sarah shot him a look of sympathy, and another wave of guilt passed over him.

'She won't. She's there for another two weeks at least, and we'll be gone. You could send a telegram?'

'I guess.' He tried to figure this out. Going home at this point wasn't something he'd even considered; he needed to sort his life out. Much as he loved his home country, he wanted to do the right thing with Pippa, face her and tell her the truth, and then…well, then he'd try to see

Grace again. The very thought filled him with dread. If he wound up alone, it was probably what he deserved, but he could no longer go on living a lie, that was for sure.

'Hey, Richard, I have an idea. How about we tell Daddy about it, and he might come up to see you getting the award? It would have to be something that big to get him to set foot across the Mason-Dixon Line, but he'd do it for you. It would be nice to see him, wouldn't it?'

'It would, especially now. Sure, let him know, tell him we'd both love to see him.'

Richard and Sarah walked the next morning to the post office. The man there eyed them greedily now that he knew they were 'Yanks' and had access to all sorts of goodies denied the locals.

'My missus loved those chocolates you gave me…' he said ingratiatingly.

'Good. It's a shame we don't have any more. Things are getting tough over there as well now,' Richard said, shutting him down before he could ask for another hand-out.

Sarah sent a message to their father, and he sent one to Pippa, just saying he was going to New York and would write from there. He should send one to Grace too, he knew, but he didn't because he didn't want to elicit another lecture from Sarah. He'd write from the States.

The flurry of organisation meant there was no time to write a detailed letter but they managed to embark on the *SS Valiant* at Southampton at the appointed time. The ship had been full to capacity with troops and supplies coming over, but like the last time they went home, it was empty on the return trip, and they had a very comfortable crossing. Richard worked on his novel and tried to relax. All he could think about was Grace, though. He wondered how she was getting on. Had she gotten her job and house back? One part of him hoped she had, but another was relieved her ties to Knocknashee were not as bound fast as they had once been.

To their delight, their father sent a car to pick them up from the port, and the driver had instructions to take the three of them to the St Regis, where he'd reserved three rooms. Jacob normally would have complained about the price and waste, but he had the good sense and manners to just accept the generosity. That night, they and their father had dinner in the elaborate dining room, with the impeccably clad waiters. They'd invited Kirky, who hadn't changed a bit.

'You know they have their finger on the pulse,

right?' Sarah admonished the editor gently. 'You tell them not to write this or not to cover that, but the thing is, they get what people want to hear. Ordinary people don't care about troop movements or political speeches – they want to know about the common man or woman on the street. So you're much better off letting them write what they like. They have an instinct for it.'

Richard caught his father's eye and shared a secret smile. Sarah Lewis was no Southern belle, there to look pretty and not have an opinion. She had many opinions, most firmly held, and she'd argue the dickens out of any man, regardless of who he was.

Kirky looked exactly as he had when Richard last met him, still short and bald, with blue eyes and saggy skin on his face. He wore a crumpled suit that was creased so much he might have slept in it, and his large, soft body seemed to spill over the sides of his chair. He was a tough New Yorker with an accent to match. He sat next to Richard's father, and the contrast was undeniable. Arthur Lewis stood over six feet and was as hard and athletic now as he'd been when Richard was a child. He held himself ramrod straight and exuded confidence and money. He'd shaved off his moustache, which made him look a bit more approachable, Richard thought.

'I agree with you,' Kirky said, to their amazement. 'Richard here knows how to reach people. He has an instinct for what they want and gives it to them.' Then he nodded at Jacob. 'And you take the pictures.' He allowed a slight wink at Sarah, which made her laugh.

'You know perfectly well he's a genius. Would it kill you to say so?' she challenged.

'I pay him, don't I?' Kirky replied, helping himself to more French fries.

'I think all three of you are marvellous, and I've even started reading your Yankee rag, Mr Falkirk,' Arthur said, with a smile to bely his words. Sarah glowed under their father's praise.

'Kirky please. The last person to call me Mr Falkirk was Sister Josephine in the fourth grade when she pulled me up by the ears.' He wheezed when he laughed, and Richard thought the man might be the unhealthiest person he'd ever met. He smoked incessantly, drank in the office as well as after work and only ate fried food. He was smart as a whip and married to the long-suffering Lottie, whom they'd heard about but never met. 'But yeah, my Yankee rag is doing quite well down in your neck of the woods. I guess war don't care if you're a Yankee or a redneck, huh?'

'I think you're right.' Arthur tucked into his Cobb salad. 'But I'm mighty proud of these young people doing what they're doing to bring the real story to us at home. Without the valuable work they do, I don't think we'd really have much of an understanding of why it's so necessary.'

Kirky shrugged, which Richard took to be agreement, as Jacob seethed.

'So this award, Kirky, tell me about it?' Arthur asked.

'It's the Bustemer Award for Journalistic Excellence in Foreign Affairs. They got it for the piece they did in Singapore, though how they managed to get their sorry asses captured by the Japanese when that part of the jungle they were in only had a handful of Japs remains a mystery. It would take these guys…' He rolled his eyes.

'Ah, Kirky, you were worried sick, admit it,' Sarah ribbed. 'You telegrammed me every day wondering if I'd heard from them, and when they turned up, you were very emotional, you know you were.'

'I was trying to figure out how to get them out of there – bad for the image to lose two staff. Besides, I'd just paid for his new camera. I wanted my money's worth.' He gave that wheezy laugh again.

The dinner went on in a happy vein, Sarah able to tease and admonish Kirky in a way Richard and Jacob wouldn't dare. He asked them in great detail about the events after the Fall of Singapore, and Richard and Jacob gave him plenty of information on other newspapermen in London, for which he had a voracious appetite. He knew absolutely everyone.

'So you guys are booked back on Sunday?' he said as he raised his hand for the check. Though Arthur had offered, Kirky insisted on paying.

'But you're coming to the awards ceremony, right?' Richard asked.

'Nah, I've got plans. Lottie wants to go to some thing in Brooklyn. I mean, I said to her, Lottie, I said, Brooklyn might as well be Bangladesh as far as I'm concerned. I hate to leave the island of Manhattan, but her girlfriend is in a play or some crap like that. It's gonna be torture, but I'm facing worse torture if I don't go, so…' He shrugged, resigned to this fate worse than death.

Richard found he was disappointed; he would have liked to have had Kirky there to see their work acknowledged. It was a very prestigious award, and he was proud not just of himself and

Jacob but of Kirky for taking a chance on two kids with not much experience.

'About that...' Jacob began. Richard knew he and Sarah really wanted to spend some time in the States, maybe even get down to Savannah, see their old friends; it had been so long. 'We were wondering if we could extend the trip a bit...'

'What? Are you nuts? There's a war on, kid, if you didn't notice. I need you back there filing copy and taking pictures. As it is we're down a lot of stuff because of the travelling. No way. Back on that boat with you three the second this dumb shindig is over.'

'Well, come now, Kirky,' Arthur interjected. 'My children and Mr Nunez here have been working very hard for you and your newspaper, and I think a little vacation is justified. I know the war is still on, but who knows how long that's going to be the case, so I feel it's really time they took a break, don't you?'

Kirky signed for the food and stood, heaving his heavy body up. It was sweltering outside, and Kirky was sweating profusely. 'One week, that's it. Now try to stay out of trouble, OK?' He patted Sarah's shoulder as he walked away.

'Did we just get a week's vacation?' Jacob asked with a grin.

'We sure did.' Sarah was giddy with the excitement. 'Let's go home right away after the ceremony – what do you say, Richard? See Esme, and maybe go to the King and Prince one night, catch up with everyone…'

'I sure would love to have you home for a spell,' their father said. 'Y'all need feeding for a start. You've gotten so thin, Sarah. If you stood sideways and stuck out your tongue, you'd look like a zipper.' He laughed, and Richard noticed he'd slipped into his old Southern accent now that Kirky was gone.

'Now then, Mr Nunez, tell me a little more about yourself.'

'Well, sir, I'm a Jewish communist who loves your daughter,' Jacob said, with a smile.

'Well, I'm only interested in the last part of that sentence, son. So long as you treat her right, we won't have a problem.' Arthur drained his glass of red wine.

'I certainly will, sir. We take care of each other, and Richard too,' Jacob answered, softening.

'I'm like their baby.' Richard chuckled as he wiped his mouth with the napkin and swallowed the last sip of beer in his glass.

'Well, I have some people to meet since I'm

here, so how about you young folks have some fun this evening and I'll see you all tomorrow?' Arthur said as they walked out of the restaurant. He had the doorman hail a cab.

'Are you happy to go home?' Sarah asked, linking Richard's arm as they crossed the lobby.

'Sure, sounds good.' He desperately wanted to get back, but he could see what this would mean to his sister. 'I'm sure looking forward to Esme's cooking and a little bit of heat.'

'We're going to head out to hear some music – you coming?' Jacob asked.

But Richard wanted to get back to his room, write to Grace and try to figure out his next move. 'No, I'm beat. I'm going to go to bed.'

Sarah headed for the door. 'OK, Grandpa, catch you later…'

'You go on, I'll catch up,' Jacob said, falling into step with Richard as he made for the elevator. 'I forgot my wallet in the bedroom.'

As they entered the gilded, mirrored space, Jacob looked shifty, shuffling from foot to foot, his jaw clenched. 'What is it?' Richard asked. They knew each other so well now, they were tuned to each other.

Jacob reached into his pants pocket, pulled out a small box and flipped it open to reveal a diamond solitaire. 'I got it from my uncle's shop this morning. I'm going to propose to Sarah. I asked your father this afternoon, and he gave me permission but said she'd probably turn me down. What do you think?'

Richard smiled. 'I think she'd be a very foolish girl if she did. But she might. Not because she doesn't love you, she does, but you know how she is about marriage and all of that. But I wish you luck, my friend.' He clapped him on the shoulder.

As he walked to his own room, he wondered what kind of engagement ring he would buy if he was proposing to Grace. Pippa had said she didn't want one; she wasn't able to wear it at work and she wasn't a big ring kind of girl.

He remembered her telling him ages ago in a letter about the claddagh ring, a special Irish ring with a crown and a heart held up by a pair of hands, and how if you wore it one way, with the point of the heart facing inwards, it meant you were spoken for, but if you wore it another way, you were 'on the lookout'.

A warm glow passed over him. Only Grace could make him feel like that.

CHAPTER 2

ST REGIS HOTEL, NEW YORK, USA

20 AUGUST 1942

Dear Grace,

Greetings from the Big Apple. I think you told me before why it's called that, but I forget. I'm here because Jacob and I are getting an award for journalism for the piece we did on the Fall of Singapore. It's all very exciting, and Sarah and Jacob have even managed to get an extra week's vacation out of Kirky, so we're going to the ceremony Saturday night and then down to Savannah. She "flailed him to flit-

ters," as you said once, which I remember because it's such a great phrase, as so many of your Irish phrases are. Anyway, she gave it to him hot and heavy about how we should not be directed, that we had an innate sense of what people want, and how he should be much nicer to us. He won't be of course, he's sour by nature, but it was good to watch Sarah in full flight. She's as fearless as you are, blessed am I amongst women!

Our father came up to New York and went to bat for us to get some time off too, and eventually Kirky had to back down. I'm looking forward to seeing Esme and having some home-cooked Southern food. I guess I should go and see my mother, but to be honest, the thought doesn't fill me with delight. She'll probably just reject me again, and though I tell myself I don't care, I guess I do really. While I was in London, I could kind of switch that off, but now that I'm back, I guess I have to face her. Or maybe I don't. What would you do? She hasn't written or made any contact, and she's allowed my father to leave her rather than support us, her grievance is mostly with Sarah and Jacob. But still, I don't know. Go there and be a dutiful son to get another emotional kicking? Or don't bother? Any advice welcome.

Hey, guess what? Jacob is going to propose to Sarah. He just showed me the ring. His uncle is a jeweller here in NYC. It reminded me of the time you told *me about claddagh rings. He'd asked my father, who said "I wish you luck, but I don't think she'll go for it." She's no demure Southern belle, my sister, and being a happy little wife at home with babies and the help is never going to fly, but Jacob doesn't want her to be like that anyway. I hope she accepts, but like my father, I'm doubtful.*

I'll be back in London in two weeks' time, so I'll write again then, or I might send you a postcard from Savannah—I think I've sent you a few over the years. I'd love for you to come and see my city. It's really beautiful and full of character and stories; I think you'd love it. I hope we can do that someday.

Did you get your job and house back now that the canon is gone? Write and tell me everything.

Lots of love,
Richard

He folded the letter and stamped and addressed it. He knew he should write to Pippa as well, but everything he'd say would sound like a lie. He couldn't tell her the truth about what he wanted, and he couldn't pretend everything was fine either. Maybe he'd send her a postcard from Savannah, a nice view of River Street or Forsyth Park or something.

He wrote a quick note to Esme to say he

couldn't wait to see her; he hoped it would get there before they did.

The next day and a half flew by. Richard spent time with his father and told him about his experiences in the Far East and a bit about Grace. They walked around Central Park, his father every inch the Southern gentleman, with cane, cashmere overcoat and trilby despite the heat, smelling of old leather, and the talk flowed easily; it was the most conversation they'd ever had.

'Sounds like you were lucky to get out alive. I'm sure glad you did, Richard. I know the times we live in and all of that, but can you please try to be more careful?' his father pleaded. 'I was out of my mind with worry. I telegrammed Sarah every day for news.'

Richard smiled, unused to this new version of his father. 'She said.'

'I think I was driving her crazy, but I...' He paused. 'Look, son, I know I haven't been the most...well...hell, I don't know what the word is, but not the best kind of father for you children. I should have been there more. I should have communicated more when I was at home, but I guess I just didn't know how to. Children, where I came from, were women's work – men provided and women nurtured. But your mother is not the nurturing kind, we both know that. I should have stepped up, but I didn't, and I want to apologise.'

'There's no need –'

His father held up his hand for silence. 'There is. I failed, and maybe I can't ever make it up to you at this late stage, but I'd like to try.' He stopped then and faced Richard.

'You don't need to try, it's happened already.' Emotion made his voice crack.

His father just nodded, but Richard could see he was choked up. That little speech would have been hard for him.

Pulling himself together, Arthur changed the subject. 'So you reckon our Sarah is going to accept Nunez? 'Cause I sure don't.'

'I don't know, probably not. But not because she doesn't love him – she really does and he loves her. They are a great team, and I think they'd go the distance. But she's against the way marriage ties women down, and maybe she got it from Mother, but she hasn't a maternal bone in her body.'

'Well, I've told him to take his chance, but I don't know…' Arthur shook his head and chuckled. 'She's something else, isn't she?'

Richard smiled. 'She sure is.'

That afternoon he gave Sarah some time alone

with their father while he paid a surprise visit to Mrs McHale, whom he took for a drink at the sports bar Toots Shor's. He thought the St Regis or somewhere fancy would have been more to her taste, but she said she was dying to go to the bar across from Radio City Music Hall, where all the celebrities were known to frequent. She needed a young man to take her because it wouldn't be the done thing for an old lady to go to a sports bar alone.

They had a wonderful two hours. He told her all about Grace and the canon, and she'd clapped and hooted with delight when he told her of his final denouement. She was a riot. She started stories, but meandered off on tangents that were as entertaining as the original story so many times, he could hardly remember a time he'd laughed so much. She drank gin and tonic and was ecstatic when she saw Joe DiMaggio deep in conversation with some other men. Richard loved baseball and missed it since he'd been away, so he shared her enthusiasm but did dissuade her from approaching him.

He invited her to attend the awards ceremony, and she accepted as if he'd offered her the crown jewels. His father would probably not thank him for having to escort an old Catholic lady, but he'd get over it.

When he got back from his outing with Mrs McHale, it was time to dress. He'd had a rented black tux delivered to the hotel – he had no need of evening wear in this new life. After dressing, he met Sarah, who was wearing a midnight-blue silk trouser suit with a men's shaped jacket and heels that looked like she would break her ankle if she walked even a step. She'd had her hair done, which was so badly needed, and wore a little make-up. She was very pretty, he thought, but he didn't tell her because she would not react well to such a remark and would ask him if that was all men thought about when they saw a woman, was she pretty or not. It was safer not to bother.

She whistled when she saw him. 'Looking sharp, little brother,' she said as she gave him a nudge.

'You clean up well yourself.'

'I do, don't I?' She gave a mock curtsy. 'Daddy is in the bar. He's ordered cocktails, so let's go in. Jacob is still getting ready.'

'In his own room?' Richard murmured, with a wink.

'If he had his way, he'd sublet his bedroom and

give the money to the communists, but yes, for the purposes of getting dressed, he's in his own room.' Sarah shot him a wicked grin. Richard knew there was no way they were going to be separated.

She wore nothing on her left hand, so he assumed either Jacob had proposed and she'd turned him down or he'd not asked her yet.

Their father was reading the paper in a corner of the bar, with a bottle of Taittinger on ice and three glasses beside him. He put it down as they entered.

People here grumbled about the war, how certain things were now hard to get and how labour was in short supply as so many men had joined the forces, but Richard knew they had no real concept of it. He hoped it never came to it, that American cities, like London, would be flattened by bombs, citizens hungry, bereaved, maimed, medical supplies perfunctory at best. He realised he'd been changed fundamentally, that the war-hardened man who came back was not the wealthy, entitled boy who left.

'Well, well, well, don't you two look as fine as a frog's hair split four ways?' Arthur grinned as he poured them a drink. 'Now, I want to raise a toast to you both and say how proud I am of you. I wish Nathan was here – I called him, but he's deep in training army medics so can't be spared. I'm very proud of my children.'

'Thanks, Daddy. I'm so happy to be home again, even if just for a while. We love London, and it's good to feel like we're doing something worthwhile, but it sure is nice to be home too.'

Arthur waggled his finger and looked at her in mock disapproval. 'This is New York, Sarah Elizabeth Frances Lewis. This is not home.'

'Well, back in the United States then and going home tomorrow. Though the rail journey isn't what I'm looking forward to…'

'Well, funny you should say that, because today I went and bought myself a little toy.' Arthur sat back with a self-satisfied smile, looking very pleased with himself.

'What kind of toy?' Richard took a sip of the cold champagne.

'Well, over the last few months, I've been taking flying lessons. I passed the test for my pilot's licence three weeks ago, and today I bought an Aeronca five-seater touring aircraft, so if you'll risk it, I'll fly us home tomorrow.'

Something about his father's enthusiasm, the boyishness, touched Richard. He'd wanted to surprise them, and he had.

'I'm in,' Richard said. 'If you say you can fly, I

believe you.' He meant it. His father did nothing by half measures.

'I've never been in a plane in my life,' Sarah said. 'I'll be terrified, but I trust you, Daddy.'

'Well, that's two votes of confidence.' Their father grinned again, topping up their glasses.

'Aren't you having one?' Richard asked.

'No, I'll be keeping all my wits about me for tomorrow.'

As he spoke, Jacob appeared in a tuxedo. He looked very handsome, his chestnut hair oiled back, his green eyes shining. Arthur poured him a glass as Richard and Sarah teased him playfully and told him about the plan to fly.

'Amazing, I'd love it, thanks,' Jacob said, accepting a glass.

The bar was almost empty – it was early yet. And as Richard settled deeper into his seat he saw, to his surprise, Jacob get down on one knee. Was he going to do it now?

Sarah looked confused then shocked as he opened the box and showed her the ring.

'I know I should pick someplace more romantic, and probably we should be alone, but I can't wait another second. This box is burning a hole in my pocket. Sarah, if I promise that you'll never have to do anything I say, that I will never want a baby, or drapes and comforters in matching chintz, or a house to put them in, come to that, that I'll never say "my wife does that" about any domestic chore, that I won't expect you to change your name or anything else about your perfect, lovely, beautiful, kind, brave, strong, terrifying self, would you please, please, please marry me?'

Richard and his father shared a smile. It was a genuine plea, and they were both rooting for him.

'But why? We never talked about –' Sarah began.

'Because if I die, or if you die, I want to be your next of kin and I want you to be mine. I love you, Sarah, you know that. You are perfect in every way. And I know you think marriage is outdated and only a method of enslaving women and taking their rights away, but if I swear here in front of your brother and father that I would never dare even think about doing that, will you please let me be your husband? Hell…I'll change my name to Jacob Lewis to prove it if you want. You can wear the pants, I promise.' He laughed then. It had been a running joke ever since some man, who'd had a deserved tongue-lashing from Sarah, told Jacob that he should put his foot down about his woman smoking and drinking and wearing trousers.

Jacob had said he would, just as soon as he'd finished the ironing.

Sarah thought for a moment and then looked down at Jacob Nunez, the great love of her life, on his knees before her. 'OK, but I'm going to make you stick to every one of those promises, and if you even try…' She was beaming, though, and her eyes were bright with tears.

Jacob slipped the ring on her finger and stood, took her in his arms and kissed her. Richard and his father clapped, and the bartender sent another bottle of champagne to their table.

CHAPTER 3

CORK CITY, COUNTY CORK, IRELAND

AUGUST 1942

Grace looked around the cavernous church as everyone gathered for Mass. The walk to the front door had been a wet one. It felt like it would never stop raining, despite it being summer, but she was determined to be here, to hear Father Iggy celebrate Mass. She was enjoying the last weeks before school began again and was paying a long overdue visit to the Warringtons. They had been so kind to her since she first arrived to their hospital as a sickly child, and she'd neglected them of late. They never complained, were always delighted to have her visit, but she knew they missed her. It was one of life's many sadnesses that they never had a family of their own.

Hugh and Lizzie had invited Father Iggy to share in their Sunday dinner, which was so kind of them. People always assumed priests were inundated with invitations, but Father Iggy had let slip the day before yesterday when they had tea that he would be alone in the parochial house once he'd said the noon Mass.

Another of the priests was on call, but his sister lived close by so he'd be at her house and everyone knew where to find him in the case of an emergency, and the other two priests in the parish were going home to their families out in the countryside somewhere.

Father Iggy had family, but they were up the country, so once Grace knew he'd be alone, she asked Lizzie if they wouldn't mind inviting him, and of course they'd obliged.

She'd always enjoyed the Saturday evening Mass. The canon had put a stop to it in Knocknashee, claiming people came after the pub and it was blasphemous, but that wasn't true, not really

– it was more that he didn't like to leave his warm fire and his bottle of brandy. Poor Father Lehane had been run off his feet since the canon was arrested as no replacement had yet been sent, so nobody liked to ask him to do more than he was doing already.

As Father Iggy came onto the altar in his brightly coloured vestments, Grace felt a wave of affection for the small chubby priest with the jam-jar-thick glasses. They had an unlikely friendship, she supposed, but friends they were, and she knew he valued her highly.

To his left, an enormous, beautiful flower arrangement had been placed on the altar, the sweet aroma filling the church and mingling with the fragrance of the incense and beeswax. The smell brought her back to earlier years, and she felt a pang of sadness. When she was a little girl, her mother would take her shopping on the first of October, the feast of St Thérèse of Lisieux, known to everyone as the Little Flower, to whom her mother had great devotion. Part of their day out, which always involved getting tea and a cream bun in the Imperial Hotel, was a visit to the Holy Cross Priory, the Church of the Immaculate Conception and finally St John's, to say a prayer to the saint. They would light a candle at each one for Mamó and Daidó, her grandparents – most churches had a special altar to St Thérèse set up – and it was a lovely time.

She thought she would light some candles after Mass; there were so many souls for her to pray for now, so many people she had lost.

The choir sang 'Veni Creator Spiritus', and though the Mass was in Latin and Father Iggy had his back turned to the congregation, there was a beautiful sense of peace and community. The church was filled to capacity, mostly adults as the children were tucked up in bed. People here looked hungry and cold, even more so than in Knocknashee. She knew from personal experience and from the children in school how everything was hard to come by now as the war dragged on and on and on. Even the basic requirements for living were stretched to the breaking point, and luxuries were really a thing of the past. Parents in Knocknashee managed, just about, but up here it was a different story. This was a poor parish, and before the Emergency ever happened, things were tight, but now hunger and cold and lack of access to medicine or even proper sanitation was a real issue. Father Iggy did his best, but the parish wasn't in much of a position to help. She knew it broke his heart to see the people hungry, children especially, but there was little he could do.

He intoned the words of the familiar Tridentine Mass, and soon it was over. The choir sang 'Tantum Ergo', and everyone filed out into the dark, still night. The sky was cloudless now that the rain had finally stopped, and the stars twinkled overhead. Hugh had said he would drive over to collect her; he was working late in the hospital, so he would be out anyway. She waited for him on the steps of the church as the crowd dispersed.

As the congregation thinned, she heard Father Iggy's voice behind her. 'Warm enough for you, Grace?' He grinned, and she saw his black clerical coat was thin and frayed and his shoes were the worse for wear too. 'God never got the reminder that it's supposed to be summer in Ireland.'

'It could be warmer but it's lovely. Aren't the stars so bright tonight?' She looked up. 'That was a beautiful Mass, Father.'

'Well, if you wouldn't have bright stars at the moment, when could you have them? God knows we need cheering up.' He gazed upwards beside her.

'Come hungry tomorrow.' Grace smiled as she

turned to him. 'Lizzie is cooking like she's feeding fifty, not four.'

'Indeed I will, but where is she getting it, or should I not ask?' Father Iggy whispered theatrically with a conspiratorial chuckle. 'People are saying stuff can't be got for love nor money.'

'Well, Lizzie applied for an allotment and she was given one, so now she grows vegetable and even rears chickens, and so one of them… Well, less said about it, the better.' She laughed. 'And the parents of one of the children in the hospital sent a big ham – they keep pigs apparently – and she's forever growing things from seeds, and Tilly sent up some stuff with me. So there'll be a fine feast for us tomorrow.'

'Are you sure I'm not imposing, Grace? I'm fearful I am.' His brow furrowed and his blue eyes looked worried behind his thick glasses.

'Not in the slightest, we are delighted to have you. Please, Lizzie is really looking forward to it and so am I. We'll have a lovely day. There'll be music on the wireless and a roaring fire despite it being August, and wait till you smell the apple crumble – my mouth is watering at the thought.' Grace groaned as the rain started again.

'Will we step in?' he suggested with a rueful

smile. 'At least we won't get soaked inside. We can see out the window if Hugh comes.'

'Good idea, but you don't need to wait with me, Father. I'm sure you've other things to do.'

'Grace, having you come to Cork is the nicest thing to happen for a long time, so of course I'm not going to let you stand outside in the rain on your own.'

They stood into the porch and watched the rain coming down in sheets.

'Do you like it here?' she asked.

He paused before answering. 'It's not really a matter of liking it or not liking it. We go where we're sent, and we do the best we can.'

Something about his demeanour worried her. He seemed to have lost his sparkle or something. In Knocknashee he was jolly and cheerful, always ready with a kind word or a trick or a joke for the children; here, he seemed to be more serious or something.

They had a close bond from the time he'd spent in her parish, so she felt she could ask. 'Is something in particular bothering you, though? You seem a bit…I don't know…sad?'

He looked conflicted, his mouth in a firm line as he exhaled through his nose. She knew priests were supposed to be removed from their flock;

they were not really meant to have normal human feelings.

'You can tell me, if it would help, and I promise it won't go any further,' she said softly.

'Oh, Grace…' He sighed. 'I…I shouldn't complain. I've it much easier than so many others have, but…'

'But what?' she asked, but before he could answer, Hugh's car drew up outside.

'Ara, I'm fine. Don't mind me and my moaning, big pity about me.' He smiled but it didn't reach his eyes.

On impulse she reached over and hugged him. He wasn't much taller than her and she was tiny, but he was twice as wide as she was. To her surprise, he hugged her back. They released each other and she waved at him and went out to Hugh.

CHAPTER 4

The following morning, she was peeling potatoes in the kitchen with Lizzie while Hugh made his famous stuffing for the chicken. The rain ran in rivulets down the window.

'Have you heard from Richard lately?' Lizzie asked.

'Yes, he wrote from the boat when he left, just all about that business with the canon and everything.' The thought of the other letter, the one that had been delayed by two years and that might have changed everything, she pushed from her mind.

'Whatever happened about that?' Hugh asked,

picking sage from one of the pots of herbs growing on the windowsill.

'We never heard another word. When Eloise was arrested, it was the same. Mary was Tilly's next of kin, so they had to tell her something. But on the canon, we've not heard a peep.'

'And the other pair, Sheehan and the other fellow, they went without a word?'

'Anthony Nolan, yes. Father Lehane put his foot down apparently, hard as that is to envisage.' She laughed. 'So they're gone and that's all there is to it. I wrote to the Department of Education outlining the situation, which on paper looked like I made it up, it was so outlandish, but I got a letter back saying since I had never been formally dismissed, I should just continue as normal. No reference to the mad story I told. Eleanor got a letter too, so we're both back in school and they're gone and not another word said. It's ridiculous really, but I suppose with the war on…'

'Loose lips sink ships,' Lizzie said with a wink as she scooped the peelings of the potatoes into a basket for the hens.

'Does the local sergeant have any news about it?' Hugh asked as he expertly chopped onions to fry in precious butter from Tilly; the onions would then be added to breadcrumbs and sage to make the stuffing.

'I don't think so, or if he does, he's not telling us. To be honest, everyone was so happy to see the back of the canon, nobody cares.'

'I can just imagine.' Lizzie had never forgiven him for all he'd done. She was a compassionate woman, but Canon Rafferty was a nasty piece of work, priest or not.

'He could be hanged if he's found guilty of treason,' Hugh said.

'I doubt they'd go that far,' Lizzie set the lid on the saucepan of potatoes. 'I'd say the Church and the State would like him out of the picture completely, and they won't want any publicity at all, so hopefully he'll just be kept in jail indefinitely or sent to the missions, God love those poor people.'

'Let's hope so,' Grace agreed as she took cutlery from the drawer to lay the table.

'So is Richard still in London, Grace?' Hugh asked. 'I'm going over next month to Great Ormond Street Hospital. They want to see if we can take some children, as hospital beds in England are stretched to capacity and they need to clear space for servicemen. The board allowed me to volunteer some paediatric beds here.'

'As far as I know.' Grace tried to keep her voice light.

Lizzie and Hugh shared a surreptitious glance that they thought she didn't catch.

'I was thinking I could meet him – maybe we could go for a drink or something?' Hugh suggested. 'I'm sure he'd like to hear news from here.'

Grace knew what he was doing. Part of her felt frustrated. She knew he meant well, and that they thought there might be a hope of something romantic between Richard and her and wanted that for her, but it could never be, and she didn't need anyone's pity or interference. They were acting as they always did, with her in mind, so she would have to be gentle. 'I'm sure he'd love to see you again, Hugh, if he has time, but I don't really know what his schedule is like or where he even is.'

Lizzie persisted. 'I'm sure he was very cut up to be leaving after that whole business in Knocknashee.'

Grace knew she would have to say something to put a stop to this. 'He was very helpful certainly, we'd never have got the better of the Canon only for him, and it was good of him to give up the time. Especially since he's doing a very strong line – and I'd say would be due to get married soon – to a girl called Pippa.' She gave them the broadest beam she could and tried to ignore the pain on their faces.

'Oh,' Lizzie said. 'I didn't realise he had a girlfriend. I thought…well…we thought he was single.'

'Oh no.' Grace forced a laugh. 'Americans are in high demand over there, and Richard being handsome and charming, I'm sure he was beating them off with a stick. But Pippa Wills was the one to catch his attention. They've been together quite a while now. I haven't met her of course, but she seems very nice from what he's said. She's from London, lost her whole family to the war in one way or another, the poor girl.'

Hugh's face was so stricken, and she almost wanted to laugh. For a doctor, he was a very emotional man; he wasn't one of those who didn't get attached to his patients, and he was extremely protective of her, she knew that. They'd been heartbroken when Declan died, for the loss of the young man they'd grown so fond of, but for her too. Declan wouldn't want her to be maudlin, she was sure of that, so she tried to stay bright and cheery.

'So will I prepare the turnips?' she asked brightly.

Lunch was a relaxed, happy affair, and it felt so good to eat until full; they rarely did that these days. After dessert of apple crumble and custard, they all retired to the sitting room, where a fire crackled merrily in the grate and Hugh put on one of his gramophone records of the London Philharmonic.

Lizzie came downstairs with a sweater for Father Iggy that she'd knit, and though the wool wasn't the nicest colour, kind of puddle brown, it was all she could get. He was absolutely over the moon; it was as if she'd given him diamonds.

He'd brought the Warringtons a lovely tin of biscuits to thank them for inviting him, regifted from a parishioner, he explained, and he'd brought Grace a leather-bound copy of *Little Women* by Louisa May Alcott. The green cover was embossed, and the title and author were in gold foil. It even had a gold satin ribbon as a bookmarker. It was the most beautiful book she'd ever owned.

'This is like Christmas,' she said, a bit embarrassed that her friend had spent so much money on her.

'Well, it was for your birthday, but I didn't see you so…' He blushed pink.

'Oh, Father Iggy, it's gorgeous, but you needn't have,' Grace protested. The book must have cost a fortune, and she knew the priest hadn't a shilling.

'Well, I'll tell you something now, it's a little secret.' He grinned.

'Go on,' Lizzie urged. She was very fond of the little priest.

'There was a short story contest in a magazine, to write a ghost story for Halloween, and one night, for the want of anything more productive to do, I had a go. I told nobody, but I wrote a story my father used to tell me about a true thing that happened near where I grew up. It was my uncle, my father's brother, a priest, who told it to him.'

'And what happened?' Lizzie asked.

'Well, what happened was I won it.' Father Iggy chuckled. 'It's going to appear in the October special edition. I entered using my middle name Dermot, after my uncle, so nobody knew it was me. It wouldn't do to have priests going on with that sort of thing – the bishop probably wouldn't think it becoming of a member of the clergy. But the prize was a book token for Liam Russell's bookshop on Oliver Plunkett Street. I was racking my brain on what I could get as a little gift for you, Grace – I wanted to get you something because you've been so kind to me – so this was perfect. The Lord works in mysterious ways, you know.' He winked. 'So I took myself in there with my book token, and sure enough there it was. You said it was one of your favourites.' He beamed pink with pleasure that his gift had been a success.

'But you should have got something for yourself,' Grace protested.

'I did. The token was for more than the cost of that book, so I got myself a lovely book of poems by WB Yeats, which I love, a present to myself. And now here I am with a lovely new warm jumper as well. I'm like King Croesus.' He chuckled again.

'Will you tell us the story?' Grace sat on the sofa opposite the blazing fire in the Warringtons' cosy sitting room. It was dreary and dull outside, the rain not letting up at all, but they were happy and as full as ticks after the wonderful dinner.

'Do please, Father Iggy.' Hugh smiled, throwing another log on the fire, sending sparks up the chimney.

'Well, 'tis a strange one, right enough, but if you want, I'll tell you.'

Father Iggy was a natural storyteller, and he and Mary O'Hare had spent many the long winter's night exchanging tales when he was a priest in Knocknashee. Grace couldn't help but think he would be so much better suited to their rural parish than here in the city.

They settled in, Hugh on the armchair, Lizzie on the couch with Grace and Father Iggy on a kitchen chair they'd brought in beside the fire.

'Well, my Uncle Dermot was a parish priest up in County Cavan – this would be going back now, oh, I'd say around fifty or sixty years ago, so the 1880s or 1890s. He was only a young curate, but the old parish priest was riddled with gout, so my uncle was called upon to do everything.' He leant forward, resting his elbows on his knees. All he was short was a flat cap and a pipe, and he'd be exactly like the *seanchaí* who'd come visiting around the houses of Knocknashee with their stories in return for bed and board.

'Now in the town at that time, there was a big house in the middle of the main street, and it was always given to the bank manager. The bank owned it, you see, and the banks don't like to have local men managing, for fear of favouritism or pressure being brought to bear on them by friends or relations, so the manager was always selected from some far-off place. So there was a change of management, a common enough occurrence. The last incumbent, who had served five years in the town, only stayed in that big house for a week, and then he and his family found a different place further out of the town for the duration of his time running the bank. He never said why, but everyone thought the house was haunted, and over the years now and again, people would say they saw a child standing in the upstairs window overlooking the street. Now my uncle was a man of the cloth, but he was fine and practical at the same time and so dismissed all that auld talk as an old *pisheóg*.'

Grace glanced to her right. Lizzie was enthralled and so was Hugh.

'Well, a new bank manager was appointed when the old one left, and he said that haunted or not, he and his family were going to live in the house. He said it was only auld *rawmeis* and he was not going to take a tack of notice of it. So he and his wife and two young daughters moved in. The building was fine, well looked-after and plenty of space. There were three storeys and four large bedrooms. But there was a room on the top floor for which the key was supposedly lost. Now the agent had no knowledge of the whereabouts of the key, so short of breaking the door down, there was no way of opening it, a big solid oak door.'

Father Iggy glanced around at his audience before resuming. 'The man said they had enough rooms anyway and it didn't matter, but one night he was working late in the small office on the second floor when he heard footsteps upstairs. His wife and daughters were all asleep on the same floor, so there should be nobody up there, so he decided he'd better investigate.

'Now this was a big man, from Dublin, well over six foot and powerfully built, and he used to play rugby, so he wasn't afraid of anyone, and up the stairs he went. He got to the top landing, off which was a corridor, and as he stood there, he saw a youngish woman in a long old-fashioned dress, fair hair pinned on top of her head, no hat. She walked by him. She never looked at him – she was reading a letter – but her skirts brushed off his shoes. He was about to speak to her, ask her what she was doing in his house, when she approached the locked door and, with no difficulty at all, opened it and entered. Well, the man was shook, I needn't tell you. He didn't know what to do. But he pulled himself together and walked up to the door.'

Father Iggy paused then for dramatic effect, and Grace found she was holding her breath. Slowly she exhaled, the only sound in the room apart from the tick of the clock and the crackling of the dry timber in the grate.

'Well,' Father Iggy went on, 'he turned the handle, but nothing worked – the door was locked fast. He rattled it and put his shoulder to it, but still it wouldn't budge. He went to bed, and all that night, he could hear footsteps overhead and the sound of scraping, as if something was being dragged along the floor. His wife heard it too and was terrified, and she begged him to leave the house. He was not for retreating, though, so the next morning, he found the local carpenter and had him break the door down. He was more furious than scared, you see. He was not going to sit by while something invaded his home. But when the door finally broke and could be opened, what met them was just a room full of cobwebs, entirely empty of furniture, rugs or anything else. But out of the corner of their eye, didn't they see a small white bird, pure white. Now the carpenter was a bird expert, and he said to the banker, "That's a white blackbird. I heard tell of them but never saw one, but you can see it's a blackbird with the yellow beak and the eye ring.'"

They hung on the little priest's every word.

'But before the man had a chance to examine the bird, it flew past them, out the door and out an open window on the landing. They entered the room, and there was nothing to suggest anyone had been in there for decades, so they agreed to close the door and give the man a chance to think about what he would do.

'Well, that night he was lying in bed with his wife, who was scared out of her wits and begging him to give up and move out, when the sound of scraping and timber being spilt and cracked filled the room again. It was coming from the floor above.'

Grace could feel cold sweat between her shoulder blades.

'The man, determined to get to the bottom of it and still convinced someone was playing a trick on him – maybe someone who wanted the house to be sold for a pittance – got the carpenter back and instructed him to lift the floorboards. As the carpenter used a crowbar to loosen the floorboards, he called the man over to see. Beneath the timbers was the skeleton of a child.'

When the Warringtons' tabby cat Archimedes leapt from the sideboard onto the couch at that exact moment, it made Grace jump. She let out a squeal and everyone smiled.

'What happened then?' Hugh asked, fascinated.

'My uncle was called and so was the coroner. But when the coroner saw the remains, he deemed them to be so old, there was no need of an inquest – it would all have been in the far distant past, he thought. So my uncle blessed the room, and the bones were removed and buried in the graveyard where my uncle did the burial rite. They even put up a little stone, with an inscription "The Child of the Bank House. May they rest in peace."'

'And what happened then?' Lizzie asked.

'Well, the sounds upstairs stopped, but the bank manager's youngest daughter, who was only three or four at the time, years later asked her parents who the nice lady was who came into her room every night and stroked her hair till she fell asleep.'

Silence hung in the room until Hugh broke it. 'I'm not surprised you won, Father. That's a spooky story right enough.'

Father Iggy beamed. 'My father was a great man for the yarns.'

'So 'twasn't from a stone you licked it then,' Grace said, exhaling after the tension. 'You'll have to tell Mary O'Hare that one.'

'Oh, I'm only in the ha'penny place compared to Mary,' Father Iggy replied. 'She'd put the heart crossways in you with her tales, so she would.'

CHAPTER 5

SAVANNAH, GEORGIA, USA

23 AUGUST 1942

'So we never thought we'd see the day, but Sarah Lewis is joining the rest of us in marital bliss.' Miranda slid into the seat beside Richard at the yacht club bar.

The flight down had been wonderful and his father a confident and competent pilot. They'd landed at Daffin Park and had a driver pick them all up and take them to the yacht club, where they were given a hero's welcome. Everyone was following their success and the award had made the papers in Savannah, so they were being congratulated everywhere. The unwritten rule of Jews not being allowed in the club seemed to have been overlooked, and Richard knew his father would have had something to do with that. Nobody would dare challenge or insult Arthur Lewis, and Jacob Nunez was his soon-to-be son-in-law.

Miranda looked her usual self, polished, slim, expensive.

'I hope it is bliss for you, Miranda,' he said, after asking the waiter for a lemonade. He'd had three beers and that was enough for him.

'Algy is away a lot, so yes, it's…bearable, I suppose.' She sipped her cocktail.

'That's hardly a ringing endorsement for the state of matrimony.'

Miranda moved closer to him. 'Why did I let you go? I'm kicking myself. I only did it because I was sure you had no prospects as a writer, but now look at you. Infuriating.'

Richard laughed out loud. That was the thing about Miranda – there was no pretence. What you saw was what you got, and it was refreshing.

'Is it too late? I'd leave Algy in the morning…'

She winked, and he suspected she was only half joking. He wasn't conceited, but Algernon Smythe had never been a man who attracted women, and the years since his marriage to the beautiful Miranda had done nothing to improve the situation. If anything, he looked even more red-faced and jowly, with his soft round body, booming voice and endless nautical chatter. Richard could see why she was regretting her decision.

'You'd hate my life, Miranda, war-torn London, terrible food, cold and damp...' He accepted the glass of lemonade from the liveried waiter as she ordered another vodka martini.

'If I had you in my bed, Richard Lewis, I think I'd cope.' She clinked her glass off his. 'Now tell me. Sarah says you have a sweet English rose on the go, and I thought your heart belonged to the wee Irish lassie.' She did a terrible Irish accent, even worse than his.

He sighed. 'I think wee lassies are Scottish, but anyway...'

'Tell me, I swear I won't blab.' She fixed him with her sapphire-blue gaze. 'You can trust me. There is something amiss, Mr Lewis. You don't get to be someone's teenage sweetheart – dare I be so bold as to suggest first love – and not know a thing or two about them, and I know you are not happy, so spill. Tell Auntie Miranda...'

He smiled but shook his head.

Her demeanour changed, no longer flirty or a bit tipsy. 'I mean it, Richard. We're old friends. I'm not joking when I say you'll be the one that got away for me until I'm an old lady, but we're friends, so if a woman's perspective could be helpful, then I'm all yours. And I promise it will go no further.'

He stood then and offered her his arm, leading her out to the terrace and around the corner, away from the boisterous crowd. There, sitting on a stone bench overlooking the ocean, the tinkling of rigging against masts hanging in the still evening air, he told her the whole story.

She sat and listened, without interrupting or teasing, and when he finished, she was silent for a few moments, then spoke. 'Richard, here's my two cents worth. You love that Irish girl, you have since that first letter, and I think you always will. Pippa sounds nice, but she deserves better, and so do you. So go back, tell her the truth, and then find a way to get your little red-haired beauty into your life and your bed. Put a ring on her finger because you're that kind of guy. But don't settle for less – it's not worth it.'

'And if I'm too late? She loved her husband who died so much, and he was a great guy, so she was right to. What if her heart is just too broken and I've blown it?' He rested his forearms on his knees and stared at the ground between his feet. He felt her rub his back.

'Then you are. But at least that's only making *you* miserable, not some other poor girl who might kid herself and get you up the aisle, when in the end, she will know she made a terrible mistake and married the wrong man.'

Richard sat up and took her hand. 'Since when did you get so wise?'

Her normally sanguine and serene face slipped ever so slightly. 'Since I was that girl.'

He put his arm around her shoulder and gave her a hug. 'Leave him if you're miserable, Miranda. Life is too short. My folks split and the world didn't stop spinning.'

'Maybe not, but your mother isn't acknowledging it at all. As far as everyone at bridge is concerned, she and Arthur are still married.'

Richard snorted. Caroline Lewis was not going to give the upper crust of Savannah the satisfaction of knowing her husband left her, even if the dogs in the street knew he did.

'Are you going to see her?' Miranda asked gently.

'Nope.'

'I think you should.'

'To get another cold shoulder, to hear how she never loved me, how she's ashamed of Sarah for marrying a Jew, how ungrateful I am for not wanting to go into the bank? No thanks.'

'I know she's difficult, but you only get one mother, and I think even if she does go on with all of that, at least you tried.'

'I tried before,' he said.

'Your daddy is putting a brave face on, but several of the ladies, widows, divorcees and what have you, have tried their luck with him and gotten zip in return. He's not interested, and it wasn't for want of trying. He's a catch, your pa…'

'So what?' Richard didn't like to hear his father discussed in these terms.

'Just that he isn't interested in anyone else. For all her contrary nature, he wants to patch things up with your mother, but she's stubborn as a mule and won't back down. I know Nathan tried and got nowhere, but she might listen to you.'

Richard laughed out loud at that idea, a bitter sound. 'Listen to me? She can't stand me.'

'She doesn't mean it, Richard. Give her one more shot?'

He looked at her then and remembered how when she was his girlfriend, how much Caroline liked her. Maybe it was mutual. Maybe Miranda saw a side of her hidden from other people. 'I'll see. I don't know.'

'I think Sarah would like her to go to the wedding. For all the ups and downs, every girl wants her parents there, beaming and proud.'

'Beaming? Seriously? You have *met* my mother, right? If she beamed, her face would crack.'

'Well, maybe not beaming, but there. It would mean a lot to Arthur and Sarah, though they'd never admit it. If you won't do it for Caroline, do it for them.'

'Miranda.' Algernon came around the corner, looking mutinous. 'Ah, Lewis. Was about to fire a shot across the bow, looking for my wife. Should have known she'd be holed up with you.'

Richard had always known Algernon to be a bit of an idiot, although basically harmless, but there was a nastiness to him tonight.

'We were just chatting about my sister's upcoming wedding. How have you been, Algy?' Richard tried to keep it jovial.

'Miserable.' He shot Miranda a withering glance. 'Stay single, Lewis. No good can come of marriage. They all show their true colours in the end.'

'Oh, shut up, Algy, you're drunk as usual.' Miranda stood and gathered her wrap and bag.

'You shut up, you cold-faced tart...' His words were slurred, and Richard decided he had to intervene.

'Algy, we'll see her home, how about that? Sarah and my father and me, we can drop her off on the way –'

'Oh yes, you'd love that, wouldn't you, Lewis? Have a go at my wife just like so many others...'

Richard didn't expect the slap from Miranda across Algernon's face, but he got in just in time to stop the wild swing Algy made at her in return. Richard pulled Miranda out of the way as Algy fell forward.

'OK, you're coming home with us,' he said, escorting her out. 'You can stay at my father's tonight.'

Arthur was ready to go, as were the newly engaged couple, so they all piled into the Chrysler. Richard explained what had happened quietly and succinctly to his father. Arthur drove, Richard took the passenger seat, and Jacob and

Sarah sat in the back with Miranda, who cried softly as Sarah comforted her. The car was otherwise silent until his father spoke.

'No man should ever hit a woman, ever, for any reason, so if that's been happening, then you need to pack your bags. If you need help, financial or otherwise, please let me know.' And that was all Arthur Lewis had to say on the matter.

CHAPTER 6

CORK CITY

AUGUST 1942

Grace stayed with the Warringtons for a week. Hugh and Lizzie did all they could to make her welcome, but despite her best efforts to present a cheerful face to the world, her heart was heavy as she sat on the bus back to Tralee.

Loss and grief, her usual companions, but also guilt.

She felt guilty because everyone assumed,

correctly to a point, that her sadness was about Declan. It was still early days, but if she was honest, a lot of her misery wasn't because of her late young husband; it was more because she couldn't stop thinking about Richard with Pippa. She'd given up on the idea of him, or at least resigned herself to it, until that old letter arrived; it had knocked her into a world of what-ifs and maybes. She wished she could turn it off, but she couldn't.

Images of him and Pippa Wills getting married ran in her head like a film. Surely he would have told her if he and Pippa had married? She replayed the last time she saw him in Knocknashee, when through his intervention, they revealed Canon Rafferty to be the person on the German payroll, feeding information to the Nazis and indirectly causing Declan's death. It was afterwards, when they were alone, walking to the beach on a warm summer evening, that she got the impression that perhaps she meant something to him. But maybe she'd imagined it because she wanted it to be true. But of course it wasn't. Not now anyway. Maybe two years ago, but everything was different now. She was Declan's widow. The word sounded strange, but it was the truth, and Richard was with Pippa. How could he have feelings beyond friendship now, after all this time?

So much had happened. It was hard to believe that first letter was sent in 1938, and then how almost two and a half years ago, Richard Lewis got off the bus in Knocknashee with a baby in his arms. Odile was walking now and talking, albeit in a babbling Irish that only Tilly, Mary and Grace could fully understand. She had no idea that she should be a little French girl.

She had to give up on the idea of her and Richard being a couple, of course she did. He was committed to someone else. If Richard still loved her, he would have said something. He didn't, so he must not feel like that anymore.

Tilly's words rang in her ears. It was on another subject – Eleanor Worth's sadness at not getting a birthday card from her husband when he was able to write easily enough. Eleanor had made excuses for him, saying he was so busy and all the rest, but when she was gone and Grace mentioned how hard it was for Eleanor but how Douglas was probably so distracted with the war and everything, Tilly had answered, 'People do what they want to do. If he cared enough, and he wanted to cheer her day up, he would have found the time. We can make time for things we want to do, and we can always find excuses to avoid things we don't.'

Grace sighed as she stared out of the window of the bus as it wound its way over the county bounds from Cork to Kerry. The path, an old sheep track through the mountains, had been expanded to allow motor vehicles, but only barely, and the view outside was spectacular. It was still unseasonably cool for August, but the sky was blue and cloudless. Few trees grew up here anyway, so the landscape was wild and rugged, dotted with moss, lichen-covered rocks and hardy mountain sheep. An odd cottage with blue-tinged smoke from a turf fire dotted the fields, separated by dry stone walls.

Ireland was so heartbreakingly beautiful, its history tragic but heroic, and thanks to Mr de Valera, it was spared the devastation Britain was experiencing. She loved it here. Could she picture living anywhere else even if things had worked out with Richard? Probably not. She'd loved New York, the busyness of it, the way people from all over the globe congregated there, the activity and opportunity, but she could never imagine staying there forever.

She thought about Brendan McGinty, the big New York policeman who had taken a shine to her when she and Declan went over there to find Declan's stolen sister. Siobhán McKenna had been sold by the canon, but she now lived happily as Lily Maheady in Rockaway Beach, New York. It made Grace so sad to think Lily would never know Declan as her big brother. Brendan McGinty, who'd become their friend and unofficial tour guide, had said proudly how he was Irish, but not only had he never been here, nobody back as far as his grandfather had been either. What if she'd accepted his impromptu offer of marriage? Could she now be the wife of an American cop, living on Long Island or in Queens? He was a sweet man, but the idea was as outlandish to her as someone suggesting she go to live on the moon.

But Richard is American, the little voice said. And she could imagine living with him. In fact, she imagined little else. And as to where? She didn't care. She realised that if Richard Lewis were to ask her, she'd follow him to the ends of the earth.

She mentally berated herself as the bus slowed for a herd of cows being driven home for milking. The farmer was in no rush, so the bus just had to wait. This was how it was here.

Mooning about Richard would have to stop. Tilly was right. If he wanted to tell her he loved her, he would. And he hadn't.

She was looking forward to getting home in case there was a letter. She'd been gone for a week, so it might have come. She had to be nonchalant with Charlie, because as the postman, he knew what she got and what she didn't, and she would hate him to think she was desperate for a letter from Richard when his dead son was meant to be the love of her life.

She wondered how Eleanor was getting on. She'd love a letter or something too, she'd said. She'd not seen her husband since she and the girls moved over to his parents' house after their school and home in Liverpool were bombed in the summer of 1941. Over a year ago. The Worth girls, Joanne, Olivia and Libby, had completely assimilated; it was hard to tell them apart from the local children as they ran wild over the peninsula with their friends, and Eleanor had finally learnt to relax and let them go. It was so different to England here. No harm would come of them, and children roamed freely.

The Worth house, Douglas's late parents'

place, was three miles from Knocknashee, so Eleanor had saved and saved to buy three second-hand bicycles for the girls last Christmas. Charlie had collected them for her and had given each one a new coat of paint, so they looked new. A green one for Joanne, a blue one for Olivia and a pink one for Libby. They'd been the envy of the town. All any child ever wanted, as far as Grace could see, was a bike. She'd got polio at age ten, and riding a bike was never something she could consider, so the craze was lost on her, but she could feel the excitement when the Worth girls sailed into the town on their new wheels.

Grace smiled at the memory of Kate and Paudie's little faces, naked longing, as they saw Charlie painting the bikes for the Worth girls in the little yard behind the cottage where they lived. What they didn't know at the time was that Charlie had been given the opportunity to take two old bicycles from the posts and telegraphs office in Killarney. He'd brought them to Grace's house and cut them down to be the right size for Dymphna's children, and he'd painted one black for Paudie and one pink for Kate. Declan's engineering skill was got from his father undoubtedly.

Baby Seámus was thriving too, and she smiled

in anticipation of giving him a cuddle when she got back. He was so tiny yet so perfect.

She wondered how life would be if she'd become pregnant during the short marriage she'd had to Declan. She'd had such hope, she'd been a bit late with her period when he drowned and she thought she might be, but no, it wasn't to be. Maybe that was her one chance of being a wife, a mother, having a family of her own.

Sadly, she watched the landscape change as her thoughts meandered like the ribbon of road through the hilly patchwork of fields.

She must have dozed off because the next thing she knew, the driver was shaking her awake. 'Are you going to Knocknashee? Because Bobby the Bus is leaving there now, so you'd better get a move on.'

'Thanks…' Grace was flustered but gathered her things and bolted to the far side of the station, catching the Knocknashee bus with seconds to spare.

Finally, having endured the packed bus to Knocknashee, she opened her front door. All the way back, she'd had to listen to Jack Collins, one of the five brothers who were forever fighting. Unlike his brothers, Jack had a shock of pure-white hair. People said he saw the ghost of a young woman with hair to her waist walking up the strand one night when he was tending to his lobster pots and the shock of it turned his hair snow white overnight. Everyone had scoffed at the story, but Mary O'Hare had told her that many years ago, a girl was engaged to a boy but his mother got a better offer for him, a girl with a bigger dowry, and so on the day he married the second girl, his first love walked into the sea at that exact spot. Plenty of people claimed to see her, but it had put the heart crossways in poor old Jack anyway.

'I'll tell you now, Miss Fitz, what had me in Tralee,' he'd droned. 'Didn't I have to go to the hospital with an infected big toe. So I washed the toe and, indeed, the entire foot in preparation for the consultation, but nobody told me he'd have to take the other sock and boot off too.' He seemed genuinely perplexed by this turn of events.

Grace listened, in the absence of any other option.

On and on he went. "The doctor said he needed to compare to see how swollen the bad toe was. And sure, I never washed that foot at all.'

'And says the doctor to me that the smell made his job impossible!' eyes wide in outrage. 'But it was hardly my fault now, was it?' he demanded of Grace, showering her in a light spray of indignant spit. She agreed with him just for the sake of peace. She hoped it might shut him up, but alas no. On and on he went about his toe, before changing tack.

'You see, I have another complaint as well. I've a draught in my back, which I suspect is being caused by the wind in my stomach. I gets very bad wind, you see.' Which he demonstrated by breaking wind loudly and noxiously, forcing them to open the windows of the bus despite the rain which had just begun to fall in a dull mist. The journey felt like it took a fortnight.

On the mat was just one letter, not from Richard, and her heart sank. Weary and sad she picked up a thick cream envelope with elaborate handwriting she didn't recognise.

As she boiled the kettle on the gas stove to make a cup of tea, she opened the strange letter. The address was the bishop's palace in Killarney, and the letter was short.

Dear Miss Fitzgerald,

I would be most grateful if you would come to the palace for afternoon tea on Saturday, the 17th of October, at three o'clock. There are some matters I wish to discuss with you.

Yours in Christ,

Deacon Paul Byrne
Secretary to Bishop E.H. Buckley

The bishop's secretary wanted to meet her for tea? What on earth for? She'd never had any dealing with the bishop except for his bi-annual visits to the parish to confirm the children, and even then her conversation was at the most perfunctory. Why would he or his secretary want to speak to her now?

She folded the letter and replaced it in the envelope. She'd have to go. There was a time when she would have been anxious until the day came around as to what it was about, but she'd been through so much by now, she found she was ambivalent. Surely she wasn't to be replaced again? Father Lehane was a nice young priest, and he was growing in confidence now that he was out from the critical gaze of the canon. If he, as chairman of the school board, was unhappy with her, surely he would have said something? She could ask him if he knew what it was about, but she would probably give him a heart attack. He was still very nervy. No, she'd just have to wait and go to see for herself.

She made her tea and gazed out of the window into the small yard behind her house.

She should really do her exercises, she knew,

but one night without would be all right. She dressed in her flannel nightie, the bedsocks Mary O'Hare had knit her, the polio meant her feet were cold winter and summer, and an old jumper of Declan's that no longer smelled of him, despite her not washing it.

She set the cup of tea on her bedside locker and eased herself into bed. Her bad leg was always cold, and Declan used to have her put it over his to warm her up. She would never have that again. Tears pricked her eyes. Was that it? Her one chance at happiness? Was this her life now until she died, alone in her childhood home?

She settled down with her book, a novel Lizzie had enjoyed and had given her, and tried to not think about Richard.

CHAPTER 7

KNOCKNASHEE, COUNTY KERRY, IRELAND

4 SEPTEMBER 1942

'What do we think William Butler Yeats meant when he said "now and in time to come, wherever green is worn, all's changed, changed utterly, a terrible beauty is born"?'

Grace was teaching the older class today because Eleanor wanted the little ones to do some art projects. They loved making collages with autumn leaves and Eleanor had taken on the role of always having some little project on the go. Easter, Christmas, Samhain – she found something in every month, and every child participated. In these glum times, it was nice to see the school so cheery.

Tessie Cunningham, a thin, timid child with white-blond hair, raised her hand. 'I think he means that since the Easter Rising, nothing will ever be the same again, that it was the first step on the road to freedom and from that point, there can be no going back.'

'I think you're right, Tessie, that's what he meant. What about a terrible beauty? What does that mean?' She pointed to Dathai O'Sullivan, who was messing with Gus Walsh down the back of the class by using a pea shooter to land spitballs in the hair of the girls in front and not paying the slightest attention to Yeats or his poetry.

'Er…what he means is…' Dathai flushed, as all eyes were on him. He wasn't a popular child, inclined to bully and make little of others, so nobody rushed to his aid. Grace marvelled, not for the first time, how schools were just little microcosms of the world. Friendships worked in a nice child's favour, where bullies who might seem on the face of it strong, ultimately were weak because their alliances were based in fear and intimidation, not mutual respect and cordiality, so they ended up standing alone.

Grace waited, making him squirm a little; it was no harm for children like him to see what his behaviour led to.

'Gus, have you any idea?' she asked, turning to his partner in crime.

He pouted. 'No.'

'About what?' Grace remained sweet but was not going to let this go. They'd been outside in the yard at morning break, and she'd seen them picking on Ann Molloy, a shy child who stammered when nervous. They were mocking her stammer, and Grace had overheard it. It was not helpful to the child being bullied to create a big scene there and then, in fact it often made things worse, but she was going to ensure they knew their behaviour would not go unchecked.

'What?' His eyes were downcast, his voice sullen.

'What was I asking you about? What was the question?'

She heard a few sniggers, but a raised eyebrow from Miss Fitz was enough to stop that.

'I don't know,' Gus finally admitted.

'Well, maybe if you were paying attention, you'd have more information, so while everyone else is outside playing at lunchtime, you two can stay in here and read "Easter, 1916", and we can have a class discussion afterwards.' She smiled as if this was an ingenious solution to a particularly tricky problem.

She allowed everyone else to go outside – it was a bright sunny day – and even gave the girls some chalk to draw a hopscotch and the boys the school football to kick around.

She had a word with Eleanor to say she'd stay in to supervise her pair of criminals, and she settled into her desk to do some paperwork as Gus and Dathai read, mutinously, the poem.

She'd seated them four rows apart on the side of the classroom that overlooked the yard so everyone could be witness to their incarceration. She seldom punished the children, so when she did, it was big news.

Charlie had put the post on her desk as usual. There was a circular from the Department of Education about the teaching of Irish, a bill from Mahers Coal Merchants in Dingle and a letter seeking a recommendation for a boy Agnes had taught years ago who was applying for a position in a bank in Galway.

It wasn't until she'd read the others that she saw two letters from Richard, partially hidden under a large envelope with a catalogue for school supplies. Her heart sang. She recognised his writing, but the stamps were American. Was he back in America? Why? How?

She was delighted to have twenty minutes to read them, so she slid the letter opener under the flap of the earlier postmark and extracted a short letter. She tried to suppress the relief and joy she felt, because every time she looked up, either Dathai or Gus was staring defiantly at her.

'Please take your exercise book out and write the poem out,' she commanded.

'All of it?' Gus spluttered indignantly

'Yes, all of it. Legibly. And if it's too sloppy to read, you'll stay behind after school and write it again.'

'But that's not fair!' Gus, who was an expert at playing the victim, whined.

'Oh, for the love of God, would you shut up,' Dathai hissed. 'You're only making this worse.'

He began writing, neatly and with great care. Reluctantly Gus had no choice but to follow suit.

The first letter, with the earlier postmark, was written from New York, and he told her about a journalism award he'd been given and that Sarah and Jacob were engaged. This letter must have been delayed; Charlie was always saying there was neither rhyme nor reason to the way post went astray or got waylaid these days. Military took priority, and civilian needs were a very poor second.

The second letter was longer.

Savannah, Georgia, USA

August 28, 1942

Dear Grace,

As you know, I'm back in the States. I mentioned in my last letter how Jacob and I won an award—I've attached a clipping of us getting it, all dressed up like a pair of penguins. It was great, though, and the president of the Bustemer Foundation said some very kind things about us. Kirky was his usual insouciant self, telling us that we'd won it in about three words and summoning us to New York. Then he said he couldn't go to the ceremony because he had other plans.

My father took Mrs. McHale, which was a hoot. He'd never met anyone like her, and they got along like a house on fire. She's an old lady, but boy, she's a firecracker. She flirted outrageously with him and had him crying with laughter.

Anyway, as we went up to get the award, Sarah went to the back of the room to get some good shots of it with Jacob's camera, and guess who she saw, lurking in the back? Kirky. She swears he was wiping a tear from his eye as we were on stage. He denies it, of course, but I think there's a five percent chance he's quite proud of us.

We managed to inveigle a week's vacation out of him. Sarah can, as you would say, "charm the birds from the bushes" when it comes to him, while Kirky is totally impervious to my or Jacob's wishes.

I mentioned Jacob was going to propose—well, he did, and Sarah said yes!

The wedding was today, and we head back to London tomorrow. It was all done really quickly, but my father insisted he wanted to walk his daughter down the aisle, and so he did. They married in city hall of course, since Jacob is Jewish and we're not particularly religious, and we had a party afterward at the yacht club. I'll enclose a photo—Jacob got some friend of his to develop them today. This is the bride and groom, me and Miranda as best man and maid of honor, and my parents. Nathan is busy training army medics so couldn't come.

Grace looked at the small black-and-white picture and felt a pang. Miranda was as beautiful as ever; she was like a film star. She had her hand on Richard's shoulder, and he had his arm around her waist. Sarah and Jacob looked blissfully happy, and Richard's father had a big beam on his face. His mother looked, if not miserable, then neutral. There was another picture of Richard beaming at the camera, his hand on the shoulder of a small coloured lady who was looking up at him with such adoration, it was almost palpable.

My mother wasn't going to go to the wedding, but Miranda convinced me to go and see her, which I did, reluctantly. I basically said, "Mother, this is your last chance to make it up with Sarah and with Father. You won't get another. We both know you don't want to divorce and have the shame of it all, and you also know there are plenty of women circling your husband who'd snatch him from under your nose without a second's hesitation, so this is your one and only opportunity. Also if you let Sarah down today, then any hope of reconciliation will be gone. She loves Jacob and he loves her, and the sooner you just accept that fact, the better. It's now or never."

I swear I've never spoken to her like that before, and I was quaking inside—she's kind of an intimidating person. Imagine Snow White's cruel stepmother from the movie, and you have a good mental image. And she didn't break down in my arms and admit she's been wrong or anything, but she showed up and nailed a smile on her face. As the bride and groom, who were too delirious with love and joy to notice, walked out to cheers and confetti, she looked like she was being put on the rack, but she made a big thing of taking my father's arm and walking like a sergeant major in lockstep beside him. It was a clear signal to any and all ladies who might have had the idea of snapping him up that Arthur Lewis is not on the market. It was kind of funny, but it looks like they might be patching things up.

Their relationship is a mystery to me. Maybe there's more to it than what's visible to the rest of us, but if it's what they want, then I'm happy for them.

I've enclosed a picture of me and Esme too. I really missed her, so it was wonderful to be reunited. She fed me up like a prize pig and fussed over me all week. I loved it. She means a lot more to me than my mother does, and I can't wait for you to meet her—you'll love her. She's so funny and wise and kind.

Grace thought for a moment. Richard often said things like this, that he wanted to show her places in America, or introduce her to people there, as if that was something that was going to happen. But why would he say that? Was he planning on wheeling her out there in her dotage like some old maiden aunt, or did he imagine she would visit with him when the war was over, and if so, how would Pippa feel about that? It was an odd one.

I hope things are good with you. If you wrote, and I

hope you did, I'm sure it's in London waiting for me, so I'm looking forward to hearing all your news.

Lots of love,
Richard

A wave of relief passed over her. He was all right, he hadn't stopped writing to her, Pippa hadn't forced the point – though maybe she would once he got home. She got the impression Pippa didn't go to America with him. Was that significant?

She sighed at her own stupidity as she put the letter back in the envelope and then released the prisoners for the last five minutes of playtime.

As they made to leave, she stopped them. 'Mocking another person is not nice and won't win you any friends. Nobody who is happy and confident feels the need to pull another person down, so bullying says a lot more about the bully than the person they are picking on, do you understand?' She fixed them with her famous stare, one she'd learnt from Agnes.

'We do,' Dathai said immediately, the less malevolent of the two, before Gus could object and start his whining again.

She dismissed them, wondering if the message sank in.

CHAPTER 8

LONDON

SEPTEMBER 1942

*R*ichard lay in bed feeling awful. Poor Pippa was so unwell. She looked like a ghost, and she was throwing up all the time. He lay with his hands behind his head as the horrible sounds of retching came from the bathroom. She was embarrassed as well as ill.

Their conversation that first night he was back in England three weeks ago went around and around in his head like a record on repeat.

She'd been waiting in the flat when they got back, and instantly he knew something was wrong. She was pale as a sheet, with none of her usual bubbly exuberance.

She'd asked him to go for a walk. A wave of relief had passed over him. Was she going to break it off with him? Save him having to do it?

But it wasn't that.

She'd walked with him to the end of the street, and then just stopped, turned to him and said, 'Richard, I'm pregnant. It's yours of course. And I'm keeping it either way, but if you don't want to…'

The blood had thundered in his ears. *No. No. This cannot be happening. No!*

Somehow – maybe it was his firmly ingrained Southern manners – he managed to recover, on the surface at least, and take her in his arms and say all the right things.

It would be OK. They'd get married. She wasn't going to be alone. Of course he wasn't going to abandon her.

There was nothing else he could say. For such a monumental thing, such a huge decision, there was remarkably little conversation.

Sarah guessed right away and told Jacob. That night, once Pippa was asleep, they found him sitting in the kitchen, drinking tea, staring into space.

'You OK?' Sarah had asked, pulling up a chair.

He exhaled and shook his head.

'What are you going to do?'

'Marry her. I have to.'

'Wasn't that the plan anyway?' Sarah asked, barely audibly, Jacob shutting the door into the hallway.

'She's not the one I love, Sarah,' he whispered. 'I'm sorry... And I've made a mess of everything, and this is all my fault, I know, so there's nothing you can say that I haven't already said to myself a thousand times, but I love Grace. I think I always have, but I realised it when I was over there. I intended to come back, break off the engagement, tell Pippa the truth. But when I got back from Ireland, she was in Manchester, and then we were at home, and now...well, now this.'

Sarah had rubbed his back and Jacob sympathised, but neither of them had any words of comfort or solutions to the mess he was in. They knew he was right; he did have to marry her.

He looked up as she half walked, half crawled back to bed, her face the colour of porridge.

'Would you like a cup of tea? Some toast maybe?'

She groaned. 'I can't, Richard. I don't think I can even face swallowing water. I'm so sorry. I know you had planned we'd have an outing today, but I just can't...'

'That's all right, don't worry.'

'I know I'm being rubbish. We've hardly spoken properly about everything since you came back from Ireland, but I feel so awful, I just can't...'

She bolted to the bathroom again, and he wondered what could possibly be left in her stomach since she hadn't eaten anything and all she seemed to do was throw up.

Two days ago, when he'd been out on a story, she'd had a bit of what she called spotting. He had no idea what that meant, but Sarah explained. Pippa and Sarah decided to go to the midwife clinic four streets away, but by the time they got there, it had stopped. The nurse said it wasn't uncommon and there was nothing to worry about.

He hated the surge of hope he'd felt when Sarah told him that evening, thinking this nightmare might be over.

They needed to marry, but there was no way they could with her so ill. Every time he suggested they set the date, she said she couldn't leave the flat let alone get married. She wasn't exaggerating. She was so sick, he'd never seen anything like it.

He got up. He was no use to her, and he knew she hated him lying there listening to her retch, so he went to the United Press office. He had some stories to file, and being a Saturday, it would be quiet, so he might get a chance to work on his novel. Anything to take his mind off his terrible predicament. Most of his journalist colleagues were out drinking by this time on a Saturday. Maybe by the time he got home this evening, she'd be feeling better. He slipped out while she was in the bathroom, leaving a note on the bed.

He was right, the office was almost deserted, and he filed his copy before settling down to a few hours of writing for pleasure. Richard tried to bury himself deep in his novel, a story of intrigue and betrayal in the upper circles of Savannah's society.

Every time he tried to focus, though, his mind wandered.

He had no option but to marry her. Pippa was carrying his child; he had to do the right thing. His plans to finish with her and declare himself to Grace would have to go out the window. He couldn't abandon Pippa. And the baby. *Baby.* The word thundered in his brain. A real baby. A child. His child. A boy or a girl. He felt bad enough planning to break up with Pippa when she wasn't in trouble, but if she was, then there was no way. He was trapped. He ran his hand through his hair, feeling the sweat tingling on his scalp.

He forced down the crushing pain in his chest.

He had to tell people – his parents, Grace, Kirky. He couldn't even begin those letters.

CHAPTER 9

LONDON

OCTOBER 1942

'You look beautiful,' Richard said as he stood in the doorway. Pippa was standing in front of the mirror in their bedroom, wearing a cream skirt and jacket she'd borrowed from her workmate Joanie.

There was a bit of a wait for the registry office because so many people seemed to want to get married, but eventually the wedding date had been set for the tenth of October. Sarah was to be Pippa's bridesmaid, and Jacob, best man.

Pippa smiled weakly, 'You're not supposed to see this before the wedding,' she said.

She'd lost even more weight due to being sick all the time, and it meant her four month pregnancy was visible just as a tiny bump in her otherwise concave abdomen.

She winced.

'Are you all right?' he asked. He was aware she'd been having pains all night.

'Yeah, it's nothing, I think. I've just had this ache for a few days. I think it's from the constant throwing up – my insides are aching.'

'You're sure? We could go back to the clinic?'

'Nah, there's not much they can do anyway. They said I was alright last time.' She placed her hands on her tiny bump. 'I can't believe I'll have a little boy or girl of my own soon. It's amazing, isn't it?' Her eyes lit up with the possibility of it all.

'It really is,' he said with a smile.

'I know all mums-to-be are excited, but for me, it's even more than that. I don't even have a photo of my family, everything was lost in the bombing.' She stared up at him with tears in her eyes, 'I know it's not ideal Richard, but it's a *baby*, *our* baby, my son or daughter, someone who needs me, that I can call my own. It means everything to me, everything.'

Richard nodded. He knew how excited she was. Sometimes he would wake at night and hear her whispering to their child, about what a wonderful life awaited them. She gently poked him in the chest.

'Now then, baby Lewis, Daddy should not have been here last night, you know,' she said with a grin. 'It's bad luck.'

'We don't do things the conventional way, so why would we stick to the old traditions?' He winked at her in the mirror as she stared at her tired face. She was pale and her hair was limp, but she was still very pretty.

They'd gone last week to a Jewish ceremony to commemorate those who had perished at the hands of the Nazis. It was attended by many of Sarah and Jacob's refugee friends, and a kindly British lady asked Pippa where she'd escaped from. Pippa had laughed and said she was British, but Richard knew what the woman meant – Pippa had that hollowed-out look that refugees often had.

The doctor assured her when Richard took her to see him that the baby was all right, that infants in the womb were quite selfish and would take what they needed, leaving the mother in deficit, and he'd given her extra rations for milk and orange juice as well as a ration of cod liver oil, which she declared disgusting.

Richard even tried to feed her the sweet things his father sent back with them, but she was still nauseous most of the time and couldn't face food.

His father. Richard had finally written but had yet to mail the letter containing the news that Arthur was going to be a grandfather, that he was getting an English daughter-in-law, that she was penniless and had no family at all. He tried not to assume what his father's reaction would be. Before they'd left for Europe, he would have said his father would be mad at him, would probably have offered to pay the girl off to get rid of her, but now it was different. Arthur would most likely ask him if he was sure this was the right thing to do. But to be honest, he wasn't.

PIPPA HAD ASKED him last week if he'd written to his family or to Grace about the upcoming wedding, and he'd said he hadn't had a chance because he was so busy. Something about the way she'd looked at him made him feel like such a louse.

'I wrote to my father yesterday,' he said, straightening his tie.

'How will he be, do you think?' She looked worried.

'I'm sure he'll be happy for us. He gave me some advice a while ago, to marry someone kind. Clearly he didn't, but you are, and he will see that when he meets you, and he'll love you as much as I do.'

'You reckon? I dunno, Richard. From what you've told me about your family, I think they might have set their sights a bit higher up the pecking order than me...' She fixed a stray wisp of blond hair.

'I had that chance – remember, I told you about Miranda – and my father told me I was right to walk away, that marriage is a long road, and for it to stand a chance of working, you have to at least marry the right person to begin with.' He chuckled. 'And Miranda Logan was not the right girl for me.' He sighed. 'She married the wrong person too and is dealing with the consequences now. Luckily she had my father to help, because her own family refuses to accept the breakup even though Algy had become violent.'

'And you think I am the right person for you?' she asked pointedly.

'You know I do.'

Her eyes met his in the mirror. 'Still time to back out.'

'Pippa, I wish you wouldn't say things like that. Of course I'm not going to back out. We're in this together, you and me and our child, and we're going to be fine, OK?' He crossed the room and put his hands on her bony shoulders, turning her to face him. He felt like a giant bear beside her.

She wouldn't meet his gaze, but he placed a finger under her chin and gently lifted her face to his. 'OK?'

'I'd have it anyway, you know that, don't you? I wouldn't have an abortion even if you did leave me,' she said, a trace of her old feisty self still there.

'That's not something we need to think about, because I'm not leaving you, ever. I'm going to marry you later today and you're going to marry me, and we'll be a family, Pip, you and me and our baby. And who knows, we might even have more, and you'll have the big, loud family you always wanted.'

'Richard...' She led him to the bed and sat down, pulling him beside her. 'I know I've said it before, but I want to say it again. You don't have to do this.'

'Pippa, what part of this don't you get? I love you, and I think you love me, and we're getting married. We agreed to do this before you ever got pregnant, so why all this doubt and worry?'

She took his hands in hers. She looked like she was deliberating whether to tell him whatever was on her mind. Eventually she spoke. 'Because I know I'm not the one you really want,' her eyes on the faded rug on the floor. 'I know you love Grace. And please don't say I'm imagining it, or you two are just friends, because you're not as good a liar as you think you are. And I asked Sarah to tell me straight out if you were in love with her, and she couldn't say you weren't.'

'Pippa...' He sighed and ran his hand through his thick blond hair, and then, like her, he fixed his eyes on the floor between his feet. 'OK, since we are going to be man and wife – and we are doing this, by the way – I'll be honest. There was a time in the past when I thought maybe things might work out between Grace and me, but that was a long time ago. She married Declan, and I met you, and things are different now…'

She put her hand on his shoulder, and he straightened. 'Look me in the face, right into my eyes, and tell me you love me more than her.'

Richard felt his heart thump. This was it, the moment that would define his life. He met her gaze. She was so vulnerable but so very brave and stoic and strong, and in her body that had endured so much was a child, his baby boy or girl, his son or daughter. He couldn't abandon either of them, no matter what she said.

Richard placed his hand on her abdomen and said, 'I love you both more than Grace.'

'And you won't regret it, you are totally positive?'

'I won't,' he said quietly. 'It's all going to be fine, Pippa. We're going to be fine.'

She sighed and stood, giving him a weak smile. 'Right then, time you buggered off. I'll see you at the registry office. Let's keep one tradition at least, eh?'

CHAPTER 10

Killarney, County Kerry, Ireland

17ᵀᴴ OF OCTOBER, 1942

Grace sat in the parlour of the bishop's palace in Killarney, the aroma of lavender wax polish pervading the warm, still air. It was a beautiful sunny day, the leaves beginning to turn red and gold and orange as summer was giving way to autumn.

A dour housekeeper had told her to sit in here and wait; she'd been here almost twenty minutes already without anyone coming next nor near her.

The three lakes of Killarney, made famous by

a visit from Queen Victoria in the last century, were azure blue; small whitecaps scudded across the surface, and the water lapped the pebbled shore. She'd told Richard that when he visited next time, she would take him through the famous lakes on a boat, and then by pony and trap through the mountain pass in the MacGillycuddy Reeks called the Gap of Dunloe. They could take a picnic, spend the day, and she would feel proud of her beautiful place. She couldn't imagine how that could ever happen, but it was a nice dream.

Her reverie was interrupted by the sound of the wide oak door opening, and the housekeeper appeared again. She reminded Grace of a witch in a story book, white hair, thin face, bony fingers, dressed in black.

'His Grace will see you now. Follow me.'

Grace stood, her stomach twisting in anxiety. She had no idea what this was about, but something told her it wasn't a good thing. Was her job, her home, in danger again, even now after everything with the canon? Was Francis Sheehan to be foisted on her again? The bishop wouldn't summon her for that, though; he'd just appoint him and have him turn up. She'd met Bishop Buckley twice over the years. He came to Knocknashee every four years to confirm the children.

A priest could give First Holy Communion, but confirmation had to be given by a bishop. She found him to be pleasant. He did the job and left, and he seemed happy enough to be the prince of the Church in the eyes of the poor people of the peninsula. He was a tall, handsome man, with longish silver hair brushed off a high forehead, warm brown eyes and skin that took the sun well. He was apparently an excellent golfer and spent much of his time in the picturesque town of Waterville, playing golf on the course there that overlooked the sea. This house, that life, was as far from the experience of the people of Knocknashee as it was possible to be. Ireland might not have royalty, lords and ladies and all of that, but the high-ups in the church lived a life every bit as opulent.

As Grace followed the woman who walked too quickly for her to keep up, she tried not to limp, but it was impossible. At the end of a long corridor, lined with portraits of previous bishops in their ceremonial vestments, the woman knocked on yet another large oak door and waited. The wait allowed Grace time to catch up, and as she approached, she heard a voice from inside.

'Come.'

The woman opened the door without a word to Grace. 'Miss Fitzgerald of Knocknashee, Your Grace.'

'Thank you, Mrs Mulligan,' the sonorous voice inside replied.

The woman gestured that Grace should enter and pass her by; she wasn't joining them.

Grace found herself in a large book-lined study, where a blazing fire crackled with dry logs despite the heat of the day. The bishop was seated on what looked like a small throne beside the window, and Grace walked forward and kissed his proffered ring. It was gold and set with a purple amethyst. She'd learnt as a child that the bishop of Kerry's episcopal ring dated from the thirteenth century, where it had been removed from the finger of a cleric who was later canonised. To her frustration she couldn't remember his name. The ring would at one time have been the bishop's seal for letters so would have had the initials of the long-dead bishop engraved on it. To kiss it when meeting a bishop was a symbol of respect for the office and the man.

Bending so low was difficult because of her leg, and he raised his hand up when he saw her struggle.

'Thank you for coming, Miss Fitzgerald. Please take a seat.' He gestured to a much lower and more ordinary chair opposite him on the other side of the bay window that overlooked the palace grounds. 'Mrs Mulligan will bring tea shortly.'

Grace decided to wait to reply until he explained the reason for the summons.

'You must be wondering why I asked you here?' He raised an eyebrow and gave her a small smile.

She could hear Declan saying, *You didn't ask me, you summoned me.* But she pushed it away. 'Yes, Your Grace,' she managed, her voice husky.

'Well, let me get right to the point, Miss –'

Something made her cut across him. 'It's Mrs McKenna , Your Grace. I'm Mrs McKenna…not Miss Fitzgerald.'

He paused, and she doubted anyone had ever interrupted him before, let alone with a correction.

'Mrs McKenna, I apologise,' he said graciously, but didn't enquire further.

She nodded.

He seemed to be gauging her now, maybe reassessing her. 'I have asked you here today to discuss a delicate matter, one you have thus far been a party to, I understand.'

Grace waited.

'The matter of Canon Rafferty, and his apparent unfortunate association with forces that would seek to do harm to our country and its citizens.'

'What do you want to discuss about it, Your Grace?' she asked, surprised at her own daring.

'Well, the manner in which the discovery was made and the background information you gleaned from a friend of yours, an American gentleman, I believe, that led you to…well, the unfortunate discovery, as I've said.'

'Would you like me to tell you what I know? Is that it, Your Grace?'

'Well, no,' he responded smoothly. 'I believe I have been apprised of the facts of the matter adequately by the authorities, but I have a request for you, Miss…Mrs McKenna, and it is this.' The tone suggested it was more of a decree than a request. 'I would prefer that all details, information or speculation be placed under a seal, as it were, that you would not discuss the situation with anyone, even your close contacts and associates, because the reputational damage is something we are obviously trying to ameliorate…'

Grace felt her blood boil. Was he serious? He wanted to shut her up to protect the canon's good name? 'Are you referring to Canon Rafferty's reputation, Your Grace?' She would not be bullied. She'd been through too much.

'Well, yes...and that of the Church of course. I understand you think you know what you saw, and you have reason to believe your American friend, but trust me, Mrs McKenna, you do not know the whole story and it would be best that you discuss the matter no further. And in the event of it becoming, well, a trial or something of that nature, I might suggest you don't testify on matters about which you can't be certain...not being privy to all the details as such.'

A long pause hung between them, and Grace knew he expected her to bow and scrape and say of course she would follow his instructions. But that wasn't right. Nobody cared for Tilly's or Eloise's reputation when they were wrongfully arrested and held in captivity on the word of Canon Rafferty – where was the Church's concern for them? And was he honestly asking her not to tell the truth? To save the canon's miserable skin? And suggesting that she and Richard had it all wrong and he somehow knew more than she did? The sheer gall of the man caused anger to bubble up inside her. Everything – the way the canon took Declan and Siobhán and almost destroyed Declan, the selling of babies, the way he manipulated Agnes – all felt overwhelming.

'Your Grace, I'm sorry, but my conscience will not permit me to do any such thing. I know what I saw, and I know that what my friend told me is true, so I will, if I'm asked, tell the truth –'

'Mrs McKenna…' His tone was so patronising, she felt like screaming, but she gritted her teeth. 'This is a complex issue, and I'm asking you to accept my word that there is more to this than you might appreciate. Canon Rafferty is a –'

She couldn't help it. 'A what? A good man? A good priest? Do you really want to know what kind of man he is, Your Grace?' She was standing now, heart thumping in her chest, past caring how she offended him. 'He's the kind of man who led an impressionable young girl to believe she had some sort of romantic attachment with him, and he extorted money from her, my money as it happens. And I can't ever be sure what the exact nature of their relationship was, but I feel sure Church authorities would deem it inappropriate at the very least.

'The kind of man who stole children from their loving father when he was bereaved, for no good reason, and broke his heart and theirs. He sold – yes, sold – babies to childless couples in America. I have proof of this, written proof. Three thousand dollars was the going rate, I believe. I have this first-hand from a lady who is closely connected to the diocese of New York.

'He's the kind of man who refused a grieving widow and her young children the dignity of a Catholic funeral for her husband because he believed the man took his own life.

'He brought a man called Francis Sheehan to our school, a person who delights in causing physical pain as well as humiliation and shame to little children, children who just want to learn. And God alone knows what else the canon has been up to.

'So no, Your Grace, Canon Rafferty is not a good man, he's the very opposite, and the discovery that he was working for the most evil regime to ever blight humanity is no surprise whatsoever.'

She stopped abruptly then, shocked at her own audacity. The bishop remained completely still. She tried to control her breathing. He was immobile as a statue, and she felt he saw her as a typical overemotional female.

On and on the silence went, second by excruciating second ticking by. A gold carriage clock on the mantel was the only sound, that and the crackling of the logs.

Eventually he steepled his fingers and fixed her with a penetrating gaze. 'I'm sorry about what happened to Declan. That's the first thing I want to say.'

Grace was stunned. She didn't think he even knew who Declan was.

'And since we are apparently being frank with each other, I happen to agree with you.'

Grace was confused. Why the sudden about-turn? He agreed with her about the canon? Surely not.

'I know it might seem like I am talking out of both sides of my mouth – most unbecoming of a bishop, I'm aware. But more of my role than anyone realises is damage limitation. But since that avenue is, clearly, from your reaction, no longer an option, I am going to be candid with you, as you just were with me, and I have to hope the conversation stays between us.'

Grace would not commit to that, so she remained silent.

He sighed. 'Very well. I know about the dealings that Canon Rafferty had in America, and I also know about the…if not untoward, then certainly unfitting friendship he shared with your late sister. I am also aware of the other cases you cite, and frankly, there *is* more.'

'So how can you still defend him?' Grace heard herself ask. Speaking so directly to a bishop simply wasn't done, but she was too angry for the usual expected deference.

'I'm not. Neither is the Church defending him. If Canon Rafferty is going to offer some defence for his actions, then that is entirely his prerogative, but he will be doing so in his capacity as an individual. What I was trying – and clearly failing – to do is to lessen the reputational damage to the Church by his affiliation, and that is why I asked you to remain silent. Canon Rafferty has, to use the vernacular, made his bed, and now he must lie in it, but it is very important that the Church is not seen as supporting his viewpoint, and so that is why I asked for your discretion.'

Grace wasn't sure if that was better or worse, but either way the Church wasn't going to change. She remembered what Charlie said, how they closed ranks and would never admit wrongdoing.

But if she was called to testify, in the unlikely event of a trial, she would be compelled by the rigours of the law and the decision would be out of her hands. Besides, the gardaí knew everything she knew anyway – she and Richard had given Sergeant Keane a detailed statement at the time – so there was nothing further she could add. But she had an idea.

'Father Ignatius O'Riordan was a wonderful parish priest in Knocknashee. The children in the school loved him, and he was so kind and gentle and really embodied what the Church should be.' She paused to let the impact of her words sink in. 'He was a source of support and help and spiritual guidance in the good days, but more importantly in the bad. I think if you were interested in limiting reputational damage to the Church, reinstating him to the role of parish priest of Knocknashee would be one way of doing that. Father Lehane is struggling to manage the workload alone, and while he is a wonderful man and a very conscientious priest, he isn't as comfortable interacting with people the way Father O'Riordan is.'

A ghost of a smile played around the bishop's lips. He knew exactly what she was doing, offering him what Richard would call a deal. Her discretion in return for Father Iggy back.

The priest had written to her only last week, and she sensed once more his anguish. Hugh Warrington told her why, because Father Iggy couldn't, but there was a convent in his parish, a place for unmarried girls who found themselves in trouble, where they went to have their babies. Hugh knew of medical colleagues who refused to attend patients in those places, but he'd been called twice to attend to girls who were pregnant and had polio to add to their woes, and he'd been horrified at the conditions and the cruelty. He and Lizzie were sure that ministering in that environment was taking a heavy toll on kind-hearted Father Iggy.

It had all come to a head two weeks ago, the story again from the Warringtons. A young girl in the convent had died in childbirth. The nuns were going to bury her in the grounds, as was normal, but her family demanded her body and that of her child be returned to them. Apparently, she came from a somewhat notorious family in the city, not to be crossed, and the girl's mother threatened the Reverend Mother with physical harm if she didn't release her daughter's body. The nun acquiesced, and the girl's body was prepared for burial, but the parish priest bolted the church gates to the hearse. He refused to give the girl a Catholic funeral or bury her in sacred ground because he said she died in mortal sin. The whole family were outside, all in distress. The mother was not a violent woman normally, and she just wanted her child laid to rest in the proper way, so Father Iggy had taken pity on them, went out and with a pair of bolt cutters, cut the chain, defied his superior and welcomed the grieving family into the church. He performed the requiem Mass and proceeded on to the cemetery, where her uncles had dug a grave, and they buried the poor misfortunate girl and her baby in consecrated ground. The whole incident was the talk of the city. Father Iggy had been reprimanded by the bishop of Cork and was miserable by all accounts. He was to be sent somewhere else as punishment, and the bishop was going to make sure it was not a desirable posting.

Grace thought of her dear friend, his inherent kindness and his bravery to stand up against the might of his superiors. If he could do it, knowing the dire consequences that would ensue, so could she.

'And is it your contention, Mrs McKenna, that were Father O'Riordan to return to Knocknashee, his presence would have an…emollient effect on the recent happenings and could serve to…'

'Play it all down?' she finished for him.

'Well, I might not put it quite like that but…'

'I think that's exactly what would happen, Your Grace.'

CHAPTER 11

LONDON

OCTOBER 1942

He had to write to Grace. And mail it. Putting it off wasn't helping. And the many efforts that ended up in the wastebasket were of no use either. He would just have to tell her the truth. There was no other way. She'd written three times, two letters and a card, and he'd not replied to any of them because he was scared and ashamed.

Jacob and Sarah were fast asleep; he could

hear Jacob's gentle snoring through the wall. He sat up against the pillows. It was getting too cold to be out of bed; the gas was cut off, a burst main or something, so there was no heating. London had enjoyed an Indian summer, but October had arrived with a cold snap. His notepad rested on a copy of *For Whom the Bell Tolls* by Ernest Hemingway that he should love, he knew, but found heavy going. Probably because he'd been so distracted by everything.

Dear Grace, he began, for what felt like the fiftieth time.

I'm so sorry it's taken me so long to write, and I'm sorry if you thought I didn't want to or that something bad had happened. I hope you weren't worried. A bit presumptuous of me to assume you would be, so if you weren't, then great, and if you were, I'm sorry. God, this letter is gobbledegook already. I'm supposed to be a professional, but I don't know why, I don't seem to be able to write coherently. Well, I do know why. But anyway...I didn't write for a long time and I'm sorry.

When I left Knocknashee, I... He paused. He what? Was heartbroken? Was determined to go back to London and break it off with Pippa and then declare his undying love for Grace and they would all live happily ever after like some kind of a fairy tale?

I had a plan. I had some things I needed to sort out in London before I spoke to you again.

He stopped again. Here was the hard part, the part that might shock Grace.

What was he thinking? This would definitely shock Grace. And that wasn't the only reason he found it hard to talk about, but he had no option. Especially now. He would just have to say it straight out.

As you probably guessed, Pippa and I were together. I might not have made it clear that we were in a relationship, in the sense that we were living together as man and wife and I had asked her to marry me. Twice.

I guess I never told you because I didn't want you to think I was the sort of man who slept with women before marrying them, or that Pippa was...well, that kind of girl. It was more complicated than that, but then I suppose you might say, he would say that.

I asked her to marry me the first time because I was going to Singapore and I wanted her to be safe and under the protection of the United States if anything happened to me, so rightly she said she thought she might hold out for a more romantic proposal. Then I asked again, another time, and she agreed.

It felt wrong to be doing what we were doing without a license kind of thing, though it's quite normal over here. The war has changed so much, and people just live for the moment as far as I can see. I know it's not like that in Knocknashee, or in Savannah either, come to that.

So I was planning to marry Pippa and be legal, as it were. You were married to Declan, and so happy and in love, and I guess I felt it was the right thing to do. But when I came back to Ireland, and met you again, after poor Declan died...

He paused again. How to say this without sounding crass and insensitive? He was this far in; he had to keep going now. No matter how it sounded, he was never going to be able to write the truth of this whole mess without being brutally honest, so he might as well get on with it.

I knew it was wrong for me to marry Pippa. I didn't love her, not properly, not the way she deserved. So I decided when I was there with you that I was going to go right back to break it off.

Should he say the reason he wanted to break his engagement to Pippa was because he was in love with Grace? He couldn't bring himself to write the words. What he had to tell her next would be bad enough

I returned to London, and Pippa was sent to Manchester for her job. But then we got the award and had to go to the States.

He exhaled. This was further than he'd gotten in any previous letter, so at least that.

I came back to London to meet Pippa, to tell her the truth, but she had news for me first. She was pregnant.

The baby was mine of course, so I said we had to get married right away. Even here in London, which is not like Knocknashee or Savannah, where gossip is rife, it isn't alright for a girl on her own to have a baby with no husband to support them. She wasn't sure, even tried to break up with me, said I didn't have to marry her. She said she knew I didn't really love her.

This was so hard to write, but he had to keep going. The pain of the memory of those conversations washed over him like a cold shower. Pippa, pale and ill, asking him if he was sure, and him lying and saying of course he was, and she somehow knowing he was lying.

I told her to stop being so silly, that we would get married and all would be well. But honestly, Grace, I don't think she ever believed it, not for one second. Pippa is clever and astute and intuitive; she wasn't fooled.

But I must have convinced her enough, and so we went to the registry office and set the date. I know I should have written to tell you all of this at the time, but...I just couldn't. Pathetic, I know. I should have said and done so many things. I'm thoroughly ashamed of myself.

Richard paused. The truth of the matter was that shame didn't begin to cover how he felt about that awful day and the even worse days afterwards. He had left Pippa getting ready in their bedroom, Sarah said he and Jacob needed to get out from under their feet, so they went to the AP club for a drink. He was trying to look cheerful but it was hard. Jacob didn't seem to notice though. They'd arrived to Caxton Hall Registry Office at midday.

They were there but the girls weren't. Jacob had laughed, 'looks like she stood you up buddy.'

'Apparently it's fashionable to be late, the bride I mean.' Richard answered, trying to stay calm.

'Why?' Jacob asked.

'No idea, it just is.' Richard answered wishing Jacob would just shut up.

'Dumb tradition if you ask me.' Jacob replied.

'I didn't,' Richard snapped and instantly regretted it.

Luckily Jacob took his bad temper as wedding nerves, but it wasn't that. Richard knew something was wrong, Pippa wouldn't stand him up. They'd waited and waited, let another couple go ahead of them. Eventually an hour and a half after the allocated time, they had no option but go back to the flat. He couldn't take any more sympathetic glances. Nobody was there, so by now they were both getting worried. Maybe they'd crossed paths, so they decided to go back to the registry office. The woman in charge looked at Richard like he was the last puppy left in the store that nobody wanted, when she told them that there had been no bride without a groom all day.

They'd had no choice but go back to the flat again and wait, but when they got there Sarah was just arriving home.

Having never written the words before, he steeled himself.

Pippa had a miscarriage the day of the wedding. She'd had some medical issues early on, sickness, spotting, some pain, but they thought she was all right. But she wasn't. Sarah found her collapsed in our bedroom, in her wedding outfit. She called an ambulance, and Pippa was taken to the hospital. She'd lost a lot of blood and was very weak. The baby was gone, but they had to save her. They did, thankfully, and she's all right now, but for a few days, it looked bad. We all went to the hospital, the same one they took Pippa and I to when we got caught in the Blitz, and we waited.

Eventually, when she was out of danger, they let us see her.

He closed his eyes and wiped a stray tear from his cheek – back once more in that room. She was so tiny, so pale and worn out looking in the bed. His heart broke for her, she'd lost so much already.

'Our baby is gone Richard, I think she was a girl, but she's gone.' A fat tear rolled down her pale, hollow cheek. 'I was so full of hope, I'd finally have someone of my own, but she's gone…'

The tears were flowing down his face now, but he wrote on.

She told me that even if I hadn't wanted to marry her, she would have kept the baby anyway, she'd have found a way, because she wanted someone of her very own so badly. She wasn't a person who ever went on about her sad circumstances, so for her to say that to me took a lot. She gave confidences rarely and reluctantly.

He paused again. The guilt and shame were his ever-present companions now and never more than at this exact moment. He'd visited her every day, staying for hours, she slept mostly, and barely spoke when she was awake.

He tried to be positive.

'The doctor says you are doing great Pip, that you'll be fine, it will just take a bit of time. And we can reschedule the wedding, and we'll have other children, and I know we'll never forget this one but...'

'No Richard,' She said. 'that's not going to happen...'

'Of course we will...' he'd tried to reassure her.

She shook her head, her skin almost the colour of the pillowcase,

'Listen to me Richard, we won't. It's over. I found the letter you wrote to your father, the one you never sent...'

He tried to explain but she held her hand up for silence.

'I know I don't have much, but I do think, even now, I'm worthy of someone who loves me and only me, and I won't play second fiddle, Richard. I don't deserve it. And we couldn't be happy, because she'd always be there, in the background. I'm not blaming you, but Grace is who you love, not me, so this wouldn't be right.'

'Pippa, I told you, Grace...'

'Is just a friend. So you say. But she's not Richard.' She cut across him. 'Admit it to yourself if you won't admit it to me. You love her, you want her, and I can't compete, I won't.'

He swallowed. Even if he couldn't be honest with anyone else, he could with Grace. He had to be. He was going to tell her the truth.

I visited every day, told her we'd reschedule the wedding, but after about a week, she said she was letting me go. I argued of course, said I wanted to marry her. I had full intentions of doing it, Grace, but she knew.

He inhaled and exhaled slowly.

I'd written to my father, telling him everything about Pippa and the baby, but I'd never mailed the letter. I told her I had, but she found it that morning, and I think that confirmed what she knew. I'm tortured that finding that letter brought on the miscarriage. Sarah said that's not how it works, that there had been signs that the pregnancy was problematic, but I don't know.

So once I knew there was no way to convince her—and I did try to change her mind, I swear I did, Grace—I admit I was relieved she didn't want to marry me, to tell you the truth, but I would have. I did love her, I still do, but just not enough and not in the right way. Once she was discharged, she insisted on going with her friend Joanie to work up in Manchester. There is a sister factory, owned by the same company as the one she works for here, and they were offering clerical positions, better pay, easier work, and with an apartment and everything, so the boss said they were welcome to go up and do that job because he liked and trusted both her and Joanie. She said she needed a new start someplace else, and though I wanted her to at least stay in London, so Sarah, if not I, could keep in touch with her, she insisted she was going. She was discharged from the hospital last week, and she came and gathered her things and left. I wasn't home when she came; I think she wanted it that way.

So that's why I haven't written, Grace. I've felt like such a heel, and maybe you agree and are horrified. She said I was not really free to give my heart to her, and she was right, I know, but I thought what I did feel would have been enough. As usual, I was wrong and she was right.

I wanted to write to you at least once more, to explain. If I don't hear from you, I'll understand you are sickened by my behavior, and I wouldn't blame you—I make myself sick most of the time.

I pray you will write back, but if you don't, know that you have meant more to me than any other person I've ever met, and I am so glad you threw that bottle in the ocean in Knocknashee that day. Because of you, I had the courage to stand up to my father and the expectations placed on me, and I have lived a re-

markable life thus far. I have known people and places I could never have imagined, all because you encouraged me to live my own life. And I have known what it is to truly love.

If this is to be our parting, I wish you joy and happiness in your life, Grace, because you deserve it. In a world that seems so chaotic, where evil seems to be triumphing over good, where there is so much senseless death and destruction, you are the one bright light in my life. And for that I'll be forever grateful.

Yours,

Richard

He signed off and folded it without rereading, placed it in an envelope and addressed it. Then, braving the cold floor, he stood up, pulled his trousers over his pyjama pants, added a sweater on top and put on his socks and shoes. The closet was almost empty now that Pippa had taken all of her things. He took a stamp from his bureau and applied it. This letter was going in the mailbox before he had time to change his mind.

He would have to worry about Grace's reaction until he heard from her, if he ever heard from her again. But at least he'd been honest. She deserved that. Just as Pippa had.

CHAPTER 12

KNOCKNASHEE

OCTOBER 1942

Grace joined in with her class of children as they sang an old folk song. She was no longer worried about Canon Rafferty walking by and hearing them sing; children's innocent voices seemed to be one of the many things that irritated him. He didn't even enjoy hearing them sing hymns.

She'd spent last week reading them a translated version of *Beowulf,* the Anglo-Saxon story of how the hero, Beowulf, slayed Grendel the monster, then his mother and then, years later, a dragon. It was an old Norse tale, and she wanted to show them how the stories they were familiar with from Irish mythology, of monsters and heroes, kings and peasants, were reflected all around the world. No doubt the canon would be appalled if he knew about her teaching stories from pagan times, but she didn't care. Something Richard had said in a letter ages ago, about how much more peaceful the world would be if people realised how similar they all were instead of endlessly focussing on difference, had given her the idea. In her small way, she wanted to open the children's eyes to the shared humanity of the world.

'*Trasna na dTonnta dul siar dul siar, slán leis and uaigneas is slán leis and gcian, Geal é mo chroi agus geall e an ghrian...*' She sang aloud with the children, and wished the words of the song were true. *Over the waves, away, away, goodbye to loneliness and sorrow, joy in my heart and joy in the sun...*

Once the song was over, she asked Colm Murphy to come up and read his essay about the story of the shamrock. They were doing a project on different plants that grew in Ireland and this week they'd chosen the shamrock.

They all knew it of course, how St Patrick came to Ireland as a slave, held captive by the appropriately named Niall of the Nine Hostages – that always made her smile. She and Declan used to joke about the name and wonder if that was how he introduced himself.

'Hello, I'm Niall of the Nine Hostages. Nice to meet you.'

As Colm waxed lyrical about how difficult it was for poor old Patrick, up on the side of the mountain in Ulster where the weather was 'desperate altogether', according to Colm, she marvelled at how his grandfather, Batt Murphy, would never be dead. He was a great man to spin a yarn, known as a *seanchaí*, and Colm had inherited his skill. Every pair of eyes was on the boy as he told them the story they knew so well.

'And so' – Colm weaved his tale – 'didn't the bold Patrick escape, because he was a fierce smart fella, and that's probably why God picked him to be the one to convince all the auld pagans here to give those beliefs up as a bad job, worshipping the sun and the moon and what have you, and follow him to worship the one true God.'

Grace smiled as he went on to describe the misery in such graphic detail, the howling gales, the stinging nettles. He even pushed the boat out by explaining how with no toilet, poor St Patrick would have to do his business outside, and with all the thistles up there, that would have been a prickly business. The children winced and giggled in equal measure. Colm was eloquent and colourful in his description of St Patrick's life, much of it embellished as the historical record was scant, but that was not going to impede Colm. He held his audience captive as he described life in the fourth century.

Grace gazed out the window, towards the road. A car was coming down the street. There were few cars about, Dr Ryan having the only one now that the canon was gone. Father Lehane had no ability to drive or interest in cars – he went everywhere on his bike – and there was so little fuel available anyway, there wasn't much point in having a car. Lizzie and Hugh's Ford stayed in the garage most of the time now. She wondered who it was before turning her attention back to Colm.

'And one day, wasn't he trying his best to get it into their thick heads about there being only one God but three people, and they were scratching their skulls and wondering what it was that he was on about at all, when he saw the little shamrock down on the ground, growing away between the rocks.

'Well, didn't he pick it up, boy, and he showed them, right there and then. "Look," says he, "can't you see this little shamrock? Is that three plants or is it one plant, would you say?"'

Colm looked all around, and as he told the story, he made eye contact with each child, as if he were the very saint himself. 'And they looked back at him and then down at the little green shamrock they'd been seeing all their whole lives, and they said, "Well, 'tis one plant but it has three leaves."

'"Exactly!" shouted St Patrick with glee. "Now ye have it. God is the same as this little shamrock, one God but three gods within, the Father, the Son and the Holy Ghost."

'Well, the people of Ireland were thrilled to bits once they finally got it, and forever more, the shamrock became the symbol of Ireland.'

The class burst into spontaneous applause.

'Right, everyone, put away your copybooks, put them up on my desk, and I'll look at your stories of St Patrick tonight. And thank you, Colm, for such a lively retelling of the story. Batt would be very proud of his grandson.'

Colm beamed. He'd adored his *daidó* and was devastated when he died two years ago.

The children did as she asked.

'Right, you can get your lunches now, and out you go and get a bit of fresh air. And stay off the boggy bit of the yard – I don't want the mammies coming in here and eating the head off me because you went home covered in muck.'

'Thanks, Miss Fitz...' they chorused as they galloped past, as eager as spring calves to get outside.

Within seconds the room was empty. Even after all these years teaching, it always struck her how much emptier a classroom was when children were gone than any other room. They seemed to occupy every cubic inch of space, and the void when they left was enormous.

She thought she would make herself a cup of tea, and one for Eleanor as well, and they would eat their sandwiches together while watching the children play. Eleanor's class were in the middle of an art project, so they were still clearing up. Sometimes the two women cheated and just opened the window and sat inside, but today was bright and sunny and they could wrap up and sit on the bench Declan had made one summer. Underneath, where nobody could see, he'd carved a heart and put 'G and D' inside it. She'd laughed at the childish gesture, but he told her that he meant it. She was in his heart, and there she would stay to the day he died. Little did either of them think he would be dead a few months later.

The kettle whistled on the small gas ring, and she poured two mugs of tea. The leaves were suspiciously light in colour, and there were rumours going around that the tea leaves were being mixed with something else to make them go further. Biddy O'Donoghue denied it outright, but Grace would put nothing past her or her creepy husband, Tom. He had a nice little black-market business going, and people less scrupulous than she were glad to pay a bit extra to get things they shouldn't.

'Excuse me?'

The voice startled her. She spun around to see a tall, slim, grey-haired man in an RAF uniform at the door of her classroom.

'Oh, I...I'm sorry...I wasn't expecting anyone...' she said, flustered.

'I'm sorry, I didn't mean to disturb you.' He smiled, a kind smile. He had crinkly blue eyes, and she judged him to be in his forties. His accent was hard to place, not Irish but not British either.

'No, I'm sorry...' She crossed the room to the door. 'I'm Grace Fitzgerald. How can I help you?'

As she spoke, Eleanor's class were let go, and

the older children thundered past the visitor to get outside with their lunches.

'I was looking for –'

'Douglas!' Eleanor gasped. The man turned, and the normally reserved and very proper Mrs Worth ran into her husband's arms.

Grace slipped out into the yard to give them some privacy during their reunion and called the Worths' three daughters to her.

Joanne, Olivia and Libby were like locals now, speaking Irish fluently and friends with all of the local children. They ran towards her, Olivia leaving a very competitive game of hopscotch they'd drawn on the footpath with chalk. They were using an old shoe polish tin filled with sand to throw onto the different squares. And Noirín O Chinneide was left with one end of the skipping rope when Libby dropped her end to come to Grace.

'I think you should go inside,' Grace said to the sisters. 'There might be a surprise there for you.'

'What kind of surprise?' Libby, who was nine, asked.

'Just go in and see.' Grace ushered them back into the school and stood at the door to stop all the curious children now wondering what was going on. The car, a black Ford, was parked outside, and that was causing a bit of a furore among the boys.

She gave the children an extra ten minutes before calling them all back to class with the bell. Inside, in the classroom, Douglas Worth was sitting on a desk, one arm around Joanne and another around Libby, while Olivia stood in front of him telling him a story about the stray kitten they'd found, and how Mummy said they could keep it if they took care of it, and his name was Dolphin because he could jump like a dolphin in the bay. Douglas was clearly overjoyed to be reunited with his family.

'Right, Worth family,' she said, 'we can manage here – off you all go home. I'm sure you have a lot to catch up on.'

'But Grace, it's only two o'clock…' Eleanor objected.

'Don't worry, we'll go for a nature walk. Now off with you all.' She shooed them out.

'Thank you, Grace. I…I can't believe he's here!' Eleanor squealed into her ear, like she was a fourteen-year-old.

As they left with a cheery wave, the Worth girls delighted to have their daddy home, Grace called the rest of the children into her room.

'Right, get your buckets…' she called, to whoops of joy. They knew what that meant. 'Pair up.'

The nature treasure hunt was one of their favourite activities. Two older children paired up with two younger ones, and in teams of four, they had to find a list of items Grace ordained.

She wrote on the board, thinking what might be found in October. They had to remember the list, no writing it down.

Red clover

A buttercup

Five daisies

A nettle – and remember to grasp it tight so it won't sting

A fuchsia

Five periwinkles

A piece of basalt

And…a fossil

'First team back with everything will win a prize. Off you go.'

The older children were wise to this game and so divided the list up, with each child remembering two items from the list. Grace smiled to see the little ones leave, mouthing their two things over and over so as not to forget and let themselves down in front of the bigger children.

They thundered down the school path out onto the street and headed for the strand. She walked after them, more slowly because of her limp, but they were quite safe; this was their place, and everyone knew everyone.

She saw Nancy O'Flaherty leaning on the post office half door and went over to say hello.

'Ah, Grace, the fine weather is nice, isn't it? No harm too after the wet summer we had.' Nancy said with a cheery smile. 'You're on your own today?'

'I am, just for the afternoon. Eleanor's husband turned up, so I sent her and the girls home with him. They're over the moon. I don't think they had any idea he was coming.'

'Ah, isn't that lovely. He's in the British army, isn't he?'

'Air force. He arrived in his splendid uniform and everything. The children didn't see him, because if they had, they'd have made a show of us.' She laughed.

'Young Benny O'Rahily joined the air force as well. You know his sister Mary, would have been one age to your Agnes?'

Grace shook her head. 'I don't –'

'Ah, you do. The mother had a squint – she's

dead now, God be good to her – used to clean for Dr Ryan years ago?'

In the true style of Knocknashee, Nancy wouldn't stop until Grace said she knew the person, though she had no idea. People forgot how much of her life she spent in hospital, and when she came home, Agnes more or less forbade any contact with the locals. She considered them beneath her for some strange reason Grace never understood. Grace and Tilly used to joke about it all the time. *You know Mickey the nose? Ah, you do, his sister had yellow ears, the mother only spoke Swedish? You do know them – had a giraffe in the back acre?*

They would have each other in paroxysms of laughter as they made up ever more outrageous descriptions of fictitious people.

'Oh, I think I do now...' she lied.

'Yes, well, Benny had a bit of a nasty incident in the pub in Dingle when he came home of leave. He ran into the Keohane brothers – you know one of them is doing time for IRA stuff...' She dropped her voice, though there wasn't anyone within earshot.

This, Grace did know. There was a significant anti-English feeling here – the long and bloody struggle for independence was fresh in the community's memory – and she'd heard of men who enlisted in the British armed forces getting a hard time from local diehard republicans who were still fighting the War of Independence in their heads if nowhere else.

It was a complicated thing. Ireland was definitely on the side of the Allies – they gave all sorts of assistance to the British and Americans – but memories ran deep, and people had a visceral reaction to British uniforms, so wearing one around the streets of Ireland would not be wise. It was only twenty years ago that very uniform brought chaos and destruction, and people didn't forget.

'He got a bit of a hiding,' Nancy said. 'He's all right, but still, not nice.'

'I hope nobody says anything to Douglas Worth…'

'Ah, he's Protestant, he'll be left alone. Of course he would have gone. You know the way it is.'

Grace knew exactly. The Protestants were considered by almost everyone to be half English even if they'd lived in Ireland for generations.

'You must be glad to get Richard's letter this morning?' Nancy said kindly.

'I didn't get any letter,' Grace said, 'not for a few weeks?'

'Oh, Charlie was running a bit late this morning. Seámus spat up all over him as he was going out the door, so he had to change his uniform.' She chuckled. 'Maybe he missed you. There was post for you.'

Grace couldn't help but beam. 'I'll have that to look forward to later on so. Now I better catch up to the children before they take to the high seas.' She laughed and waved goodbye to Nancy.

CHAPTER 13

Treasure hunt complete, the children resumed playing outside. Each team had managed to gather all of the things, so she would have to do a draw tomorrow for the prize, which would be a jelly baby each for the winning team. One sweet was hardly a grand prize, but with the sugar rationing, children hardly ever got a treat, so the jelly baby would be sucked slowly.

She offered up a prayer of thanks to Mr Boyle, the school supplies salesman, who gave her a precious box of sweets when he came with the delivery and to take the next order. He visited twice a year, and she would have been lost without him.

As she leant on the school wall, the warm sun

on her face and the tangy brine on the air, she was in fine form.

'Nice day, Grace.' Jamie Keohane walked by with a smirk. He was slight, with a receding hairline and, Grace always thought, a bit ferrety in his features. His eyes were too close together or something. He wore a flat cap, an old shiny-with-age suit jacket, a grandfather shirt and work trousers that had seen better days. Most people addressed her as Miss Fitz when she was with the children, and him using her first name felt overly familiar.

She never spoke to the Keohanes. They were older than she was and, based on what Nancy said, best avoided. They were one of the families still fighting the war against the British, though it ended long ago.

'I see you had an RAF man here today,' he said, stopping in earshot of all of the children, who found reasons to be over by the wall.

'Pardon me?' She turned. She'd heard him clearly, but she needed time to think.

'An RAF man came here to the school today. I hope he wasn't looking for recruits.' He smiled but it didn't reach his eyes.

She responded coldly but politely. 'No, he was here on personal business.' The children were all 'flappy ears', as Eleanor called it, where they went silent if something interesting was happening.

'Because no Irish boy or girl has any business going over there.' He turned to address the gathered children. 'Sure you don't, fighting their war for them. We owe them nothing, 'tis they owe us...'

Grace was not going to get into this. There was something menacing about him, and she wanted nothing to do with him. 'As I said, it was personal business. Now if you'll excuse us.'

'Did you know my brother Sean?' he asked.

Grace wished he'd leave her alone, but something told her not to be rude. She did not need to make an enemy of the Keohanes.

'No, I don't think so?' she said, stopping to face him. The children were still gathered around.

'He's serving five years for offences against the state.' He shook his head. 'This isn't the republic we fought for, that's for sure.'

'Well, I'm happy to say I didn't fight for anything.' She gave him a quick smile. 'I wasn't even born. Now I'll have to get on.'

'And who was that RAF man so?' Keohane persisted.

Grace had no good reason not to tell him –

he'd find out in two minutes flat either way – but something about this questioning wasn't just chit-chat. 'His name is Douglas Worth. His wife teaches here.'

'Well, I hope he's not planning on sticking around. We're a neutral country, and you might mention to him that the wearing of that uniform around here might not be the healthiest of ideas.' It was clearly a threat.

She was at her door now and turned. 'I'm sure he just is back on leave to enjoy a peaceful few days with his wife and children, so I think we should let them to it.' She used her best teacher voice, one that normally brooked no argument.

'You'd say that, would you, Miss Fitz? Would you indeed?'

Before she could respond, Sergeant Keane crossed the street. The sergeant seemed to have an uncanny knack of being where he was needed.

'I'm assuming you're on your way to see me, Jamie?' he asked pointedly. The main reason people like him had a regular appointment at the barracks was if they were on bail and needed to check in every day. Grace suspected this was the case; she'd not seen him around for a while, and all the Keohanes had been in prison at one time or another.

'Oh, certainly, Sergeant.' He doffed his cap theatrically. 'We must keep in with the forces of the Free State.'

Grace knew it was a dig. The gardaí were formed when Ireland became independent, and there were some people, the Keohanes included, who saw the foundation of the new Irish twenty-six-county state as a betrayal of the ideals of the thirty-two-county republic. The remaining six counties in the north of the island remained part of the United Kingdom, and people like Jamie Keohane didn't like that.

He smirked and touched his cap before sauntering off after Sergeant Keane.

She decided to make a lesson tomorrow on this very topic. Too often the narrative of Ireland's complicated relationship with England was left to people like Keohane, but she wanted to teach the children that people like Douglas Worth were not the enemy, no matter what the old diehards said. Peace wasn't worth it if people still fought the war in their hearts and minds.

As Nancy had told her, there were two envelopes on the mat. One from Richard – she'd know his writing anywhere – and another a letter from a school supply company. She was too interested in hearing from Richard to open the second letter, so it would have to wait.

The evening was milder than it had been, so she didn't bother lighting the range. Dymphna had dropped over a bowl of stew. She said she made too much, although Grace suspected she made too much on purpose, knowing Grace wasn't inclined to cook proper dinners when it was just for her. She often just had a bit of bread and jam for her tea, or a boiled egg.

She set the stew to heat over a pot of water on the gas stove and then opened Richard's letter.

Dear Grace,

I'm so sorry it's taken me so long to write, and I'm sorry if you thought I didn't want to or that something bad had happened. I hope you weren't worried. A bit presumptuous of me to assume you would be, so if you weren't, then great, and if you were, I'm sorry. God, this letter is gobbledegook already. I'm supposed to be a professional, but I don't know why, I don't seem to be able to write coherently. Well, I do know why. But anyway...I didn't write for a long time and I'm sorry.

As Grace read on, the sad, awful story of poor Pippa and the miscarriage and the cancelled wedding and all of it, she was only pulled from the letter by the sound of the plate rattling under the ferociously bubbling water. She switched the ring off and sat down, trying to take it all in.

Richard and Pippa were not together any more. She was gone to Manchester. She'd refused to marry Richard because she said he was not the right person for her.

What did that mean? Was he heartbroken? Or feeling guilty? Or angry? He was certainly ashamed of his behaviour, but from Grace's perspective, he did the right thing. He was going to stand by Pippa, and he would have been a good husband and father, she was sure of that. She read and reread his letter. There was so much in it, so much to absorb, but it posed more questions than it answered. Was she shocked that Pippa was pregnant and Richard was the father? Of course she was. She and Declan had longed to consummate their relationship before they married – she recalled him dragging himself away from her with an anguished groan as he kissed her in those weeks before the wedding – but neither of them would have even considered giving into their carnal desires and making love before they were allowed to.

But they were Catholics, and it was probably different for them. Richard said his family were Episcopalian, but it wasn't what he called 'a big deal'. They went to church and all of that, but people didn't live every moment of their lives by the rules of their church, and anyway, as far as Grace could see, they didn't seem to have as many rules to begin with. She tried to imagine what people here would make of this story. They'd be horrified, no doubt. It happened here of course. Grace had heard whispers of girls who'd gone off to 'relatives in England' – everyone knew it was a euphemism for an institution – only to appear back a year or so later, looking bereft. And poor Father Iggy having to witness the awful way those girls were treated in those places that, if Hugh Warrington was to be believed, and she did believe him, were just unimaginable. But it was all in whispers and nudges; nobody ever said it out loud. It often struck Grace that the women or girls had to bear the shame alone; nobody mentioned the men. The girls hardly got themselves pregnant, but as usual the fathers seemed to get off scot-free. She was a bit shocked, but more so very sad for poor Pippa. She knew what it was like to have no family of your own and how precious a baby would have been to her.

What did she think about it being over between Richard and Pippa? Deep in her heart, she felt relieved. The idea of Richard married to

Pippa Wills was a deeply painful one, although admitting that, even to herself, made Grace feel awful. She'd never even met the poor girl and wanted her gone, even though she'd done nothing to harm Grace and had lost so much.

So now, after everything, Richard Lewis was single and so was she. But the letter was cryptic. He said she was the one bright thing in his life, but did he mean as a friend? He said he knew what it was to truly love, but that might be someone else? Miranda Logan perhaps? Or some girl he never mentioned? She would be foolishly putting two and two together to make seven if she jumped to the conclusion that he meant her.

He said that Pippa refused him because he wasn't totally free, that she wouldn't be a second fiddle to anyone. Could she have meant Grace? She thought about the letter in the box, written two years ago, long before she married Declan or he met Pippa. In it he'd said he loved her, that she was the one, but that was a lifetime ago. Did he still feel that way? If so, why not say it outright? He'd been honest about everything else, hadn't he?

No matter how many times she read and reread it, she found herself frustrated with uncertainty. She took the dinner off the pot and ate it quickly. Richard was free, and he wasn't going to cut communication with her; he was alive and well, so all of her worries were relieved. But what next? How should she reply? Should she write and sympathise at the loss of his child? Was that the right thing to do? Or should she agree that the way he treated Pippa was shabby? She could see how some people might think it was, but he didn't do it on purpose. And he would have done the right thing and married her. He was not the kind of man to get a girl in trouble and just abandon her, as so many were. Tilly would probably raise a sceptical eyebrow; she always said Grace rushed to forgive everyone everything, no matter how bad the behaviour. That was true in the case of everyone except the canon – she could never excuse him.

She would need to take some time to think about her response. She'd let the information settle for a few days.

CHAPTER 14

Two days later, Tilly put Richard's letter down, having taken what Grace felt was an eternity to read it. She'd sat there as Tilly scanned the words, and Grace had no idea what she was thinking.

The children were off for a few days for the Halloween break. Tilly and Odile had called, and she had to show her friend the letter; Grace had read it and reread it and couldn't figure out what he meant.

They were sitting in her kitchen. The range was lit, and Odile was playing with a big box of coloured blocks Grace kept for when she visited.

'Well, at long bloody last,' Tilly said eventually.

'What does that mean?' Grace put her hands on her hips, demanding her friend explain.

'It means' – Tilly spoke slowly, as if addressing a dimwit – 'that at long last, you two can get together. Thanks be to God. It took long enough.'

'It doesn't mean anything of the kind. What makes you think that?' Grace longed for it to be true, but she thought Tilly was reading too much into it.

'Because he's saying so, more or less.'

'Where is he saying that? More or less?' Grace demanded, and Tilly shrugged. 'Are you shocked?'

Tilly smirked then. 'About what?'

Grace could feel herself blush. 'Well, about the…baby, that he and Pippa were…'

'At least he'll have a bit of experience by the time you get to ravage him.' Tilly hooted. 'Ah, Grace, if you saw your face! Of course I'm not shocked. It's not the 1800s for God's sake.'

'Well, we're not all as worldly-wise as you clearly are.' Tilly's words and tone of voice hurt. She knew she was parochial and old-fashioned, but there was no need for Tilly to make fun of her.

'Ah, I'm only messing. But seriously, Grace, of course he was sleeping with her. But that's not important. What matters is she's gone and he's single, so jump in there and show your hand, for the love of God. Tell him you love him and you want him and all the rest before some other English one snaps him up and the whole snakes and ladders starts up again.' Tilly sighed and ran her fingers through her messy hair in frustration with the whole thing.

'Well, I can't just write and say that!'

'Why not?' Tilly pulled off the crust of the freshly baked barmbrack on the table and smeared it with a thin scrape of butter from the dish. The traditional Halloween fruitcake was a bit light on fruit and peel this year, but Dymphna had done her best.

'Well, because I have no indication he feels the same way any more, and also because there's the small matter of his broken engagement and the loss of his child, for God's sake. I'd be like some kind of Grim Reaper, swooping in on his grief to try to trap him.'

Tilly let out a growl of frustration. 'Grace McKenna, would you listen to yourself? You're supposed to be the clever one in this village, but for a smarty-pants, I must say you're being fairly thick. Of course he loves you. You told me about the lost letter! He wrote it all before…'

'Yes!' Grace cried. 'Two years ago! Before Declan, before Pippa. And he was with Miranda, his old girlfriend, just recently – he sent a picture of her with his arm around her. Maybe he went back and realised she was the one he loved. It would make more sense, she's much more suitable.'

'More suitable than you? Ah, will you stop. And anyway, isn't she married to some other fella?' Tilly cut another wedge of the brack.

'Well, yes, but he's awful now or something, I don't know. And you can get divorced in America…' Grace said miserably.

'Grace you're losing your marbles now. Of course it's not Meringa or Minerva or whatever she's called.'

'Miranda.'

'Right, Miranda. Please, if you trust me on nothing, trust me on this. It's you he loves. Anyone with eyes can see it.' Tilly's tone was softer now. 'I wouldn't lie to you now, would I?'

'I know but…' Grace sighed heavily, her eyes downcast, her shoulders slumped.

'But what?'

'Well, even if that's true, and I'm not confident it is, how would it even work? There's a war on. I live here, he lives in London. And when it's over, he'll go home, I suppose. I've got polio. He's Episcopalian, whatever that is, and I'm a Catholic. I speak Irish, and he hasn't a word of it. He's rich and I'm not – his family would probably be horrified –'

'Write to him, Grace just write to him. You're trying to look ten miles down the road and around six corners. Nobody knows the future, especially now, so one step at a time, eh? Just write, sympathise about the baby, wish Pippa luck, say she sounds like a lovely person, and see where it goes from there.'

Grace looked into the eyes of her best friend, who she was certain would never steer her wrong. 'All right, I'll write.'

'Good. Odile and I are going to Dublin in the morning, so you better have written and posted it by the time I get back or I'll cover you in jam and set the drooler on you.' She jerked her head at Odile, who was gnawing a block, drool running down her chin. She was cutting her back teeth and was very grizzly.

CHAPTER 15

LONDON

DECEMBER 1942

Richard fought the initial panic he felt and tried to be as enthusiastic as Jacob was at the latest development. They were sitting in the Dog and Duck, the nearest pub to their apartment because the gas was off again and their place was arctic cold. Warm British beer and fish and chips wrapped in newspaper were what he needed to soothe his frayed temper.

After a week of hard work, sourcing interviews and tracking down people in the know all around London, getting their reaction to the ongoing Battle of Stalingrad, the piece was rejected. He was furious to have all their hard work bumped in favour of a story about Bing Crosby's Christmas tree.

No explanation from Kirky as usual. But Richard knew it was because it was too grim and maybe because it showed the Russians in a good light. He remembered Kirky warning him not to send too much 'stuff about commies and Jews' when they were first sent over here. They'd hoped Kirky would be more relaxed about what they wrote now, after the award and Sarah's lecture, but it wasn't the case, and even if Kirky had become a bit more lenient, he'd drawn the line at good Russians. The Stalingrad piece was too technical and far away and miserable, and people were sick to death of war news. This was the latest of several stories Kirky had rejected. He was particularly resistant to stories of Jewish refugees, but Jacob persisted nonetheless.

Richard had seen the latest edition of the *Capital* but didn't share it with Jacob – he'd see it soon enough. Jacob was getting more and more frustrated with the job, and Richard didn't want to rile him further.

He'd not heard a word from Grace, and she surely had received his letter weeks and weeks ago by now, so he was growing increasingly glum. Obviously she was appalled – he didn't blame her – and was cutting contact. So neither Pippa nor Grace was speaking to him. No more than he deserved.

'So what do you think?' Jacob asked, his eyes bright.

'I think Kirky is getting soft in his old age.' Richard vied for time, dragging his attention back to his friend, who had little patience for Richard's complicated love life. Jacob thought he was crazy to let Pippa go, and while he liked Grace, he told Richard the idea of him living happily ever after with a widow who spoke a different language, lived on a peninsula on the west of Ireland and had no intention of ever leaving her community was sheer madness. Sarah was a confidante of Pippa's as well, and he knew, though she never admitted it, that Sarah thought Pippa had done the right thing. Sarah was kind to him, and understood he never set out to hurt anyone, but she also felt for Pippa and was sure his love for Grace was never going to amount to anything.

They were both right. So talking about it further wasn't going to help anyone.

Sarah would be joining them shortly, and he wondered if she knew of Jacob's latest idea.

'I know. I think I just pestered him so much, he might be hoping we get shot down.' Jacob laughed, then drank a mouthful of beer and grabbed a hot, salty chip.

'So explain it to me, slowly this time, what's happening?' Richard had had so much on his mind of late that he knew he wasn't as focussed on the job as he should be.

'OK, the US Air Force has agreed to allow a select number of journalists – Andy Rooney, Walter Cronkite and a few others, and us – to go for training. We'll be given an officer's rank, and we need to know the basics in case we can be useful up there. But in a nutshell, we are finally getting to see the war up close. We'll see firsthand, eyewitness accounts of bombing missions and report them. We'll have to wait – the training won't be for a while. There are loads of newspapermen who want to go, but we're on the list at least.'

'And we fly with the bombers?' Richard kept his voice neutral.

'Yes, at last. Instead of waiting for the guys to

come back and asking them how it was, we'll see for ourselves.' Jacob's eyes were lit up like he was a kid going to a fairground, not into the treacherous dark night to drop bombs over Germany.

'Assuming we don't get ourselves killed.'

'Well, yeah. But if we were just regular civilians, we'd have been drafted by now probably anyway and be risking life and limb every single day.'

Richard knew Jacob was right about that much at least. 'Right, so we train as airmen and then we go up with them. Is it a one-time thing or do we do it regularly?'

'Well, I guess they'll want their money's worth out of us, but I don't know.' Jacob paused and fixed Richard with a stare in that disconcerting way he had. 'Don't you want to go?'

'It's not that...' Richard replied, only half truthfully. 'I guess I'm just getting used to the idea.'

'Are you in or not?' Jacob asked as Sarah walked in the door, her nose pink, her dark curls covered with a hideous cat-vomit-green hat she'd knitted to protect her from the cold. She also wore a dark donkey jacket she'd found in a rummage sale. It used to belong to a docker, she thought – she'd found a payslip for the Liverpool docks in the pocket – and it was far too big, but the leather shoulders protected her from rain and she said it was really warm. She used to have a coat that their father had sent, beautifully cut wool in powder blue, but she gave it away to a refugee woman, as she did with most of what he sent. Under the donkey jacket she wore an orange cardigan that looked like it had been rescued from a puddle. It clashed horribly with the hat, but Sarah couldn't care less. Both Richard and Sarah did not like standing out with their fancy, expensive American clothes, so they wore things to tatters and it felt better, less conspicuous.

'In for what?' Sarah asked, hanging the donkey jacket on the back of a chair and swiping one of Jacob's chips, her dark eyes darting from Jacob to him.

'I might as well tell you…' Jacob began, and Richard went to the bar, knowing his sister would have strong feelings about her husband's plan and not wishing to be dragged into the argument.

What did he think about it? He considered as he waited his turn to be served. Life had been chaotic and confusing in recent months, and he was so conflicted on so many things, he wondered if he was even capable of making a decision at this stage.

He'd written so many letters to Grace, each one ending up in the wastebasket. And then when he finally got the guts to tell her the truth, she was disgusted and cut him off. Maybe it was for the best. If Jacob had his way, they'd be up there, on a bombing mission over Germany, with the Luftwaffe doing its darndest to blow them to kingdom come, so maybe all his angst and worry would be for nothing. Maybe his time was going to be up.

'What can I get you, darlin'?' The barmaid wore a lot of make-up and had hair dyed a bright yellow. He suspected a bleaching effort gone wrong. Lots of women had taken to administering their own beauty regimes, and the results were sometimes not what they wanted. Sarah and Pippa had done a piece on that very topic that Kirky had loved.

Pippa. Her face swam before his eyes.

'I ain't got all day, love?' the barmaid urged impatiently.

'Sorry. Ah, two pints and a gin and lemon please?'

'Ah, a Yank. You lot take your own sweet time to do everything, don't ya?' She laughed at what was clearly a dig at how long it took the US to enter the war. He was used to it, and besides, it was mostly good-humoured.

At another time he might have made a joke about Yanks being worth waiting for, but he hadn't the heart. He took the drinks, paid for them and went down to join Sarah and Jacob, attempting to read the situation. Sarah was quiet, and Jacob was staring into space.

'Thanks,' Sarah said as he handed her the gin. 'So you're going along with this scheme, I take it?' Her tone challenged him to resist.

'It's a wonderful opportunity, Sarah,' he heard himself say, and it struck him that it really was. 'We talk to guys our own age all the time, guys who risk life and limb daily, and they talk about it, or if they've lost a comrade, they just all head straight to the mess, but they are really seeing it, up close. Jacob and I are sick of sitting on the sidelines. We want to be there, to see it all happen, and hopefully to live long enough to report on it.'

Jacob shot him a grateful glance. It was an ongoing issue, Jacob constantly trying to 'get himself killed' and Sarah trying to keep him safe.

'We'll be fine. We're going on a bombing mission, not on a fighter plane.' He couldn't think of a way to explain it that was less terrifying or dangerous, so he didn't elaborate further.

She took a sip of her drink. 'Just one time, right?'

'For now, but we'll see...' Jacob was nothing if not brutally honest.

'So not just one time,' Sarah said flatly.

Jacob reached over the table and took her hands in his. 'Sarah, all over the world, young guys like us are doing this stuff daily, on naval ships, in the air, not to mention the ground troops. Their mothers and girlfriends and wives don't know week to week, month to month, what's happening, but they do it because they have to. We see the results of Hitler's plans. We've met the refugees, people who escaped. We've heard first-hand what he wants to do, and he won't stop by us asking nicely. The world has to fight back, as hard and as ruthlessly as we can, and that requires sacrifice. Ours and yours and everyone else's. We're not special. Why should we be safe and others not? And if us reporting about what it's like for these guys, what damage they can do to the German war machine, encourages others to come, fortifies women to be brave and let their men go, well, it's important, Sarah. We're not just doing it for the hell of it.' Passion burnt in his eyes.

'I get it, I do. I just…' She shook her head. 'I don't want anything to happen to either of you. You were lucky to get out of Singapore that time. I was so scared not hearing anything for months, and then I at least had Pippa with me.'

Richard sipped his beer, not saying anything.

'I don't mean… Look, you know what I mean.' She shot Richard an apologetic look. 'Just that I wasn't on my own dealing with the worry and the fear and the not knowing is all I meant to say.'

Richard nodded. He did know.

'When will you be going?' she asked, accepting it was a fait accompli.

'We don't know. We'll just wait for notification to report for training with the Eighth Bomber Command.' Jacob kept his voice down even though there wasn't anyone within earshot. Living in London all this time made them acutely aware of how spies were everywhere. 'It's just a week of training, shooting weapons, adjusting to high altitudes, parachuting and identifying enemy aircraft.'

'I thought there were rules about noncombatants carrying weapons?' Sarah said quietly.

'Overridden for us, I guess.' Jacob shrugged.

Richard wished he looked a bit less gleeful at the prospect.

'And we'll definitely be on bombers?' he asked. His nerves might just about hold on a bombing mission, but the tales of those men who came back from dogfights put his hair on end.

Jacob nodded. 'B17s most likely.'

'OK, I'm in,' he said with a smile.

His friend winked. 'I knew you would be.'

CHAPTER 16

London, November 4th, 1943

The following morning, after dressing, he lay down on his bed and reread Grace's letter for the hundredth time.

Dear Richard,

I'm so sorry about everything that's happened. I don't really know what to say. Poor Pippa. What an ordeal she's endured, and she sounds like such a nice person. I'm so sorry. And to lose a child... Well, I have no personal experience, but it's a very unique type of grief, I'm sure, so my deepest sympathies to you both.

I hope you and Pippa find peace now and that she enjoys life in Manchester.

There is nothing new to report here honestly. Life just trundles on.

Speak to you soon,
Grace

It was so cold, so unlike her. He'd been overjoyed and relieved to see a letter from her on the mat when he came home yesterday. He was beginning to give up hope he'd ever hear from her again. It took over a month to be delivered he realised looking at the date, but that was how it was these days.

But as he read this stilted letter, offering sympathies like she didn't really know him, not like her at all, his heart sank. She must be appalled at his behaviour, that was the only explanation. At least she'd not cut all contact. Maybe in time they could become at least friends again. But it was only a maybe, and it could take years.

He tried to distract himself. He'd been up most of the night working on a piece on the Beveridge Report that was a blueprint for a post-war welfare state in which healthcare and social security would be offered to everyone. Jacob thought it was wonderful, and Richard had to agree it did sound good if a little bit unworkable, but he also knew Kirky would reject it as more 'commie nonsense'.

He'd covered Mussolini's first public appearance in eighteen months, in which the fascist dictator told the Italians that 'the last word has not yet been spoken' but in the same breath, told them to evacuate the cities, causing mass panic and hysteria as there seemed to be no plan as to how that would be achieved. This was something Kirky would love, the enemy thrown into chaos. Especially as the news that American bombers attacked Naples, which while necessary, did not go down well with the Italian American community.

He'd written of the retreat of Rommel from Tunisia despite Hitler demanding he make a stand, and several other stories of human interest, but his heart wasn't in it. He was moping, he knew, but nothing could pull him out of his dark mood.

A gentle knock on his bedroom door made him look up.

'Can I come in? I have coffee…well, you know, coffee substitute.' It was Sarah. Jacob had gone to the House of Commons to take photographs of Foreign Secretary Anthony Eden as he read a declaration on behalf of the government condemning the persecution of Jews.

'Sure.'

She handed him the cup and extracted a cookie from her pocket. Chocolate chip, made by

Esme, wrapped like it was fine bone china and sent over.

'I thought they were for your birthday, a special treat just for you?' He smiled as he accepted it.

'They are, but desperate times call for desperate measures.' She pulled a stool over and sat beside the bed.

'What's wrong?'

'Well, indeed. That's what I've come to ask you.' She cocked her dark tousled head to one side, a single eyebrow raised.

'Nothing, I'm fine...' he lied.

'OK, so it's a guessing game? Sure thing. Pippa?'

'No. I'm fine –'

'The baby?'

'Honestly, Sarah, I –'

'Not Miranda?' She furrowed her brow disapprovingly at that idea.

'No, of course not.' He was getting exasperated now.

'Then it can only be one thing, the same thing it always is – Grace.'

'No...everything is fine with Grace. She wrote to me. Everything is fine...'

'Except it very obviously is not.' She put her

coffee cup on his nightstand and folded her arms. 'Come on, tell me, because I can't look at your miserable face for one more day. So you can tell me willingly or I'll torture it out of you.' She smiled but he didn't respond. 'You told her about Pippa and the baby. And how you are single now and how she is the girl you've always loved and all of that?'

'I did, and she wrote this back.' He handed her Grace's latest letter, and she scanned it.

'OK, she's sad for you about the baby and sends her sympathy to Pippa, but no mention of your outpouring of love, is that the issue?'

'I guess,' he finally admitted.

'And you definitely told her that you love her and that she is the one for you?'

'I did. Well, I said I now know what true love is, and that Pippa knew I wasn't going to be able to love her completely because I really wanted to be with someone else…'

'And you specified, in actual words, that this person you were speaking of was Grace?'

His silence said it all.

Sarah exploded. 'Oh, Richard, I oughta kick you into next week – for a smart guy, you can be so dumb! Jacob is right, you know. He said you two want your heads knocked together. No wonder you two can't get together with all this code and whispers and almost-but-not-quite conversations.'

'I didn't want to scare her off. She was probably disgusted that Pippa and I were sleeping together. She's very traditional, very Catholic, and so I thought that was enough of a shock for one letter – it sounded so crass. Like, oh, Pippa's gone and the baby very conveniently died, so come on over – there's a vacancy in my bed.'

Sarah groaned. 'Well, obviously you don't say that, but the woman isn't a mind reader, Richard – you need to spell it out. In words. Using names. Just do it. For once and for all. And if she rejects you, then she does, but at least you'll know.'

Richard paused before answering. 'I don't think I could bear to lose her,' he said quietly. 'I've been so dumb, so naïve. I…'

'You're right. You've been incredibly dumb, but you can fix it. I suggest you do.'

She patted his shoulder and left.

CHAPTER 17

KNOCKNASHEE

DECEMBER 1942

*L*ater that evening, Grace pushed the envelope with the colourful stamps that had arrived that morning across the table to Charlie and Dymphna. This one was something she needed help with, someone to talk her down. Because all she felt now was hot rage.

'Will I read it aloud?' Charlie asked, putting his glasses on.

Grace nodded, not trusting herself to speak.

The letter had so shocked her, produced a visceral reaction so overwhelming, she needed to get another perspective on it.

"'Dear Grace. You won't know me, but my name is Patricia, and I am the wife of your brother, Maurice. I realise this news will come as a shock, and I do apologise. I am writing to you without the knowledge of your brother, who feels we should not burden you with our troubles.'"

Charlie stopped and looked first at his wife, then at Grace. The colour had drained from Dymphna's face, and she swallowed. Grace said nothing.

He exhaled loudly and read on. "'Maurice left the priesthood eleven years ago, several years after he and I fell in love. We met when he was a seminarian – my parents were the cook and caretaker at the seminary in Cork. We were forced to break contact, but we reconnected eventually through a mutual acquaintance. I was living in England – I'd been sent there – but when he was released from his vows, I went to Manila, where, once he was laicised, we married. We now have two children, both girls, aged six and four, called Kathleen after your mother, and Mary after mine.'" Charlie paused again, struggling to take it all in.

Baby Seámus slept peacefully in his crib.

'Go on,' Grace said tightly.

"'Maurice never felt it was right or fair to inform you, as to do so would put you in a difficult position in your community at home, that is the reason you do not have regular contact with your brother."

"'Thank you for your letters and cards over the years. We treasure them, and I know it means the world to Maurice when they arrive. He was so sad at the deaths of your beloved parents and then your sister. Even though it is from this distance, he felt the losses keenly and longed to connect with you in a more meaningful way, but as I said, he feared you would be horrified and ashamed, and also that your community would be shocked and somehow that would reflect badly on you, or might harm your position in the school."

Charlie looked up and caught Grace's eye before going back to reading.

"'I want to assure you that your brother behaved impeccably through the entire process. He and I fell in love many years ago, but we did not allow our relationship to develop until he was free to do so. It's important you know that. Also, any donations that came from your parish to him were all handed immediately to the church here – Maurice has some former brother priests he is quite close to – so nothing untoward has ever happened in that regard, I can assure you."

"'That said, I am quite sure you are reeling now as you read this.'"

'That's for sure,' Dymphna interjected. 'Grace, I'm… I don't know what to say.'

'I know. I had absolutely no idea, nothing ever. And when I think of all the years… I'm so angry. Anyway, carry on, Charlie.'

"'My parents are both dead now too, and believe me when I tell you they did all they could when I was young to dissuade me from taking a priest off course. They did not approve of our marriage.'"

Charlie smiled ruefully at that part. 'I'm sure not.'

"'The purpose of this letter now, as well as telling you the truth – something I feel should have been done many years ago, but it was not my place to do so – is to beg for your help.'"

"'I don't know how much you are aware of the fate of Manila, but this beautiful city we've come to think of as home was known as the Pearl of the

Orient. After the Japanese attacked the American base in Hawaii, they went on to attack Manila; it was an important administrative city and a critical port. We here in the Philippines are an archipelago of over seven thousand islands, and we were a territory of the United States since the turn of the century. In recent years, before the war, we became a commonwealth with alliance to the United States, so when we realised the Japanese were coming, we had to try to protect ourselves, with the help of the American army stationed here. But the reality was we never stood a chance. The Japanese wanted to get to the resource-rich Dutch East Indies, and we were not going to be able to stop them. The fact that we held out as long as we did is a testament to the bravery of our soldiers, and that of our American allies."

"'We managed to get out of the city, along with many thousands of other civilians to the more rural areas where we have been hiding, but I fear it is just a matter of time before we are overrun. Manila has been declared an open city in the hopes that it will not be destroyed, but we have heard already of atrocities against civilians, including women being forced to work in brothels for the Japanese soldiers. As a woman, and a mother of two little girls, I am terrified."

"'This is why I am defying my husband's wishes and writing to you, as one woman to another, as a sister-in-law. If we can escape, and that is a large if, but if we can, can we get sanctuary in Ireland? There is a chance we can get passage on a US merchant marine ship leaving soon. As Irish citizens, Maurice and I and our children are entitled to go home, but if we knew we could come to Knocknashee, have a place to stay, then it would make our decision easier. We have no resources. I would not ask if I was not fearful for our lives, for mine and your brother's, but more so for your little nieces.'"

Grace tried to steady her breathing. Her nieces. She had nieces. And a sister-in-law and a married brother. It was too much to take in.

"'So I am throwing myself on your mercy Grace. If you can, please respond to Father Alfonse Lopez at the address on the top of this letter. If we get the opportunity to go, we will, and so I might not receive your letter, but we will try to make our way to Ireland. We have a very dear friend here in the American forces who will help us to get passage on a ship if we have somewhere to go. And Grace, time is of the essence. Every day our future looks more perilous."

"'I enclose a photograph, taken in happier times."

"'Your sister-in-law, Patricia Fitzgerald.'"

Grace then silently showed them the photograph of the family: a tall, broad, handsome man, who looked so like her father, it almost took Grace's breath away; Patricia, small with straight dark hair and a heart-shaped face; and two serious-looking children in frilly dresses. They looked more like their mother than Maurice, she thought.

Charlie folded the letter and handed it back to Grace. 'Well, it certainly explains why he was so distant,' he said eventually.

'I...I'm so angry, Charlie. All these years, when I needed a brother...when Mammy and Daddy died, when I got sick, when Agnes...' Her voice betrayed her, and she started to cry. Hot, salty tears ran down her cheeks. 'Why could he not say it. Why not just be honest instead of living a lie all these years? What did he think I'd do? I don't understand. And now he's only telling me because he wants something...'

'Well, to be fair, he's not telling you at all, she is. I can see why you'd be upset, but she explained that he felt it would be making things bad for you…' Charlie was trying to be fair, she knew, but his defence of her brother just upset her more.

'I know it's a shock, Grace.' Dymphna reached over and put her hand on Grace's. 'But he had his reasons, and all of them were to protect you. And remember, he doesn't know you – maybe he thought you'd be like Agnes and, well…she would never accept this if she were alive.'

Grace nodded and placed the letter in her bag. She inhaled deeply and let her breath out in a ragged sigh. The point Dymphna made was a good one, she had to admit. 'I just wish he could have, but I suppose…if he knew the reception he'd get from Agnes…and he probably assumed I was the same. I only have scant memories of him, so…' She was trying to be reasonable. 'But still, I wish he'd have tried, at least once.'

'So what will you do now, Grace?' Dymphna asked as baby Seámus stirred. She picked him up and soothed him back to sleep.

'I'll do the only thing I can do. I'll write and say of course they must come.'

Charlie frowned. 'You have to, but the jaws will be wagging around here, so you'd better get ready.'

'I know, but it's what my parents would do, I

think. I should telegram first. I'll write too, but I'll telegram now, and that way at least if they get the opportunity to leave, they can take it knowing they have a home to come to.' Grace was sure she was doing the right thing. 'But when he gets here, if he ever does, he'll be getting a piece of my mind.'

'You're dead right. It's exactly what Eddie and Kathy would have done,' Charlie said quietly.

'And at least the canon is gone, so you won't have to put up with any of his… Well, you know how he'd be,' Dymphna added, stroking Seámus's head.

'There is that,' Grace agreed. The idea of Maurice coming home as what was called unkindly 'a spoiled priest' would be something he would relish – another stick to beat her with.

'I know it's a shock, Gracie, I'm shook myself reading it, but I think you're doing the right thing,' Charlie said.

'I am, I know, but I just wish he'd said something sooner. I wish *he'd* written to tell me. And it's hurtful, I suppose, that he was never going to tell me, that his wife had to be the one. But he's my brother and they're my family. I can't even imagine what he's like. I was so young when he left for the seminary, and he only came home for short visits, and he was a bit of a mystery to me.'

'He was like your parents from what I remember. I liked him as a lad anyway. Agnes was different, but Maurice was always friendly and had time for everyone. A lot of years have gone by, but people don't really change, so you'll like him a lot. I'd say if you went over to Nancy now, she'd send the telegram for you. She said there's no time to lose.'

'I can have them here, can't I?' Grace felt nervous.

'Of course you can.' Charlie stood and put his arm around her shoulder, reassuring her as he always did. 'Sure you're rattling around that big house on your own – it will be lovely to have the company. And try to focus on the good. You're getting a family you never knew you had, and after all you've lost, that's a good thing. And sure, you know how it goes around here, 'twill be a nine-day wonder. Today's news wraps tomorrow's chips. There'll be a bit of guff, you know that, but he's one of our own at the end of the day, and that will be all that counts.' As it always did, Charlie's sensible, kind approach soothed her.

'You're right. I'll go to Nancy now. She won't mind, I'm sure, once I explain.'

'Indeed and she won't.' Charlie helped her on with her coat.' She opened the door. 'Thanks, Charlie, I'd be lost without you.'

'Ara, you would not, Gracie, but I'm always here to help you, no matter what.'

She and Charlie weren't demonstrative really, it wasn't their way, but he loved her every bit as much as her own father had and she loved him. There was never need to put it in words; they both just knew.

CHAPTER 18

Nancy was listening to the radio when Grace knocked on her door. Raidió Teilifís Éireann had a programme of waltzes and foxtrots on at this time. Nancy and her late husband were great dancers according to everyone, and she'd once confided to Grace that she loved to tune in as it reminded her of Ned, and sometimes she danced by herself in her little sitting room. Something about that revelation broke Grace's heart, and she'd said a prayer that night for Nancy to find some nice man to dance with sometime in the future.

'Ah, Grace, 'tis yourself. Come in. I was just listening to my programme.' Nancy ushered her into the house beside the post office.

'I'm so sorry to disturb you at this time of the evening, but I need to send an urgent telegram.'

'Divil a bit of disturbance. I'll do it now. Come on in with me this way.'

Grace followed Nancy through her parlour and through a door into the post office, now closed to the public.

The wonderful thing about Nancy was she wasn't a gossip. It was important for her job, and while she was naturally friendly and chatty, she would never reveal a confidence or betray a secret. When the postmistress told her last year about the telegrams from the canon to Anthony Nolan, it would have been after much deliberation and soul-searching, Grace was sure.

Grace was sure Nancy knew more about the private lives of families around here than anyone. There was no bank nearby, so everyone put their money – if they had it – in the post office. It was through Nancy all the telegrams arrived, notifying of deaths, marriages, babies and everything else. Not much happened in Knocknashee that Nancy O'Flaherty didn't know about, but she never said a word about anyone's business.

Grace filled her in on the letter and showed her the photograph from Patricia as Nancy set up the telegram machine. To her surprise, Nancy wasn't at all shocked.

'Well, Grace, that explains a lot, doesn't it? Maurice was always a nice lad, quiet, but very polite and decent. Sure how could he be any other way with the lovely people he came from. But it always struck me as very peculiar that he was so…well, sort of distant when he wrote to you… and I often did wonder why it was so. Especially after poor Eddie and Kathy died, God rest them, and Agnes too. I was a bit vexed with him, to tell you the truth. He could have been kinder to you, and you only a girleen, left on your own to manage everything.'

'I used to wish he would send something other than "a Mass will be said for your intentions", and I still don't understand why he couldn't tell me the truth.'

'Well, look, you know now and you're going to make contact, so have a think about what you want to say there while I set this up.' She took the letter and set the address on the machine. 'It won't be cheap, mind. The Philippines is a long way.'

'I don't mind. And I'll keep it short. All right. Dear M and P,' Grace dictated. 'Please come. I look forward to welcoming you home. Grace.'

Nancy typed it out and turned to Grace with a smile. She hadn't changed a bit in all the years, salt-and-pepper hair pulled back in a bun, a warm, open face, pink cheeks and a pink nose. Every day she wore the same outfit, a brown skirt, a cream blouse and a cardigan. She had a squint in one eye; Grace had heard that there was an operation now to remove it, and she hoped Dr Ryan knew about it and could mention it to Nancy.

'God be with the days of the old Morse code button. I don't know myself with this thing, forty words per minute it can do…' Nancy said proudly as she stood up from her telegram desk at the back of the post office.

Grace paid the fee of two shillings and six pence, and as she was about to leave, Nancy asked, 'Will you stay and have a cup of tea, Grace? I made a madeira cake yesterday. 'Tisn't as moist as I'd like because I only had lard, no butter, but it's all right.'

'I'd love to, Nancy, thanks.'

Grace followed her back to the little kitchen off the parlour, and they chatted easily as Nancy made tea.

'I suppose I'll be the talk of the place – again,'

Grace said ruefully. She accepted a china cup and saucer and a slice of cake from Nancy as she sat at the table.

'Era, 'tis little people have to be talking about, and anyway, everyone here is very fond of you, Grace, so you won't find anyone with a child in the school who would hear a bad word said about you or your family. People don't mean to be cruel most of the time, it's more boredom.'

'I suppose so.' Grace sighed. 'And I hope they can come, but I'm not looking forward to the whispers and nudges.'

'Right now, you listen to me.' Nancy settled into her chair. 'Your brother is a good man, and I'll tell you something you probably don't know. When he was a young fella, your father did all he could to talk him out of the priesthood. Ask Charlie if you don't believe me. Your mother was pleased he had a vocation – sure what mother wouldn't be? But Eddie never thought it was the right road for Maurice, and he told him so too.'

Grace's eyes widened in surprise, Nancy was right; she'd never heard this before. 'And did my mother know this?'

Nancy nodded. 'She did and she was rightly vexed, so she was. She was a very devout woman was Kathy. She had a deep faith, not shoving it down anyone's throat, mind you, but just a quiet, strong faith, and she was so happy that her boy was going to be a priest. She and Eddie rarely fell out, but they fell out that time.'

'When he was going to the seminary, was it?' Grace hung on every word. Agnes had never told her anything about her parents and only ever mentioned Maurice as a priest, never as a brother, so this was all news to her.

'Then, and later too. He was very bright, like all of ye Fitzgeralds, but your parents wouldn't have had the money to send him away to boarding school, so when the parish priest before the last snake' – she curled her lip in disgust at the mention of Canon Rafferty – 'Father Spillane, God rest him, he was a lovely man, suggested Maurice go to Farranferris College in Cork, where he'd be trained for the priesthood, Kathy was delighted. She wanted him to have the opportunity of course, but she wanted to see him ordained as well.'

'But my father wasn't keen?' Grace asked.

'Maurice was only fourteen, so he was too young to tell, but Eddie thought he might have an eye for the girls. He was a fine-looking lad even then, and he's grown to be a handsome man, the head cut off your father.'

'And so what happened?'

Nancy sighed. 'Kathy got around Eddie in the finish. He said he didn't want it, he thought it was an unnatural way for a man to live and he didn't want it for his son, but Maurice was keen to keep going with the books, and between him and Kathy putting the pressure on, Eddie had to give in.'

'And did Maurice ever express doubts, as far as you knew?'

Nancy took a sip of tea, and Grace could tell she was deliberating on what she would say next. 'I'm only telling you this, Grace, to make the next part of this story easier on you. People will talk about a spoiled priest and all the rest, you know they will, and some people might be shocked at him breaking his vow and marrying and having children. But Maurice wanted to leave before he took his final vows. I only know this because Ned's brother Ciarán and Maurice were great friends, so 'twas to Ciarán he came that time, and they both asked Ned for advice. Maurice was twenty-five – I remember it was his birthday, in March – and due to be ordained the following May, 1929, 1930 maybe, around then. You were only a child, so nobody would have told you, but he came home to tell your parents that he'd met a girl in Cork, this Patricia. She worked in the kitchen of the seminary – her parents were the cook and gardener – and he wanted to marry her and leave the priesthood.'

Grace swallowed and tried to take this in. How could Agnes never have told her? 'Did Agnes know about this?'

A hard look crossed Nancy's face. 'Oh, she knew well enough. 'Twas her he told first – your parents were away for the day, Kathy had a hospital appointment – and Agnes made an awful fuss, said he was under no circumstances even to consider it, that the whole family would be disgraced, the name dragged through the mud if he went ahead. She told him your mother's health was failing and news like that would kill her and that he was to get back on the bus and do his duty by his family and by God and to tell that evil hussy who was tempting a priest to stay away. She even threatened to report her to the seminary and have her parents dismissed and the whole family thrown out without even a reference if he didn't break it off immediately and go ahead with the ordination.'

'And he did?' Grace's voice sounded strangled to her own ears.

'Well, he called to his friend Ciarán, sure there was no bus back till that evening. And he was in an awful state. Ciarán thought he should ignore Agnes, but Ned mentioned that Kathy and Eddie were gone to the hospital – he'd met them earlier in the day on their way. So poor Maurice thought Agnes must be right, that his mother was very ill, and he couldn't have it on his conscience that he'd let her down. And he was fearful for the livelihood of his girlfriend's family as well. So he went back…'

'And got ordained even though he didn't want to?'

'I think he did. He never let on to your parents that he had any doubts at all, and by the time he realised Kathy was only going to a routine check-up – she had a bit of a murmur in her heart all her life – 'twas too late.'

'But surely he could have –'

'Somebody made the seminary authorities aware of the relationship, and the girl was sent over to England. Maurice was heartbroken. He wrote to Ciarán, telling him everything. The parents were allowed to keep their jobs but under a cloud, and nobody would tell him where the girl was sent, and he didn't dare ask. That's why he was sent to the missions immediately. Normally they do a few years here first, but he was shipped out the minute he was ordained.'

'It was Agnes. She told on him.' Grace would put her life on it, it was exactly the kind of thing she would do.

Nancy didn't reply. She didn't need to.

'And sure, Canon Rafferty was here by then, and she was…well, whatever was going on with them, so it was not just bad-minded of her but so hypocritical as well.' That familiar feeling of hurt and bitterness washed over Grace. 'But they must have stayed in touch somehow.'

'Well, it looks like that, certainly,' Nancy agreed. 'I'm only telling you this because I want you to know he tried to get out of it. Eddie was right, Maurice wasn't cut out for the clergy, and he would never have taken his vows but for –'

'Agnes blackmailing him,' Grace finished. She exhaled raggedly. Would the bitter legacy of her sister's nastiness never end?

'Look, it's best to let the dead lie, Grace love. Maybe I shouldn't have said anything…' Nancy looked distressed at causing such pain, opening old wounds again.

'No, I'm glad you did. It's better I know.' Grace

was trying to come to terms with this new information. She felt so lonely. She wished Declan were still alive, or that Richard was there, someone she could talk to. But Tilly was in Dublin with Odile visiting her sister and Eloise, and while she had Nancy and Charlie, it wasn't the same. Why did it always feel like she had to handle everything alone?

CHAPTER 19

Nancy knocked on the glass window of the classroom and beckoned Grace out.

'I thought you'd want this, Grace love – it came very early this morning.' Nancy handed her a telegram. Janie was continuing the seven-times tables with the class, though everyone's eyes were on Miss Fitz and Mrs O'Flaherty outside the door.

Grace scanned it and read aloud. '"Thank you, Grace. Passage secured to Suez. And onward from there. P & M."' She paused. 'Well, at least they got the telegram, so all we can do now is wait and pray, I suppose. That reply was very fast.'

'It's amazing what they can do now. That would have been weeks if not months in the post. I'll light a candle for them now – I'm going to ten o'clock Mass – please God they'll be safe and will get here in one piece. They are all going in convoy now, all the ships, 'tis safer. Sergeant Keane was telling me.'

Grace swallowed, overwhelmed with it all. Her brother, his wife and her nieces were all on a ship in waters so dangerous they had to travel in convoy in the hopes of being safe from attack. Could God be so cruel as to take them from her too? She was furious with her brother, but still, the idea that the family she never knew she had could be blown to bits on the sea before she'd laid eyes on them was horrible. The ocean had never shown her anything but cruelty. To her horror, she felt salty tears on her cheeks.

'Ah, *alanah*...' Nancy rubbed her arm. 'Don't be worrying, people here will just...'

Grace shook her head. 'That's not it. I don't care what people say. But it's just everyone I've ever... The sea has taken my parents, and Declan, and now what if...'

The children's attention was glued to her, so Nancy led her away from the door and their fascinated gaze. Nancy gave her a handkerchief and tilted her chin to look her in the face. 'Darling girl, you know I can't promise you anything, so I won't, but if Maurice has been put on a big expensive American ship with his family, Mr Roosevelt won't want anything to happen to that, so they'll be sure to have it well protected. 'Tisn't like your parents coming in from the island, or poor Declan in a small *naomhóg*.'

Grace nodded. She was right.

'And Tilly is coming home today,' Nancy said brightly.

Grace was so looking forward to seeing her; it felt like ages she'd been gone. Mary O'Hare had remarked wryly how Tilly was showing much more interest in Marion and her children since Eloise came on the scene. She spent a lot of time in Dublin. Odile loved her Irish cousins, and they doted over her, and Tilly confided that Marion was happy to look after the toddler while she went out to pubs and concerts and all sorts of exotic things with Eloise.

Grace hated the feelings of jealousy she had about Eloise. The Swiss woman was lovely, so friendly. She was very close to Tilly and didn't seem to be out to hurt her or anything, so Grace couldn't even justify how she thought about Tilly's girlfriend. It was envy, pure and simple.

She was used to being Tilly's only friend, her confidante, and sharing her now was hard. It was so unkind too. Grace had had Declan, and possibly Richard, and she was being so meanspirited about Tilly having someone to love. Thinking about it made her blush.

Marion, Tilly's older sister, had married a man called Colm who had six children with his late wife. And then they went on to have two children of their own, so the house was chaotic but full of fun and love. Odile at almost three loved every second there.

'I know, I can't wait to see her,' Grace said. 'I think Mary was afraid she'd stay up there for Christmas, but I knew Tilly would never abandon her mother like that. Look, I better get back. Thanks for bringing the telegram, Nancy.'

The day went quickly, and Grace was so busy, she had little time to think of Maurice or anything else. Mary O'Hare had invited her up for tea, to be there when Tilly and Odile got home. Dymphna was still cleaning the farmhouse, and Tilly had finally given in and employed two young lads to work the farm when she was away, as Mary's arthritis was getting worse every year.

As she rang the school bell for the end of the day, Eleanor joined her in the yard. Douglas had to go back – his leave was only for four days – but it had done her a power of good to see him.

As they waved the children out the gate, Grace decided she'd start easy with the story of Maurice. Eleanor was English and Protestant and wouldn't understand how much of a scandal Maurice's sudden reappearance with a family would cause. She had to practise telling people. It would be awful for Maurice and Patricia if they managed to get here, exhausted and traumatised by all they'd lost and witnessed, to face shock and scandal. Best people knew in advance, instead of her waiting with bated breath every day Bobby the Bus pulled into the main street, wondering if today was the day.

As she opened her mouth to speak, Charlie came around the corner on his bike, back from the afternoon round of deliveries. He waved as he passed. '*Dia dhiobh a múinteoirí!*'

'*Dia is muire agat a*, Charlie,' called Eleanor proudly.

'The Irish is coming on great with you, Eleanor, keep it up,' he said in English. Charlie was bilingual as he read so much, but most people only spoke English haltingly and would revert to Irish by choice. Grace wondered if Maurice had lost his

Irish. He hardly could have, as he grew up speaking it, but she'd heard of people forgetting their mother tongue before. She hoped he hadn't. Being able to speak to the people of his own place would go a long way to reintegrating in the community. Would Mary and Kathleen come to this school? Of course they would. Her nieces. She found she loved the sound of it. Patricia sounded nice in her letter, sincere and decent, and Grace liked that she was at pains to point out that she'd not done anything wrong and neither had Maurice.

'Are you in a rush off?' Grace asked.

'No, not at all. Do you need me to do something?' Eleanor asked. She was a perfect colleague, totally capable and efficient but never overstepping. Grace was the headmistress, and Eleanor deferred to her in all things. She often said how grateful she was for the job, but Grace sometimes wondered if it was a comedown for her, to go from being principal of a huge school in Liverpool to just a classroom teacher here. She never gave that impression, but Grace thought she must feel it sometimes.

'No…well, I thought we might get some things ready for the Christmas concert. And Father Lehane has asked that the children sing the Mass on Christmas Eve. The church choir are doing the ten o'clock Mass.'

Grace felt sad that the bishop hadn't acted on her suggestion to return Father Iggy to Knocknashee. He never said he would of course, it had been a veiled hypothetical conversation, but he must have gambled that she wouldn't talk about the canon, and she didn't, and so he must have decided not to grant her request. Things were no better up in Cork for poor Father Iggy. He'd made a mortal enemy of the parish priest there for defying him about burying that poor girl who died in childbirth, and so life was not pleasant for him. He came to the Warringtons' for his tea once a week, and Lizzie said their hearts broke for him. He was so diminished – he'd got thin – and the whole situation with the convent for unwed mothers was breaking his heart. He was stoic of course and never complained, but Lizzie and Hugh both said his misery was written all over his face.

Grace wrote often, and he replied, cheery letters saying how much he looked forward to hearing from her, but he was a priest first and foremost and obedience was one of their primary vows, so he never complained. She didn't want to make it awkward for him, so she never mentioned his sadness either.

'Of course, and I thought we might do some artwork, maybe some paintings that we could put up around the place, cheer everyone up. I found a big tin of Hall's distemper in the attic – you know, that kind of strange paint with disinfectant in it or something? Douglas's father was a great man for slapping distemper on everything. Douglas always said, if you stood still, his father would paint you.' She laughed. 'It's as old as Methuselah, but I thought if we mixed a bit of the red we have here and some of the yellow as well, we'd make it go much further. I got a roll of newsprint when I was last in Tralee, and I thought if we rolled it out, they could do a lovely Christmas scene of the village maybe, Christmas trees and stars and that sort of thing, and we could put it up?'

Grace smiled. 'That's a marvellous idea. Let's do it.'

Eleanor was always coming up with ingenious ways to stretch their meagre resources. The children made models from mud, glue and sand mixed together and baked them in the range that heated the school. Then they painted them as gifts for their parents or siblings. She used gum to restore old schoolbooks for reuse and had reverted to chalkboards and chalk since paper was in such short supply. Grace had found a box of old blackboards in the school attic along with other discarded things from her parents' and Agnes's time, and Eleanor found uses for everything.

'Charlie brought me a note from Douglas this morning,' Eleanor said as she went to the art cupboard and surveyed its contents. 'He was saying Churchill was given his honorary wings to celebrate the twenty-fifth anniversary of the Royal Air Force. Everyone was very pleased, including the prime minister.'

Grace didn't mention how while some Irish people acknowledged the powerful role Churchill was playing in leading England through this war, he was not popular here. Churchill and Ireland had a long and bloody history. Nothing was ever simple.

'Cup of tea?' Grace asked, putting off the moment she had to say the words about Maurice aloud.

'That bad?' Eleanor smiled and went to fill the kettle. They had a little Primus stove they used to make tea when it was too warm for the range, so Eleanor lit it and placed the kettle on top. She took the tea caddy off the shelf and sighed. 'If they left one thing to us, it should be tea. The country runs on tea, but we've barely enough for one cup.'

'Let it steep for ages, and we'll stretch it,' Grace suggested.

While they waited for the kettle, Eleanor went back to the store cupboard and Grace tidied the piles of copybooks on the teacher's desk for marking, haphazardly deposited by the children as they left.

'Go on then. It's not your American friend, is it? Has something happened to him?' Eleanor asked as she examined a tin of ancient-looking paint.

'Well, no, he's fine. Well, he's not fine exactly. It's complicated...' Grace hadn't intended to talk about Richard. She'd promised Tilly she'd write to Richard, and she had, but when it came to it, she just couldn't write everything that was going on in her mind on the page, she was afraid of revealing her true despair, and so she just sent a short note of condolence. She knew he would be on tenterhooks waiting to hear from her.

Maybe Eleanor with her longer life experience could give her some advice. In one go, she blurted out the entire story. The lost letter from two years ago, the trip to America, Brendan McGinty, Declan's love for her, Richard turning up with Odile, her marriage to Declan, the called-off marriage to Pippa, the baby, the whole sorry tale.

Eleanor didn't interrupt; she kept working, putting old paintbrushes in a jar of water to soften. She let Grace finish and then wiped her hands and poured two cups of tea.

Eleanor examined her cup with a look of displeasure.

'It barely colours the water.'

They sat on the teacher's desk, side by side, the dust motes dancing in the dry classroom air.

'That's quite a story, Grace,' Eleanor said with a smile.

'It's a mess is what it is,' Grace replied miserably.

'Not necessarily,' Eleanor countered. 'You are a widow, and you loved your husband, but he's gone so you are free. So is Richard. Surely it's just a matter of deciding if you love him, if he's the one you want, and then finding out if what he wrote two years ago is still true?'

When Eleanor put it that way, it did sound very straightforward.

'So? Do you love him, Grace?'

'I…I think I do. I…I know I do, but I always

thought loving Richard Lewis was like loving Buster Keaton or Clark Gable, not like a real thing, not something that could ever really happen.'

'But supposing it could, is that what you want?' Eleanor persisted.

'I don't know. We… Everything is so different. I live here, I speak Irish for God's sake. He can't come and live here. I can't go there. My life here is…well, my life. My friends…my family…'

'I'm sure everyone here wants only the best for you, Grace. They want you to be happy. And with your parents gone and now your sister too, maybe it's time you made a family of your own.'

'My brother is coming home,' she said quietly.

'Your brother?' Eleanor clearly had no idea that Grace even had a brother.

'Yes, my brother, Maurice…'

'Oh yes, the priest. He's out somewhere in Asia – China, was it?'

'The Philippines. And he's not a priest any longer. His wife wrote to me a few days ago. That's one of the reasons I haven't written back to Richard – I've been so dumbfounded. I had no idea. He rarely wrote, and when he did, it was just to say a Mass was being offered for my intentions. I was so hurt and angry. When Mammy and Daddy died, the Mass, then when Agnes died, another Mass. One each Christmas, that was it. No inquiry as to how I was, his only living relative.' The bitterness in her voice was palpable.

'So he left the priesthood and got married but never said?' Eleanor was struggling to understand.

'And has two daughters.'

'My goodness, that is a lot to take in,' Eleanor said, shaking her head incredulously. 'And he's coming home?'

'He's trying to anyway. They were in Manila when it fell to the Japanese. They managed to escape, been hiding out in the countryside, and they have some friend in the American military who got them passage on a boat. They are trying to get here via the Suez Canal as far as I understand it.'

Eleanor gave a little chuckle. 'I imagined when I arrived in Knocknashee that not much could ever happen here, a sleepy little place like this, but it turns out quite the opposite is the case.'

'I used to think that too when I lived here. Once I left the hospital in Cork and I was living with Agnes, I used to try not to think about the years stretching out ahead of me, empty, nothing happening. But now that I'm living my life, a bit less excitement would suit me well.' Grace sighed ruefully.

'Well, war is strange. It causes such devastation, such loss and grief and destruction, but it also opens doors and focusses the mind,' Eleanor said thoughtfully.

'How do you mean?'

Eleanor sighed, sipped her tea, winced at the taste and put the cup on the desk. She paused, as if contemplating if she should speak or not.

'I don't usually talk about this, but it might be of some use to you, so I will. Douglas and I were about to divorce when the war broke out. Things hadn't been good since Libby was little, and he had an affair with a woman in his workplace, a secretary, much younger, pretty – the cliché, you know?'

It was Grace's turn to be shocked. 'Eleanor, how terrible for you.'

'It was. I didn't know what to do. The first summer of the war, August 1940, we were attacked in Liverpool. We'd evacuated the girls at the start. But then nothing seemed to happen, and it seemed so pointless that they were so lonely in Shropshire and I was sitting at home, missing them. Douglas had joined up by then. We agreed to hold off legal proceedings until after the war. So, I brought the girls home, and that August, on a nice sunny afternoon, I had taken them to my friend Barbara's house – her daughters were the same age. She lived on Stanhope Street. Douglas knew I was going – he was home for a while to run the local recruiting office, although we both felt it was best if we didn't spend too much time together. I was very angry with him for being unfaithful, and he seemed not as contrite as I felt he should be. I didn't even know if he was still carrying on with her.'

Grace's heart went out to Eleanor. She remembered the joy on her colleague's face when she saw her husband a few weeks ago, so something must have happened to change things, but life really was much more complicated than she'd ever imagined it could be.

'We were going to stay there, it was Barbara's birthday, she was forty and we planned to have a drink to celebrate her. I can't say why exactly, but I decided to go home that night. Libby had a bit of a cold and she was fractious, and I thought she'd sleep better in her own bed. I got the bus home with the girls instead. Douglas was out when we got back – I assumed he was with her – so I put the girls to bed and I turned in myself. He snores, so I put in earplugs. The next thing I know, someone is banging on the door, the girls are awake and crying, and it's the early hours. I went downstairs, and there is Douglas, dishevelled, bleeding, no keys or wallet, and he was distraught. He'd been working late, heard the bombers coming and it became obvious the docks were the target. He knew we were at Barbara's right by the shipyard. He ran there. Her house was hit – she died that night, she and her little girls.' Eleanor's voice caught with the emotion of telling such a sad story.

'Her husband was at sea, merchant marine. His boat got torpedoed a year later, and he went down with the ship. Probably just as well – Stan couldn't live without Barbara and his kids.'

Grace didn't know what to say; there was nothing *to* say.

'Douglas thought we were there too, the ARP man said it was a direct hit, it could be days before anyone could be found, so he ran home frantic. He cried tears of relief when he found us there.

That night we stayed up all night, talking. He was sorry for the affair. It was a silly thing, he said, meant nothing. I went a bit strange after Libby was born, got very cranky and wouldn't let him near me, he could do nothing right. It didn't excuse him, but it kind of explained it. We agreed to try again, said we loved each other, and we've made a go of it. It's not always easy, but life can take funny turns, you know.'

'And you're glad you stayed?' Grace asked. She couldn't imagine what it would have felt like if Declan had gone off with another woman.

'I am. I couldn't just turn off the feelings of hurt and anger and all the rest. But we were both sorry, and war… Well, the idea that he'd lost me and the girls, it nearly killed him too, and I realised that if he went to war with us at loggerheads and something happened to him, angry as I was, I would never forgive myself.'

'I suppose we're all just human, we make mistakes…'

'We do, all the time. But love matters, Grace. Marriage is very hard, harder than anyone ever tells you it's going to be, but love…that's not something that comes along every day, and not something you should dismiss lightly either.'

'Are you talking about me now or my brother?'

Eleanor turned to her and smiled, clinking her cup off Grace's. 'Both of you, I think.'

CHAPTER 20

Tilly was full of the excitement of Dublin at Christmas, the lights and the shops, and even though the war had caused everything to be in short supply, there was still a magic to it. The city really had enchanted her. Knocknashee by comparison must have seemed very drab.

People did their best. They'd have little homemade gifts and mothers would scrabble together the makings of a nice dinner, but that was about all people could manage.

Over a roast lamb dinner prepared earlier by Dymphna, followed by an apple tart with the top of the milk, Tilly kept Grace and Mary entertained with her stories of the capital.

Grace was awed by the change in her friend.

She still wore men's clothes, but now they were well-cut shirts and tailored trousers. Her dark wavy hair was cut to her jawline and tucked behind one ear. She was still strong and slender, but she was possessed of a new kind of elegance, and Grace saw the hand of Eloise. The only thing that remained the same was her crooked front tooth. Buachaill, her dog, was at her feet; he hated it when Tilly went away, so when she came home, he was like her shadow.

Mary eventually went to bed, leaving the two girls chatting by the fire. Odile was fast asleep upstairs; the journey had tired her out. Grace thought she'd even grown in the time she'd been gone.

'I missed you both,' she said to Tilly as she stoked the fire. They settled in the mismatched easy chairs either side of the hearth.

'We missed you too, Grace. Will you come next time? Marion said you've an open invitation, though the place is swarming with kids so it's probably a bit of a busman's holiday for you.' Tilly winked. 'Now, how are things with the handsome Yank.'

Grace smiled but didn't say anything. Tilly misinterpreted her silence.

'Ah, Grace, you did write didn't you? You

promised me you would. I know you're still so heartbroken over Declan, but he'd want you to live your life, to be happy, you know? He wouldn't want you giving up.'

'I'm not,' Grace said simply. 'I wrote and it's all fine. Now how are things with Eloise?' She wanted time to think before getting more advice.

Tilly flushed, getting the message that Grace didn't want to talk about it. 'Really good. She knows so many people. We go to the theatre and to concerts and dancing... She knows lots of women, well, like us.'

'It must be marvellous to be somewhere where you feel at home.' Grace reached over and placed her hand on her friend's.

'It is.' A shadow of something fleeting passed over Tilly's face. 'I think maybe when Mam... well, when she's gone, I might leave here, go to Dublin, or London even. I met a writer in Dublin, Kate O'Brien – she's from Limerick, but she's lived in London and Manchester and even Spain. She's a journalist and a playwright and a novelist, and she's lovely, very down to earth. She told me she never really knew what way her life was going to go. She kind of was led in various directions and had experiences, but she had no idea what would happen next. It sounded so exciting.

She knows everyone, is friends with Seán O'-Casey, people like that, and she lives such an interesting life. It struck me, Grace, that we don't have that here.'

'How do you mean?' Grace asked.

'Well, just that everyone – well, not everyone, my brother, Alfie, is an example – but most people here will live very predictable lives. Grow up here, marry someone local, have a tribe of kids and live very much as their parents did.' The way Tilly described it, it sounded like a death sentence.

'But you want something else?'

'I do. I think I would have wanted it anyway, even if men interested me. But Marion left, then Alfie, and I was the last one here. And don't get me wrong, Grace, I love Mam and I wouldn't leave her, but sometimes I feel like my choices are limited.'

'And you've Odile now as well.'

'Funnily enough I don't mind that. If I could go, I'd just take her with me. I got her the cutest little thing in Dublin, from Daidi na Nollag – it's a little rocking horse. She'll be so excited when she sees it Christmas morning. I never imagined I'd have a child of my own, you know – I knew I'd never marry so. But somehow I got Odile. To tell you the truth, I kind of dread the day her mother turns up. Obviously for her sake, I hope she does, but giving her back will break my heart.'

Grace knew what she meant. 'I often wonder if she's out there, somewhere in the world, fretting over Odile. I try to send her a message that her daughter is fine, well looked-after and loved.'

'I do too. Poor little pet to have lost so much before she even got started in life. I hope Bernadette is alive, and Constance and my brother of course. I think I'd know, I'd feel something, if Alfie was dead. Or maybe I wouldn't. Or it could be because Mam says he isn't, and you know how uncanny she can be. She says he's alive. And I believe her.'

'Hope is all we have, patience and hope.' Grace sighed. 'So one day you'll be leaving me for the bright lights, is that it?'

'One day, I think so. But you're a more seasoned traveller than I am – maybe you'd come too? Once this damned war is over and the world gets back to normal, maybe we'll both strike out like a pair of pirates and see where the wind blows us?'

Grace smiled. She and Tilly used to pretend to be pirates when they were little. No dollies and dresses for Tilly.

'Do you ever wish that you and Eloise could be, well, more public, you know, be like a couple?' Grace asked.

Tilly thought about it. 'In Dublin we kind of are. We're not holding hands or anything, but I wouldn't want to do that in public with anyone – you know how prickly I am.' She grinned. 'But in that world, with the writers and theatre people and political people, it's sort of known and nobody thinks it strange. It feels like I can breathe.'

'Tell me about it,' Grace urged. It was good to think about someone else for a while, and Tilly hadn't that many people she could be herself with.

'Well, we went to a Christmas fundraiser for this hospital, St Ultan's, and it's run by that doctor from Mayo, Kathleen Lynn, and her friend – well, more like her wife honestly – Madeleine ffrench-Mullen, who was in the Citizen Army and went to prison in 1916 and everything. Both of them were very political, but they're getting on in years now. But Grace, it opened my eyes. Women can do more than just live – we can thrive. Women like Helena Moloney, Louie Bennett, Elizabeth O'Farrell, Nurse O'Farrell they called her – she came out of the GPO with the white flag of surrender after the Rising?'

Grace nodded. She knew exactly who Tilly was talking about.

'Well, they were all there, all women like me and Eloise, doing these amazing things, unashamedly being who they are, not afraid or cowing in the corner, not just living their lives quietly in the shadows, in fear, but making a real difference. Suffragettes, trade unionists, republicans, Cumann na mBan, doctors – they are incredibly impressive. And they were so kind, so friendly to me. I never felt part of anything before. I have you – and God, without you, Grace, I think I might have walked into the sea with the loneliness of it all. I thought there was something deeply wrong with me, that I was unnatural, as the canon said. But being up in Dublin, surrounded by women like them, I felt for the first time like I was not an abomination.'

'And you are not! You are a wonderful person, Til, so brave and strong and capable. Everyone is in awe of you. But I understand – it must be hard to feel outside of things because of who you are. So I'll probably be clinging to your ankles when the time comes, but I'll let you go.'

'Well, come with me, live your life too. It doesn't have to be here in Knocknashee forever.'

'I don't know. We'll see.'

'What's going on, Grace? Something is on your mind, but you're not telling me.' Tilly had her mother's astuteness.

Tilly was her best friend, and she was open about her secrets. Grace knew her reticence wasn't in telling her friend; it was because she was afraid she would tell Eloise, and for some reason it mattered that she didn't. She couldn't put her finger on why it mattered, but it did. Eleanor's voice cut through her thoughts.

Just ask her not to say it to anyone.

Her colleague's simplistic way of thinking was refreshing. She saw things in a very clear way, not the muddled 'but what if, and what would people think' way that Grace did.

'All right. I didn't say it because I was afraid you'd tell Eloise, and I'm not ready for it to be public knowledge yet. So will you keep it to yourself?'

It wasn't that hard. She felt proud of herself. Being a child with a disability and feeling like a burden meant she was always trying to bend herself to suit others, not to be a nuisance, not to have people think she was self-absorbed. But she'd just asked her friend something and the world hadn't exploded.

'Of course, I won't say a word to anyone,' Tilly

replied, as if the request was perfectly reasonable and she was happy to comply.

So, slowly and clearly, Grace told her the whole story about Maurice.

Tilly, like Eleanor, sat and listened patiently, allowing her to finish.

'Right, well sure, that's just how it is. People will have to get over it.' Tilly shrugged 'Now more to the point, and I know you shut me down earlier, but what's happening with Richard?'

'Nothing. I sympathised and said Pippa sounded like a lovely person and I sent my condolences to them both.'

'But nothing about loving him?' Tilly gasped in exasperation 'That was the whole point, Grace.'

'I couldn't,' she replied simply. 'I just… I don't think I'll ever be able to say those words, and it felt so wrong when he was grieving and –'

'Ah, Grace, stop, will you? You're free and he's free and you love each other, so all you have to do is tell him and it will be like a fairytale ending.' Tilly beamed with delight.

'It's not that simple, though…'

'Why isn't it?'

'Well, it's just… I don't know. Loads of reasons. Firstly, she broke it off with him, so maybe if she had never done that, he would not have come looking for me. I don't want to be a consolation prize.'

Tilly howled with laughter.

'What?' Grace asked hotly, offended that Tilly was laughing at her thinking she might be worth more than second choice.

'You are the main prize where he's concerned, you donkey, you always were. But he is honourable and was doing the right thing, sticking by the girl he got pregnant.'

'Well, yes…about that.' Grace was blushing to the roots of her hair now, but she had to say it. 'I know it's not like years ago, but I'm not the kind of person who would…well, you know…before marriage, and he clearly is, so maybe we're not as in tune as I thought we were. It's a sin, Tilly. A serious one.'

Tilly sighed then. 'Grace, the Church has us all driven half cracked, and they're obsessed with sex – it must be on account of not having it themselves or something, who knows? But I think normal people should spend less time worrying about what they call a mortal sin and more time thinking about what's right. Two young healthy people, doing no harm to anyone, in a world where we could all be dead tomorrow – is having sex the worst thing you could do?'

'I suppose not,' Grace said glumly. The thought of Richard and Pippa naked in bed together upset her in ways she couldn't even begin to understand. Was her outrage because it was a sin or because she was jealous? 'I feel bad. Declan isn't dead that long and poor Pippa lost everything. It feels wrong...'

Tilly stood and knelt before Grace, taking her hands in hers. 'Grace, I feel like a broken gramophone record, over and over the same thing, but it doesn't seem to land in your thick head. Listen to me, please. All your life, you were second in the reckoning. You were the baby of the family, so nobody consulted you, then your mam and dad died, and then the polio. Agnes made you feel like you weren't entitled to much and you should be grateful for everything, and I loved Declan McKenna too, but we both know he wasn't your true love.'

Grace opened her mouth to object, but Tilly cut across her. 'You loved him dearly, and he knew it, Grace. He and I talked about it. He said he knew that Richard Lewis was the person you really wanted, but he adored you and if Lewis wasn't an option, then he was going to take his chance. He loved you and was happy to have most of you, but he knew you were never all his.'

That realisation stabbed at Grace's heart. Poor Declan.

'He wasn't sad, Grace, he was happy, I swear to you. He was sure Richard Lewis was going to sweep you away, and when it didn't happen, he decided to be brave and ask you. He told me himself that he felt he'd won the sweepstakes when you agreed to marry him, and he told me he was going to dedicate his life to making you happy. So don't feel bad – you did nothing wrong. You loved him, you made him so happy, but he knew, and I truly believe he'd be happy for you to go to Richard now he's gone. All he ever wanted was for you to be happy.' Tilly was so sincere, it was hard not to believe her. Grace wanted to believe her so badly.

'But what about Pippa?'

Tilly gave an exasperated sigh. 'Ah, Grace, come on, we've been through this. Pippa knew, like Declan knew about you, that Richard wasn't ever going to be all hers, and the girl had enough gumption to hold out for someone better. I know, you could say the same about Declan, but he was willing to marry you and have most of you, and Pippa just wasn't willing to do that. I admire her, I don't pity her. Well, losing the baby was very hard of course, but she'll have other babies. But leaving that aside, she'll be fine. Or she won't. But either way she's not your responsibility. Pippa and Richard have nothing whatsoever to do with you. They made their decisions, or she did, on her own, so don't go taking that on as well, for God's sake.'

Grace had to laugh. Tilly didn't suffer fools gladly.

'So you write again, ideally try to meet him, maybe ask him to come over. Yes, ask him to come to Dublin over the Christmas holidays. He can travel easily enough with his press pass, and we'll go up, stay with Marion. You can see Eloise and spend some time with us, I'll show you around, and you can meet Richard and have it out for once and for all and let us all heave a sigh of relief.'

'I don't know, Tilly. What if I'm imagining it and I drag him all the way over here for nothing?'

Tilly exploded. 'Well, now I feel like you need a slap of a wet fish into the chops! Of course he loves you, you absolute donkey! He's adored you since that first bloody letter, a blind man could see that.'

'So says you.'

'So says everyone.'

'There's Charlie to consider too,' Grace said

quietly. 'I'd hate him to think I just forgot Declan and moved on.'

'Charlie loves you like a daughter. And just like Declan, he'll be happy for you, you know he will.'

'So I should just write and ask him to meet me? Isn't that a bit…well…forward?'

'Yes it is, Grace. It's forward. And it's taking the initiative and it's putting yourself and your happiness first for once. So do it, woman, for God's sake. Do it before I throttle you!'

Grace smiled, and Tilly gave her a brief tight hug.

'All right, I will.' Grace exhaled. Her resolve was strong. Tilly was right. She was a free woman, and she had a right to say what she wanted to say, and maybe there was a happy-ever-after for her. 'We'll go up after Christmas? School will be off until the tenth of January.'

'Perfect. Marion will be delighted. We might even convince Mam to come. Colm bought a huge house out near the sea in Malahide. It's a massive old place, plenty of room for us. Half falling down, but he and Marion are doing it up. I'm helping too, so she minds Odile while he and I mix cement and lay blocks.'

'I can just picture you.' Grace chuckled. 'Fine,

I'll write tomorrow. I hope he can come.' What if he couldn't get away?

'He'll come. Just you watch, Grace Fitzgerald. I'd bet my eyes on it. Neither Hitler nor wild horses will stop Richard Lewis crossing the Irish Sea to see you.'

'And if I've got this all wrong, and he just sees me as a friend?' Grace hated how pathetic she sounded.

Tilly's eyes blazed with intensity. 'You haven't got it wrong, Grace, and even if it doesn't work out, you've done what you want, you've spoken up for yourself, said your piece. You are the bravest person I've ever known. You fight like a lion for everyone else – fight for yourself now.'

CHAPTER 21

LONDON

DECEMBER 1942

Richard took notes at the press conference regarding the war in North Africa.

After what felt like years of bad news, it was nice to be writing about a victory. And this was undoubtedly a more optimistic outlook than six months previously, though there was still a lot to do. They were holding the island of Malta and were happy to have established footholds in the

North African region. The army press officer called it a decisive American victory and an opportunity for Germany to see just what they were dealing with. Despite a plethora of questions, the press officer as usual walked off the podium and left. The US Army didn't take questions from anyone, least of all hacks like them.

As he and the gathered journalists shuffled out muttering, Richard knew there was as much to be learnt in the bar after these events as there was at them. The military Office of Censorship made sure that only what was approved was published, and woe betide anyone who strayed outside of that. If a paper wanted access to the military, credentials had to be sought from them, and that was on the condition that the papers played ball. It wasn't that the army told untruths about the progress of the war, but they were certainly circumspect about what they allowed people to know.

It was one of the reasons Jacob was so excited about going up with the bombers – seeing and experiencing the war with their own eyes and ears, not the version approved by the generals.

'No mention of the coal disputes, I notice,' Charles Heughan of the *Los Angeles Times* said to Richard as they shuffled to the bar. He had been their foreign correspondent since 1920 and knew everyone and everything. Richard had befriended him when he happened to mention his son was trying to buy a property in Orlando, Florida, but was running into all sorts of problems securing the financing. Richard told him to contact his father and say he was a friend, and sure enough the deal was done and Charles was grateful. Richard liked him enormously, though many people didn't. He shot from the hip, had no patience for time-wasters and assumed that all politicians and military people were lying in the first instance. He was a tall, heavy man, with a shock of white hair in need of a cut and a cream linen suit that was entirely without shape. He and his wife, who was with him in London – they stayed together all the time – had invited Richard and Pippa to dinner at the Ritz once his son got the keys to his place. Angelica Heughan was a tiny Spanish woman, the epitome of chic. They were an odd pairing, but it seemed to work.

'How bad is it likely to get?' Richard asked.

'Pretty bad,' Charles answered. 'If they can't come to some arrangement, half a million coalminers could walk off the job. FDR is saying, behind closed doors of course, that if they cause a ruckus, he'll order them back to work, and if they ignore him, then he'll issue an executive order allowing the secretary of the interior to take over the mines by force if necessary, which would go down about as well as you'd expect it to.'

He ordered a whiskey and raised an eyebrow at Richard.

'Thanks, I'll have a cup of coffee please.'

'And a coffee,' he said to the young bartender, throwing some coins on the counter. Though he lacked manners, which embarrassed Richard a bit, the bartender didn't seem to care, considering the tip was generous.

'So is that going to happen, do you think?'

Richard remembered something Jacob had observed about Charles, which was that a lot of reporters liked to give the impression they knew more than they did, but Charles did the opposite. He knew everything that happened but never let on. He'd given Richard some really great tip-offs since they'd been in London.

Jacob said that Charles liked Richard because he always came across as humble and curious. Richard wasn't sure that was true, but he didn't see the point of pretending to know about things he didn't.

Charles was one of the reporters who seemed

to hear things long before anyone else. He had impeccable sources and used them wisely.

He gave the question some thought, his mouth downturned. 'Well, according to my sources, at any one time, we've only got enough coal for about three weeks in the steel business and about ten days for the railroads, so I sure hope FDR has a plan.'

'What's the dispute about?' Richard asked, nodding his thanks to the bartender for the coffee.

'What's it ever about? Money.' Charles smiled. 'My guess is FDR will try the patriotism route, since strong-arm tactics probably wouldn't work. Remind them how their sons and brothers over here need the hardware. What are we gonna do, abandon our boys on the front?'

'Will that work?'

'It better,' Charles replied darkly, draining his whiskey in one gulp and standing up. He tapped Richard's shoulder with his rolled-up newspaper. 'Take care, kid.' And he was gone.

Richard decided to go back to the apartment to write up his piece. Kirky was anxious they report the truth, but the subtext was, focus on good news stories. He was to write a review of the comedy

Road to Morocco starring Bob Hope, Bing Crosby and Dorothy Lamour. He'd sat in the theatre alone, trying to force himself to focus on the dumb plot. How he'd find something good to say about it, he had no idea, but Sarah and Jacob had seen it too and thought it was very funny, so maybe it was just him. Nothing made him happy these days.

Richard understood what Kirky and the other editors were trying to do. As well as sell newspapers, they were doing what they could for the war effort by boosting morale. He would never say tone down the bad stuff and ramp up the good, but that was what he meant, and Richard was generally happy to oblige. Besides, work kept his mind off the fact that he'd received such a curt letter from Grace.

He drained his coffee and left his fellow reporters to their conversation, heading home. He had a lot of work to catch up on.

When he got back, he made himself a cup of tea and some toast. There wasn't any other food in the house. There were some letters propped on the table: a bill; one from Nathan to both him and Sarah – Sarah must have opened it; and a funny card from Pippa with a picture of a smiling dog on the front. It was typically Pippa, light and funny. *I'm fine, Mr America, stop fretting. Are Irish eyes smiling yet?*

Sarah appeared from her and Jacob's bedroom into the living room, reading the card over his shoulder. 'Well, are they?' she demanded.

He shook his head.

'Well, Pippa wrote to me and told me she's spending time with that Wojtec guy in Manchester. She got him a job in her factory, and he's been sent up there too – he was some kind of engineer back in Poland, so they're delighted with him. They seem to be getting on well.'

Richard grimaced but said nothing. He didn't begrudge Pippa her happiness, and Wojtec, like her, had lost everyone he loved, so they would be a good match maybe.

Sarah kissed his head as she swiped his toast off his plate. 'There are further peace talks in Savannah. Nathan and Rebecca took them both for dinner. Daddy's moved back home, and Mother even said something nice about our wedding.'

'Amazing.'

'I know. They're even talking about taking a ten-day trip on the *Arabella*, and mother hates the water.'

The *Arabella* was their father's yacht, which spent almost all of its life moored at the yacht club because Arthur Lewis was too busy to sail it and his wife detested the sea.

'Good for him.' Richard meant it. 'Though ten days in an enclosed space with our mother…well, I wouldn't sign up for it.'

'Me neither. I can't see her ever really melting, but I guess it's better if they're together. Who knows? I think I did like having Daddy to ourselves, though.'

'I know what you mean, but we thought we had two cold-fish parents, and it turns out our father is OK, he's a nice guy, so that's a bonus we didn't expect. She's got ice in her veins, and that's just how it is. I agree, it might have been better for us if they divorced. Who knows – he might have met someone nice. But they are traditionalists at heart, not just her, him too, and divorcing is "just not for our kind of people".' He mimicked their mother's snobby Savannah tones.

'I know. And if she can live with my choice, even if she's not thrilled about it, I guess I have to put up with her. I see so many women in the refugee centres, you know? Mother and daughters, mothers without daughters, daughters without mothers. And the love and grief they share if they are dead or separated is something I understand but will never experience.' She sighed.

'You would if you became a mother maybe?' Richard ventured, almost wincing at the question. He knew children were a no-go area for Sarah, but he worried she was making that decision based on their own mother.

'Don't you start. Daddy pulled me aside at the wedding and said that if I didn't want kids, that was fine by him, but that I was not Caroline Lewis, and that if I chose it, I'd be different, and that being a parent was the best thing about his life and he didn't want me to miss out on that because of the mother I got.'

Richard shrugged; no words were necessary. He secretly applauded his father for going where everyone else feared to tread.

'I'm dreading you guys going in the bombers – you know that, don't you?' she asked, changing the subject. 'Jacob won't discuss it. He says he's going and there's no point in what-ifs.'

They'd never discussed the very real danger of what they were planning to do.

'Where is he now?' Richard asked.

'He's gone to meet a man who has some eyewitness testimony of the Jews in the Zborów ghetto in Eastern Poland. Killings, disease, hunger, the endless slaughter – it's hard to hear but we must hear it. He escaped, miraculously.'

Normally the stories of refugees and escapees moved Sarah to action, to help, to resist, but something about the way she said it this time – she sounded so weary and broken.

'We will win. This will end,' Richard said, standing up and drawing her into a hug.

'Maybe, but how many more will die before then? And will you and Jacob be among the millions?' She cried then, silent, sad tears.

'I hope not, but we might be,' Richard said. 'But as Jacob says, if we were civilians at home, we'd probably have been drafted by now, so we've been lucky so far. Our luck might last.'

'Or it might run out,' Sarah said into his chest.

'It might. But that doesn't mean we don't do our bit, right?' He lifted her chin to meet her eyes.

'I guess,' she said with a sigh.

'Will you promise me something?'

'What?'

'If we don't…well, if we don't make it…go home? Please?'

She looked at him for the longest time, then nodded. 'I promise.'

CHAPTER 22

LONDON

JANUARY 1943

Christmas passed as such a non-event. There was nothing available to make a celebration, and though their father sent a big gift box, the shipping got delayed and it only arrived today. It didn't matter. Richard was glad it was over. The work was enough to keep him busy and keep his mind off Grace. But it was Saturday morning, and he was taking a break.

Dear Father,

Thank you for the gifts and treats. As usual they are much appreciated. Sarah gives a lot of the things you send away. She and Jacob still work with refugees. Sarah also writes for several magazines on top of freelance pieces for Kirky, and Jacob is taking photographs for the Capital *but also the* Daily Worker. *You're right to be very proud of her. She could be living the high life of a Southern lady, but she chooses to stay here with the scarce but terrible food and god-awful weather. It's January, and it's been raining since September as far as I can see.*

I'm busy with work. Kirky has an insatiable appetite, and most of my and Jacob's pieces get syndicated now, so the Capital *is getting its money's worth out of us. I'm glad to be busy, though.*

He couldn't tell his father about the air force training or the bombing raid even if he wanted to, and he didn't want to. He knew Arthur Lewis would blow his top if he knew his son was putting himself in harm's way on purpose. If he did go up there and get blown to smithereens, he wanted to have at least been honest with his father, but he couldn't be. Not about that anyway. But he could be truthful about how he felt. He wrote on.

I'm glad to hear things are better between you and Mother. And please forgive me if this is impertinent, but really think about it before you commit to anything again. I know she's your wife and all, but we're only getting one shot at this life, and it would be a shame to waste it with someone who can't or won't make you happy.

This war has taught me this—nothing is promised, not tomorrow, not next week, and we have a duty to ourselves to try to be happy. My friend Grace is religious. She's Catholic and very sure of an afterlife, but I don't share her confidence. Maybe there is, but maybe there isn't, and if not, then this is all we have and we should at least try to make the best of it.

Speaking of Grace, you asked me what the situation is between her and me. Well, here goes.

Richard found himself pouring the whole story onto the page. On and on he wrote, telling his father about Pippa, Grace and his feelings about the whole sorry mess.

Four pages later he stopped. He'd never in his life been so honest with anyone, except Grace of course. Maybe his father would be shocked. He had intended to tell him about the baby and the wedding and everything at the time, but that all disintegrated and he'd never sent the letter.

So there you have it. The whole unvarnished truth. I'm sorry if I'm a disappointment to you. I was trying to do the right thing. And before you say it, I know, sleeping with a girl before marrying her is not the right thing, but apart from that I was.

Pippa was wiser than I. She knew I would never be happy with anyone but Grace, but since Grace hasn't written since the short letter sympathising about the baby, I have to assume that ship has sailed.

Sarah knows how I feel, and if anything ever happens to me, I've told Sarah to inform Grace and treat her like family. She may not care at this point, but if she does, I'd appreciate it if you would do the same. I hope to survive this war, as we all do, but just in case, I want you to know that I am very grateful for that first night you came to St. Simons to see Sarah and me. It was wonderful to see you in New York and have the wedding in Savannah. I value our relationship.

I love you.
Your son,
Richard

It was the most emotional he'd ever been with his father. The first time he'd ever said that he loved him. He sealed the envelope and attached a stamp. He strolled to the mailbox across the street and thought of all the letters to Grace he'd sent. Should he try again? Try to explain more? Beg her forgiveness? He knew it would be pointless. Sarah thought his letter was unclear in its intentions, but he didn't think so. Grace would know. And she'd chosen not to respond to it. Grace was a person of deeply held principles; she'd made up her mind.

He dropped the envelope in the box, and as he crossed back to the apartment he saw the telegram boy on his bike. Some poor family was getting a 'We regret to inform you…'

Richard felt so sad for these kids whose job it was to deliver the telegrams notifying next of kin of a death in action. One of Pippa's friend's brothers did it, and Richard had asked to meet him. He did a piece on it, and though it was heart-wrenching, Kirky ran it. The boy, who was only sixteen, said the reactions varied. Some were stoic, others angry. But it was the mothers who howled like a wounded animal, or cried hard, silent tears, or refused to take the telegram, backing away from him as if by refusing to touch it, it wasn't true, those were the hardest. Their hearts were shot down over foreign fields, places they'd never been. Those were the people the kid would never forget. Those precious boys killed by Germans, and over there too, German women cried just the same as our side killed their boys and broke their hearts. That piece, the futility of it all, the sheer waste, had nearly broken Richard too.

He nodded at the boy, who stopped his bike and checked the number on the door. 'Number seventeen?' the boy asked. He was only thirteen or fourteen, thin as a rake – but all Londoners were – with spiky blond hair and freckles.

'That's right.'

'You Richard Lewis?'

'I am.'

'Telegram for you.' He handed him the small buff envelope and cycled away. He clearly didn't want to hang around to see Richard's reaction to the contents, even at his young age he knew it was rarely good news.

There on the sidewalk, he opened it, and his heart thumped in his chest.

Can you come to Dublin 8 January? Meet Shelbourne hotel 3 p.m. Grace

He half walked, half ran down the street.

The post office was just closing for lunch as he arrived.

'Please, I just need to send a telegram,' he begged.

The tall, thin postmaster with the hooked nose and enormous ears, snapped, 'Closed now till Monday.'

'Oh no…please…it's urgent…'

'Always are, mate…but so's my lunch.' He laughed, a wheezy sound.

'Please, I really need…' It was the second now. If he waited until Monday, it might be too late for Grace to make arrangements to go to Dublin; she might think he didn't want to meet her. Getting himself over there in this short timeframe would be enough of a problem.

'You're that Yank living in the mews house, ain't ya?' the postmaster asked.

'Yes, I am.' He smiled, hoping his American identity was a good thing; you never could tell.

'You got stockings?'

'Pardon me?' Richard wondered if he'd heard him right..

'Stockings, ladies' stockings…you got some?'

'Er…no…not on me…' Richard had no idea where this was going.

The man looked at him as if he was mad. 'I know you haven't got them on you, you daft beggar. I mean do you have any?' He spoke loudly and slowly as if Richard was dim-witted. 'My missus keeps carping on day and night. Her mate is going dancing with some Yanks and got some stockings, and now my ball and chain can't shut up about them.'

'Oh, right.' Richard realised. He thought of the

latest box from Savannah. He didn't think there were stockings in it.

'I don't have stockings, but' – he'd noticed the man's yellow pointing and index fingers – 'I have cigarettes, and some chocolate.'

The man beamed, and he reminded Richard of a giant goblin from a picture book he'd had as a child. 'That'll do nicely, son. You run off and get them and I'll send your telegram. Write out whatever you want there...' He pointed to a stack of old papers, previous messages written in pencil erased.

Richard did as he was told. *I'll be there. R.* And he gave the man the address.

He was back within ten minutes with a packet of cigarettes and a Hershey's chocolate bar. The postmaster took them greedily and shooed him out.

As he walked back, he passed the jewellery shop where he'd bought Pippa those earrings that she'd thought were a ring. He felt sick at the memory. Getting it all wrong again. Poor Pippa, after all he'd put her through, though he found the news that she and Wojtec were now friendly comforting.

He stopped and looked in the window at the trays of jewels that nobody had money to buy. He thought of the conversation with Sarah. Maybe the letter was not clear. Or maybe it was and she wanted to tell him to leave her alone. But she would never drag him all the way to Ireland to do that. What if… He allowed his mind to go to the best possible outcome. What if she was meeting him to tell him she felt the same?

He went in, the tinkle of the bell alerting the young woman, who was poring over a magazine that looked as old as she did.

'Hello, sir, can I help you?' She was like an eager bunny. Her blond hair was tied up in two bunches on top of her head.

Could she? Probably not. Was it presumptuous to buy Grace a ring? She still wore the one Declan gave her, a diamond. He'd seen it back in Knocknashee. Maybe he should hold off. Or even if it did go his way and he could propose to her, she might want to choose her own. Should he get one anyway, just to have on the day? Should he buy a massive one? There was one the size of a marble on a royal-blue cushion on its own, but he dismissed it. He didn't want to upstage Declan's small diamond, and anyway that wasn't Grace's style. Miranda Logan would have loved it, he realised, but not Grace.

'I'm just browsing…' he said, his voice husky.

'What does your girl, or your wife, like?' She came out from behind the counter and stood beside him. The girl wasn't going to let him out without buying something.

'Ah…do you have any claddagh rings? They're an –'

'Irish ring. Yeah, we do. Pricey, though, mind you…' She pulled out a tray of claddagh rings.

'Fourteen-carat gold, with an emerald heart, or a sapphire, or a diamond…'

Would Grace think it a bit dumb? An American buying a claddagh ring for an Irish girl? Was that a bit too cliché?

The girl persisted. 'What colour hair does she have?'

'Red. Well, copper really, curly copper hair – it's beautiful.' He blushed.

'Oh, you have got it bad.' She chuckled. 'All right then, Romeo, how about the one with the emerald?'

She took it out and handed it to him. The goldsmith had done an exceptional job. The two hands on the band had tiny emeralds at the cuff and the crown sat on top of the emerald heart, the intricate design just about visible, the cut emerald mounted perfectly.

He knew. 'How much?'

'Seventy-five pounds,' she said without flinching. 'It's handcrafted. Our goldsmith's mum was from Ireland, so he always makes them. They're surprisingly popular , we sell a lot of them.'

'Fine, I'll take it,' he said, taking out his chequebook. If by some miracle he got the guts or the opportunity to propose to her, he could use it as a temporary ring until she chose the one she wanted.

CHAPTER 23

KNOCKNASHEE

JANUARY 1943

Grace suppressed her delight when Charlie delivered the telegram on the evening of the first Saturday of 1943. *I'll be there.* Nothing more, but he'd replied immediately, and Grace allowed a glimmer of hope to build in her chest. Maybe Tilly was right and neither wild horses nor Hitler would stop him coming to see her.

She was taking down the bits of red-sprigged

holly and tinsel she'd put up around the house to make it more festive, but in truth, there was so little available that Christmas had been quiet. Everyone went to Mass of course, and the crib was there, and they went home to a roast chicken dinner if they were lucky, but the gifts and sweet treats of years gone by were a thing of the past. Dymphna managed to cobble together a plum pudding; Tilly, Mary and Grace gave her their ration of sugar and butter, and they managed to find some dried fruit. The breadcrumb was not the soft white she would usually use, it was coarse brown soda, and the pudding was not as sweet as usual, but as they all gathered at the McKennas', it was deemed a triumph. Tilly sacrificed a hen and brought the vegetables, and Grace knitted hats for everyone. She ripped out three of Agnes's finest wool sweaters, the last things she had of her sister's, and it made her smile to think of what Agnes would make of her fancy expensive knitwear keeping Charlie McKenna's head warm on his rounds.

'Good news?' Charlie asked, his kind face smiling. She should tell him, say something at least, but she just couldn't. To him, and to her, the loss of Declan loomed so large, the pain still so raw, it would feel like rubbing salt in an open wound.

'Yes, it's just from Richard. I hadn't heard from him in a while, so he's fine…' She hated lying.

The grey Atlantic was calm for once, though the cold was bitter. Charlie's face was weather-beaten from years of cycling into the sleety rain at this time of year.

'Will you have a cup of cocoa?' she asked. 'Lizzie sent me a jar for Christmas. It was so kind of her. I'd forgotten what it tasted like.'

'I should probably say no, keep it for yourself, but Grace, I'd kill you for a cup of hot cocoa.' He rubbed his freezing hands together in glee. 'I've finished my round, and Dymphna is gone into Dingle to see her mother.' He grimaced. Dymphna's mother was a sore trial, and it was tacitly decided early on that limiting her exposure to everyone, including Charlie, was for the best. A widowed postman was not good enough, but then neither was Dymphna's first husband, Tommy. For a woman who thought her daughter worthy of so much more, she showed no affection or pride in Dymphna. She endlessly criticised Paudie and Kate and only last week said she thought baby Seámus was 'a bit slow'.

'She's a saint, your wife, Charlie,' Grace laughed. 'I don't know how she puts up with that woman. May God forgive me, she's a bitter pill.'

'Same reason you put up with Agnes, I suppose – blood is thicker than water.' Charlie sighed. 'But she's a right dose, no doubt about it. Last time I met her, she told me that I'd better have made sure everything went to Dymphna when I died, and she wanted to know if my place was owned by the post office or did I own it. Clearly the implication was I'm not long for this world.'

Grace laughed. 'You'll outlive us all, Charlie McKenna. You're the fittest man in Knocknashee.'

'I hope I do. Poor Dymphna has had enough heartache.'

'Haven't we all?' Grace said as they stood side by side in her sitting room, the fire unlit. Fuel was too scarce, so she just lit the range in the kitchen. They watched the little fishing boats and *currachs* bobbing on the forbidding sea. The furze bushes along the coastline were bare and would not have their honey-sweet bright-yellow flowers for a while; for now it was just the hard spiked leaves.

'Come on into the kitchen where it's warm,' Grace said, dumping the decorations on the sofa.

'Or warmer at least. That turf in O'Donoghue's is sopping wet and only smoulders, but it's better than nothing, I suppose.'

Usually the neighbours all helped to cut each other's bog. It had always been a great day out, Grace remembered. Everyone had a picnic, and the men and boys would foot the turf and stack it on the bog to dry. The only bad thing was that the midges would eat you alive during the summer evenings. She smiled at the memory, how once the turf was dry and piled up on a cart to be pulled by a donkey, the young lads would have a competition to see who could balance upside down on top of the pile for the longest. It was great fun to watch them. It felt like a more innocent time.

There wasn't much fun these days. Turf was the only fuel source for the winter, but so many men were over in England working now – there was money to be made there doing all kinds of work – that the bogs remained uncut here. They were relying on turf from other places, and it wasn't dried out properly at all.

'Let you sit down, I'll make the cocoa. The leg looks sore with you – is it?'

'Thanks, Charlie,' she said gratefully, resting her leg. 'I've no gas for the water heater so I can't take my baths, but these are the times we live in.'

As Charlie heated milk – at least there was no shortage of that – and added the cocoa powder, she allowed herself a moment of inward glee. Richard was going to come to Dublin. She would see him in a week. And she was going to be brave. Tilly was right. She had to take a chance. Take the lead. Tell him how she felt. There was a chance he would say no, that he didn't want that kind of relationship, and if he did, she would accept it and hope, like he did when he wrote two years ago, that it wouldn't destroy their friendship.

He might say no. That thought was foremost in her mind. But somewhere behind it, like a bubble in a glass of lemonade, was a tiny effervescent thought. *He might say yes.*

The idea of it sent a wave of pleasure over her. Richard Lewis and her. They might be a couple. They might get married. She could be Mrs Lewis. Would the children call her Mrs Lewis, or would she forever be Miss Fitz? Richard had laughed when he heard that first.

'Miss Fitz, like misfits?' He'd grinned.

'I suppose so, but it's different in Irish,' she'd explained with a chuckle.

'How do you say it in Irish?' he'd asked that day on the beach.

'*Inion Nic Gearailt.*' She'd repeated it over and over so he could practise. The unfamiliar Irish words felt awkward in his mouth, he said.

Could he live here? Could he learn the language? What would he work at? Would he want to go back to America? Would she go too? What would she do over there? Teach? What about Tilly and Charlie and all her friends here? How could she leave them? And what if Maurice came back? Could she just greet him and pass him in the hallway, with a 'Cheerio, I'm off to America'?

She was getting ahead of herself as usual. One step at a time. She hadn't even spoken to him yet. And there was a war on. He'd be over in London until it was over, though it might just be on the turn. Churchill had just said that this was not the beginning of the end but perhaps the end of the beginning, which was hardly reassuring. Either way, Richard wouldn't be free to go anywhere for a good long while yet. That might be for the best, allow more time for people, Charlie especially, to get used to the idea. She could wait.

Charlie turned then, two mugs of cocoa in his hands, and sat opposite her at the kitchen table. 'No further word from Maurice?' he asked.

She shook her head. 'When Richard came back that way, it took weeks and weeks, so I don't expect to hear anything if they're at sea. I don't know the name of the ship, so even if a sinking was reported, I wouldn't know if it was theirs or not, so it's just a case of being patient and praying, I think.'

'How are you feeling about it now? Has it sunk in?' He sipped his cocoa and groaned in pleasure. 'Oh, I missed this. The simple things like a cup of cocoa.'

'I know. It's lovely, isn't it?' Grace smiled as she took a sip of hers.

So much had happened in recent times, she wondered if it had sunk in. Her brother was coming home with his family. She had a sister-in-law and two little nieces. And if they were lucky, and a German torpedo didn't get them, they would be living here, with her, in Knocknashee. This house where she'd lived with Agnes, and then with Dymphna and Paudie and Kate, and then with Declan. And now with her brother's family. Or would she? Might she leave Knocknashee altogether? It was all so much to process and everything dependent on so many other factors.

'Sometimes I think it has, but then other

times…I just can't visualise it, you know? I don't know him. I barely remember him honestly. He went off to the seminary when I was so young. He came home on holidays and so on, but he seemed to always be reading or out kicking a football with his friends. And then he was gone. I know now why – Nancy told me about the girl in the seminary he fell in love with, Patricia, now his wife, and how my father never wanted him to join the priesthood.'

Charlie nodded. 'I never knew about the girl, but no, Eddie never thought it was the right thing for Maurice. Your mother wanted the best education for him – what mother wouldn't – and she loved the idea of him being a priest. Irish mammies and their boys. I suppose if he was a priest, no woman would take him off her.'

Grace smiled ruefully. 'There may be an element of truth in that. Us girls don't seem to have the same importance with the mammies at all.'

'Ah, I don't know about that. I'm sure my Maggie would have doted on Siobhán, and I know Dymphna is very close to Kate, and Kathy was stone-mad cracked about you. I think she found Agnes…well, a bit difficult. And sure we know why now, that auld snake with his fangs in her, the poor girleen. But she and Kathy never really hit it off. But she was delighted altogether with you, Gracie, they both were.'

Charlie McKenna had been kept at arm's length from her by Agnes since her parents died, but ever since that letter from Richard, he'd been back in her life and had been such a rock of support and love. He was the closest thing she had to a father now, and she knew she owed him the truth.

'Charlie…' she began, the words struggling to form in her throat. 'I have to tell you something…'

He turned to her, his expression quizzical. 'Whatever it is, I'm sure it's not as bad as all that.' He winked playfully. 'You look like you're going to the gallows.'

'Two years ago, after he came here to deliver Odile, Richard Lewis wrote to me and told me he…well, that he loved me and that he wanted us to be together…' She swallowed.

Charlie didn't respond but waited for her to continue.

'But the letter never arrived. I don't know if you remember giving me a letter a while back, one that was battered and had been posted long before?'

His brow furrowed. 'I don't, to be truthful, but go on.'

'Well, I got it after…well, after Declan died. And so I never responded, and Richard and I never talked about it. It was all too late and…well, everything.'

This was hard but she had to continue. 'So then he met a girl, Pippa, and they were to get married but she called it off, said he didn't really love her, and that she wasn't willing to be second fiddle…'

'Wise woman by the sounds of it,' Charlie said with a small smile.

'So then he wrote and…' She stopped. Exhaled. Tried to form the words.

'Told you he loved you, and you love him too, but you were afraid to tell me in case I was upset on account of Declan,' he finished for her.

She swallowed and could only nod; no words would come. Tears pooled on her eyelids and flowed down her cheeks.

Charlie gently took the mug from her and placed it beside his on the table. Then he reached over and drew her hands into his. 'My darling Gracie, all I want is for you to be happy. Our Declan is gone, and we loved him, both of us, and he knew it, never doubted it, *a chuisle mo chroí*, and I know it broke your heart to lose him.' He looked deeply into her eyes, his weatherbeaten face kind. His rough thumbs reached up and wiped the tears from her face.

'But he, like me, would want you to live the best life you can, and if that's with Richard, then that's how it should be. He's a decent man, and a kind one, and if he's who you want, Gracie, then you should have him.'

'Do you mean it? You're not just saying it?'

Charlie laughed, taking his cup of cocoa again. 'Of course I mean it, you *oinseach*, and I'm hardly in any position to be telling you to stay in widow's weeds forever, now, am I? You're a lovely young woman, Grace, and nobody, least of all Declan, would want you wasting your precious life here grieving forever. I have Dymphna and the kids and Seámus now, and I thank God for them every day, but that doesn't mean I've forgotten Maggie or Declan or Siobhán ever, nothing like it. I think of them every single day. I hear Maggie giving out to me for not wearing my oilskins in the rain, or Declan asking me what we'll have for the dinner. And I live in eternal hope that Siobhán will turn up here some day, or I might even go over there to see her. But they all live in here' – he pointed to his chest – 'always.'

The tears came now in sobs, and he let her cry.

'Nothing real ever dies, Grace. This' – he waved his hand around – 'this comes and goes. Houses, schools, churches, our bodies even. But love…you can't see it, you can't sell it, you can only give it and receive it, and it never dies. And we'll see them again, somehow, somewhere, I know we will. But until we do, and it's our turn to go, we owe it to them to be happy. Remember how much he loved you, Gracie. Now love yourself that much in his honour, and go and live your life, girl.'

'I love you, Charlie.' It was her first time ever saying the words aloud.

'And I love you too,' he said, squeezing her hand.

CHAPTER 24

The days felt like months as she waited for the date they would go to Dublin. Mary was going to come too, and of course Odile, who went everywhere with Tilly, so it was a big expedition. Tilly had two young brothers working for her now, so they were well able to look after the farm. Ronán and Caoimhín Mac Thomáis were the two youngest of a family of six boys from a small holding. There wasn't enough land on the homeplace for them, so it was work for Tilly or face the emigrant boat. They were grateful for the work, and Tilly was very fond of them.

Mary O'Hare's arthritis was always better in Dublin. Marion and Colm's house was warmer than the farm, and it was nice for her to be taken care of for once.

Grace wished school wasn't off on holidays, because the days were dragging. She'd gone up to her parents' grave to say hello and to kill an hour in a day that seemed interminable. It had been hard at first to talk to her parents there the way she used to when Agnes was alive, because it was mostly complaints about her sister she let out up there, but knowing what she knew about Canon Rafferty and how he treated Agnes, she was more benevolent and told the three of them all the secrets of her heart.

Tilly had gone to the mart in Dingle to sell some lambs to fund the Dublin holiday, and as Grace returned to the village, Mary was walking down the street, her basket over one arm – she still baked for the shop – Odile holding tightly to her other hand.

She didn't wave or call a greeting as she normally would have done but walked straight up to Grace, her face ashen. 'I got this…' She shoved an envelope at Grace. It was a letter addressed to Mary O'Hare. The stamps were not ones Grace recognised. She extracted a single sheet of thin paper.

Senora O'Hare,

My name is Nico Gomez. I Spanish so my English no good. I friend of Alfie your boy. I know him in war in my country. Dutch soldier meet me and to tell me if I know Alfie, who is Alfie, and I say is he all right. He in France, working and alive. Helping for people coming in my country. Me also. I don't see, but soldier see him summer 1942 near Biarritz. He is different name now and looking too, but now you must know is he fine. Also Constance. Alfie tell soldier if he meet me to say is Alfie and Constance and say I write to Mama. He give me address in Spain 1936, say I write to Mama if he dead, but he no dead, no, he alive. Sorry bad English.

Saludos cordiales,

Nico Gomez

Grace read and reread it. There was no forwarding address or any other identification. This was all there was. 'Oh, Mrs O'Hare, this is wonderful. I'm so relieved.'

'I knew he wasn't dead. I just knew it in my bones.' Mary looked overwhelmed. 'He mentioned a friend called Nico in a letter, years ago.'

'Richard said a lot of people were escaping the Nazis by getting into Spain, so it sounds like Alfie is involved somehow with that, and he sent a message via one of the people he helped.'

Mary O'Hare sniffed, then nodded, and Grace knew she was fighting tears.

'Don't be sad, Mamó,' Odile said, still clinging to the hand of the only grandmother she knew.

'Mamó's crying happy tears, Odile.'

Grace picked up the little girl and gave her a cuddle.

'He's alive, my boy. I...I thought he was. I thought I'd feel it if he was gone, but then you never know. I told myself I was only saying that so as not to face the truth, it was so long since we heard anything.' She wiped her eyes with a grey handkerchief she pulled from the sleeve of her cardigan.

'I know, it's so hard not knowing...'

'But summer 1942, that's not long ago. God bless that boy, Nico. I'll ask Father Lehane to say a special Mass for him and his family, that God will protect him.'

'That would be lovely, and it sounds like Alfie is helping get people out of Nazi-occupied territory, which is so brave and good. You should be very proud of him, Mrs O'Hare.'

Mary nodded. 'He was a restless child, could never sit still. He used to drive your poor father daft, God be good to him, with his trick-acting and blackguarding when he was supposed to be doing his lessons. But my Alfie had a good, kind heart, always had. And a strong sense of fairness. Alfie wasn't big himself, but he got stuck into anyone picking on smaller children. Often he got a right hiding, but he gave as good as he got. Act first, think after, that's my Alfie.'

Grace was moved by the adoration in her voice. A mother's love. She had almost forgotten what that was like, her own mother was dead so long now.

'No mention of Bernadette, though,' Mary said sadly.

'No, but maybe he has lost touch with her or something. Richard says it's so hard to know what's going on, there's so little coming out. His sister, Sarah, and his friend Jacob work with refugees, people who have escaped from occupied Europe, and there are hundreds of them, people who lived under false identities or were hidden by friends or family. We can't give up hope.'

''Twill kill us to give her back, but I pray every night for her mother's safe return all the same.'

Grace put her hand on the older woman's shoulder. 'I know you do. She's a lucky little girl, and I'm sure if her parents could know and see how well she's being minded and loved, they'd be so grateful.'

'I think of her as Alfie's child,' Mary said quietly. 'I know she's not, but…' Odile's parentage was never really discussed. People were told when she arrived that Alfie had married a French woman and Odile was their daughter, and nobody asked too many questions. With an Irish father, she was an Irish citizen and perfectly entitled to be here, and everyone, including Sergeant Keane, was happy to leave it at that, even if they had questions. If Bernadette ever turned up to claim her daughter, well, they'd jump off that bridge when they came to it, as Tilly always said with a wry smile.

'She's your grandchild now, for life, regardless of what blood runs through her veins. She feels it and so do you, and all we can do now is be grateful for this wonderful news and pray that everyone we love stays safe and this cursed war is over soon.'

'Will it ever end, Grace? It doesn't feel like it will…' Grace could hear the exhaustion in her voice.

'It will, Mrs O'Hare. The tide is turned now, and it's just a matter of time. The Americans have the Japanese on the back foot, and the Allied push in North Africa is going very well. President Roosevelt said it's the Axis Powers that are going to be driven back now, and Churchill is over there, so between the two of them, it's all going in the right direction. We just have to be patient.'

Mary shook her head. 'I never thought I'd hear myself say a word in the defence of that man, and God knows we have nothing to thank him for, the misery he brought down on our heads back in the twenties, but he's doing a good job for them, isn't he?'

Grace nodded. Winston Churchill, as secretary of state in Lloyd George's cabinet, had sent the Black and Tans, a military group of demobbed soldiers from the Great War, many who were shellshocked and drank to excess, to fight the IRA. They were notoriously reckless and cruel, sinking to lows the regular British army never would. Any Irish person who endured life under their tyrannical regime would never forgive Churchill.

'He is. Richard says he's keeping morale up, and he attributes the spirit of the British to him, so I suppose like us all, he's got more than one side to him.'

'Well, if he wins this war and sends my boy home in one piece, then I'll light a candle for him.' Nobody but an Irish person knew how big a concession that would be.

FOLDED CORNERS

'Please God he will.'

CHAPTER 25

DUBLIN, IRELAND

7 JANUARY 1943

Grace knew Tilly had done it on purpose. The day out had been planned the night before, a stroll in Phoenix Park and a visit to the zoo with Odile. The toddler had been so excited the last time Tilly took her to Dublin, all she demanded was 'more zoo' every time Tilly so much as looked in her direction. Tilly tried explaining that a lot of the animals would be in their dens because it was so cold, but nothing would deter the two-foot dictator, as Tilly jokingly called her.

At the last minute, just as they were to get on the tram, Tilly remembered something she'd forgotten, and so she instructed Eloise and Grace to go ahead and said she would catch them up. She kept Odile with her.

Grace felt awkward and self-conscious around Eloise, and she was beyond nervous about tomorrow and meeting Richard, so the last thing she wanted was to spend a day with a beautiful Swiss woman she was, she had to admit, jealous of.

'Oh, all right, we'll go and have some coffee perhaps? Sit somewhere warm until Odile makes us trudge around looking at the animals who will be as miserable as we are?' Eloise chuckled and seemed not remotely perturbed by the change of plan, and Grace found herself envying the Swiss woman's poise as well as everything else.

Grace walked down the tram, hoping her limp was not too obvious, and mercifully found a seat. Eloise sat beside her. Grace had gone to stay with the Warringtons on her way to Dublin, and Hugh had explained how Nurse Kenny's ideas about treatment were really catching on all over the world. The demobilising of affected limbs, so long the treatment for polio, was being debunked, and heat application and physical therapy were gaining traction. He told her that she was ahead of the medical profession with her bath and her exercises, and he was so happy with how she was progressing.

She'd told them she was going to meet Richard and why, and to her relief, they were pleased for her. Like everyone, they were very fond of Declan, but they didn't see her as disloyal to his memory or anything like that. Like Eleanor and Tilly, they said she deserved to be happy and should seek it where she could.

'Odile is so funny, isn't she?' Eloise said as she slid into the seat beside Grace. 'I never really knew any babies. I have just one older brother, and my parents moved to Basel when I was only a girl, away from my beloved Alps, for my father's work. I was taken away from their families who live near the Italian border of Switzerland, so I didn't grow up with cousins.' Eloise chatted easily.

Why am I so awkward and prickly? Grace admonished herself. *Just be normal for goodness' sake.*

'Well, I didn't either,' she replied. 'I'm the youngest in my family, but my parents were teachers before me, so I'm used to little children, but not babies as such.'

'I know Tilly will be sad if Odile's mother comes back. Of course we want that for her, poor little thing, but I worry for Tilly.' Her big blue eyes were sad. Eloise Meier was an exceptionally beautiful woman by anyone's standards. Her short, blond, wavy hair and slim figure turned heads wherever she went. She dressed slightly eclectically, in tailored trousers and silk blouses, with chunky silver jewellery, not like a boy as Tilly did, but she looked delightfully exotic. That, combined with her accented English and husky voice, made everyone love her, men and women alike. What was wrong with Grace that she couldn't warm to her?

'I know, I do too,' Grace agreed. 'But if Bernadette and Alfie and Constance come back in one piece, I think she'll be so overjoyed. And who knows? They might stay here?'

'Oh, wouldn't that be just marvellous if that happened? I hope you're right, Grace, and why would someone not want to stay here in this magical, beautiful land? I never want to leave.' Eloise sighed as she looked out at the busy streets of Dublin as the tram trundled along.

'Dublin is certainly more exciting than

Knocknashee, that's for sure,' Grace conceded. They'd gone to the Abbey Theatre last night to see a production of *Juno and the Paycock* by Seán O'Casey. Grace had enjoyed it, but she liked more the conversation and fun with Eloise and Tilly's friends in Wynn's Hotel afterwards. They were all women and, Grace guessed, women like Tilly and Eloise, though there was no outward showing of it. She'd been so impressed by them. Students, women with jobs, unmarried, no children – these were women with opinions and attitudes that she found so refreshing. One girl, Jane Dullea, was a student of philosophy at Trinity College and told Grace that she came from rural County Tipperary. When she went home at Christmas, her mother said she was accepting of her mad notion to get a degree but could she please not be disgracing the family by going on about Plato or Aristotle or any of those 'other pagans' to the neighbours. Jane lived with a woman who seemed much older, a doctor, and they both found it all hilarious. It was a whole other world, and while Grace didn't understand the physical attraction, she could see how a life in the company of women such as these would be very fulfilling. She was glad for Tilly that she'd found her tribe.

'Oh, I don't know about that.' Eloise nudged her playfully. Clearly she felt none of the stiffness Grace did about her. 'Every time I go there, or Tilly comes here, something new and amazing has happened in Knocknashee.'

'Well, I…' Grace didn't know how to answer that. Especially since Eloise herself was the cause of much of the talk last year.

'I don't mean it in a bad way,' Eloise was quick to reassure her. 'Not at all…I love it there. It's so beautiful and so many characters live there, it is like being in a play.'

The stop for the zoo was next, and they got up and rang the bell.

'Will we go to that café there?' Eloise pointed at a tearoom at the zoo's entrance.

'Lovely.' The idea of paying for a cup of tea when everyone in this city had their own kitchen and their own kettle seemed mad to her, but people did it here without a second thought.

The café was busy, but Grace found a seat, and the waitress came over with a smile.

'Good afternoon, ladies, what would you like?'

Eloise perused the menu. 'I'll have tea, Earl Grey please, and a currant bun.'

The waitress noted it in her pad and looked at Grace, her face questioning.

'Ah…tea please…' she managed.

'Earl Grey?' the girl asked, but Grace had no idea what she was asking. Who was Earl Grey?

'Just black, I think,' Eloise interjected. 'Would you like anything to eat, Grace?'

She felt herself flush. Why was she being so gauche and mortifying?

'The buns are delicious,' Eloise added with a grin.

'Yes, please, a bun…thank you.' Grace handed her back the menu. 'I'm sorry, I don't know what Earl Grey is…'

'Oh, it's just a type of tea, flavoured with bergamot. My mother likes it, so it reminds me of her.' Eloise gave a wave of her hand. Her fingernails were long and painted red, and on her pointing finger, she wore a large ring with a blood-red stone. Grace felt like a pigeon beside a peacock.

'Now, tell me, how do you do it?' Eloise asked in a whisper.

'How do I do what?' Grace suppressed panic.

'Look so beautiful! Your skin, it is like cream, your hair, that colour that is so vibrant, your sparkling green eyes, and it looks like you don't even try. Every day, for me hours, trying to get my unruly hair to behave itself, make-up to hide the lines, and I have no hips or bum or bust, just like a beanpole up and down.' Eloise made two straight lines with her hands. 'The first time I met you, Grace, I was so jealous. I saw you and Tilly together, and you are both so effortlessly beautiful, so stunning , and I thought she would never want me if she knows you. I know you are not like us, I understand that, but… still…'

Was she joking? Trying to flatter Grace? For what reason? 'Eloise, you know none of that is true, so please…' Grace hated how schoolmistressy she sounded.

The other girl's demeanour turned serious. 'I'm not trying to flatter you, or flirt with you – well, maybe I am a bit – but what I said is true. But also I want you to like me, and you don't. That's the truth.' She opened her palms in a gesture to show that she was being truthful.

'I do like you, of course I do…' Grace lied, her cheeks red now. This conversation had become too intense for her.

'You don't. But I love Tilly, Grace. I know you know about us, but perhaps you think I am not serious about her, or that I am somehow trouble. I swear to you on my mother's life I had nothing to do with anything, the U-boat…none of that.' Her voice was barely audible now.

'I know you didn't,' Grace said, and meant it.

'So why don't you want me to be with Tilly then?' she asked, her face a mask of hurt confusion. 'I don't think it is because you disapprove of how we are, but perhaps you do? I want to be part of her life, and you are such an important person to her, it is driving me crazy that you don't want to be my friend.'

Grace wondered if the Irish were very repressed, but this was a most disconcerting way of going on. Were all Swiss people like this? Open and brutally honest? She didn't think they could be; it would be excruciating to live there if so. Perhaps it was just Eloise.

Grace tried to object. 'I've never said –'

'You don't have to say…I feel it. I know I can be a bit…well, too much…too forward, but I swear I mean Tilly no harm. I can make her happy, I know I can. I can't ever be to her what you are – you're her best friend, I know that. But if you can tell me anything I can do to reassure you, to trust me…I'll do it.' She exhaled. 'I asked Tilly to leave us alone today. She knows I am worried that you dislike me so much. She didn't want to do it, but I convinced her to let me have one chance to convince you I am not a terrible person…' Her voice faded away.

'I don't think you're a terrible person.' Grace

smiled now. Incredibly it seemed Eloise was being honest. 'I think you are an amazing person, and if we're being truthful, and it seems we are, I was jealous of you and Tilly. I couldn't see why she'd ever want to make time for me if someone as exciting as you was an option.'

Eloise's blue eyes widened. 'You love her?'

Grace laughed. 'Not like you do, not that, but I suppose I just didn't want to lose her to someone so…well, so exotic. And it felt like nothing I or Knocknashee had would be enough to keep her with us. She was my only friend for so long. I suppose I just hated the idea of losing her.'

'So I am afraid of losing her to you, and you are afraid of losing her to me?' Eloise smiled and reached over to take one of Grace's hands in hers.

'How about we share her?' Grace suggested.

'Yes please,' Eloise said, her big blue eyes filling with tears.

CHAPTER 26

'There, now you can look,' Eloise announced with a flourish as she brought the mirror from the wall and placed it in front of Grace. They were in Marion's house in Dublin. Tilly was sitting on the bed with Odile, who was playing with a dolly, watching Eloise work her magic.

Grace gazed at her reflection and searched for words. Eloise had set her untameable copper curls in soft waves last night, and instead of the wild mop it normally was, it was sleek, soft and elegant around her face. The Swiss woman had used precious make-up to smooth Grace's complexion; the rosy cheeks of a lifetime spent on the wild peninsula were now a touch of elegant pink. Her eyebrows had been plucked and shaped and darkened slightly, her eyelashes were brushed with mascara and her eyelids coloured with a gorgeous amber shadow. Kohl ringed her green eyes, and her lips were stained a subtle coral. She looked, even by her own standards, amazing.

'I… Are you sure it's not too much?' she asked, turning to Tilly. Eloise was so glamourous but also daring; she wore the most outlandish things but had the confidence to pull it off. Grace feared she looked like a little girl playing dress-up.

'Grace, you look so beautiful, I…' For once Tilly was lost for words. 'Not too much. You look perfect.'

Grace had borrowed a green silk wraparound dress that was almost scandalously short on Eloise but mercifully came to Grace's knees. The day was bright and sunny but bitterly cold, so Marion had offered her a cream cashmere coat to wear over her dress. She'd worn it the day she married Colm, she said, and Grace was nervous she might get a mark on it, but Marion was like Tilly, generous to a fault and didn't care about small things.

'One last thing,' Eloise said, eyeing her with a cool professional gaze. To Grace's unpierced ears she clipped gold earrings with a green stone. Grace winced as the clip pinched her earlobe.

'No pain, no gain, Grace.' Eloise chuckled in her gravelly voice.

'Give us a twirl then,' Tilly said.

Grace stood. She was going to go without her calliper today. It made her leg much more tired, but she wanted to look as normal as possible.

Eloise admired her new tan leather shoes with the brass buckle and the built-up sole and heel. 'The shoes are lovely. They turned out really nice.'

'They are, aren't they? The nicest pair I've ever had. I was just amazed when he arrived. I was correcting schoolwork one night, and there was a knock at the door, and there was Pádraig O Sé standing there. I don't think in all the years he was ever at my front door before, and he looked so sheepish, I wondered what he'd come to confess to.' Grace laughed.

'He's nice, you know, under all the –'

'Insults and rudeness?' Tilly cut across Eloise, who had a soft spot for the Knocknashee cobbler, even though he'd been so vicious when the cloud of suspicion hung over her.

'That's just a defence. He's nice, truly.' Eloise loved everything about Knocknashee and made it all sound so romantic, even Pádraig's cobbler shop.

Tilly and Grace, who'd known him all their lives, were sceptical.

The smell in his shop, of leather and linseed oil, had not changed in all of Grace's life. There was a concrete floor, with a large pockmarked bench, behind which was Pádraig with his leather apron. And on the wall behind him stood floor-to-ceiling shelves, divided into little compartments like a dovecot, each one containing a pair of shoes. In the middle of the bench was a cobbler's anvil, and strewn along the bench, a collection of hammers, awls, needles, threads and knives. Like the shop, the cobbler hadn't changed much over the years either. His huge lumbering body, bulbous nose, wild hair that stuck out at all different angles, red thread veins on his weather-beaten cheeks all served to remind Grace of the giant in the story *Jack and the Beanstalk*.

She always braced herself for some snide remark from him. He always had something cutting to say. He'd asked Mary O'Hare if she was after a razor because she needed a shave. True, Tilly's mother had a lot of dark facial hair, but only Pádraig would point it out.

'Well,' Grace explained, 'when he pulled these

shoes out of a bag and told me he'd made them for me…I…well, you could have knocked me down with a feather, honest to God. But he said he'd seen someone wearing ones like them when he went to his cousin's wedding in Killarney, and he thought he'd have a go. He knew my size because I'd dropped the one that the calliper fitted into to be heeled, and he used it as a template and made these. I hardly limp at all when I wear them, and the leather is so soft, they're really comfortable.'

Tilly wasn't convinced. 'And what did he charge you?'

'That's the amazing thing. Nothing. He said they were a present.'

'Oh, Grace, has he an eye for you?' Tilly laughed at the idea of the curmudgeonly old cobbler having romantic notions.

'Don't be daft.' Grace laughed at the idea. 'He said that he'd mentioned to Richard ages ago, when he visited that time and we stopped to chat to him when we were out for a walk, that it was very hard to get waxed flax thread since the Emergency. Richard must have asked someone back in America to send him some – his father is in a yacht club – and Pádraig got a parcel a few weeks ago. It's for making sails, I think, but apparently it will do, and he was delighted, so in return he decided to make me a pair of shoes.'

'Well, they look really lovely and they're perfect with the dress,' Eloise said. 'So now, Miss Fitzgerald, I think it's time you caught your bus.'

Tilly stood and hugged her tightly. '*Go n-eirí an t-adh leat*,' She whispered in her ear.

Odile toddled over then, and before she approached Grace, Tilly checked she was clean. Her fingers were often covered in jam or other stickiness, so it was best to be safe.

'*Is mar banphrionsa thú a*, Grace, *tá do gúna go h-allainn*,' the little girl said in awe.

'She *is* like a princess, Odile, you're right,' Eloise answered in English. '*Et en Francais?*'

The little girl thought for a moment. '*Une princesse?*' Her big brown eyes fixed on Eloise to check if she was right.

Eloise clapped. '*Parfait, ma petite.*'

Tilly beamed as proud as any mother. 'Eloise only speaks French to her now, and she just absorbs it like a sponge, and obviously her Irish is the same as any local child. She's got so many words now and understands almost everything. English is the tricky one, but we're working on it. Mine isn't wonderful either, as you know…'

'Well, how about I speak English to her, and

that way she's hearing all three languages all the time?'

'That's a great idea, Grace. We should have thought of that before. Your English is perfect,' Eloise replied as she smoothed the belt that tied the wraparound dress together.

'Does that open easily?' Grace asked, worried that the silk would come undone.

'Hopefully.' Tilly grinned and Eloise laughed.

Grace blushed. 'I didn't mean…'

'We know what you meant, but if things go the way we want them to…' Eloise winked suggestively.

'I'm going for my bus before you two corrupt me entirely,' Grace said with a rueful shake of her head. 'Bye-bye, Odile.' She kissed her dark silky hair. 'Wish me luck.'

'*Go n-ei…*'

'In English, darling.' Grace lifted the child up into her arms.

'Gluck?' the little girl said.

'That will do.' Grace gave her one last kiss before handing her back to Tilly.

'*Bonne chance, mon ami.*' Eloise kissed her on both cheeks. 'Go and get that man of yours.'

Grace left the house and walked to the bus stop. With her new built-up shoe, she felt much less conspicuous, and while she would still wear the calliper and her adapted shoe most days, it was lovely to have a choice.

A group of young men were working on a building, and as she walked by, one of them whistled. She blushed crimson. This sort of thing never happened to her, but she decided not to be upset and take it as a vote of confidence.

The bus arrived promptly for once and she tried not to look awkward as she limped down the aisle and found a seat.

On her lap was a tan leather purse borrowed from Lizzie, who was so excited she was meeting Richard. It matched her new shoes. As the bus trundled on, she recalled Lizzie's revelation.

'I hope we're not overstepping, Grace, but we don't have children and you are as close to a daughter as we have, and we so want you to be happy. What you and Richard have, it's…well, it doesn't come along every day. I know it doesn't. And in this world that seems so…well…difficult and confusing and sad, we have to find our pockets of happiness where we can and hold on to them and never let them go.'

'Well, you would know, I suppose. You and Hugh are a love story,' Grace had said with a smile, relieved she hadn't disappointed Lizzie.

'We are. And I never told you this, but I was engaged to a different chap. Rafael Loxley was his name.' She'd smiled at the memory. 'I know, what a romantic name. But he was just an ordinary chap, very nice, very funny. Oh, he used to have me in stitches. He could mimic anyone perfectly. He was in the Royal Engineers, and he died at the Messines Ridge. He was only twenty-one, and an only boy. His mother never got over it.'

'Oh, I never knew…' Grace was lost for words; she'd just assumed Lizzie and Hugh were always together.

'I don't talk about him much. He was a friend of Hugh's, that's how we met. After the war, Hugh and I started courting and we married, and we've been so blessed. Coming over here, and being able to help so many children, it's been a joy.'

'I'm so glad you did,' Grace said quietly.

'Well, the reason I told you, Grace, is even though Mrs Loxley was devastated when Rafe died – that's what we called him – she sent me a lovely wedding gift and a letter saying she was very happy for me and Hugh and that she knew Rafe would be too. It meant the world to us, it really did. There's a part of my heart that will always be Rafael Loxley's, and Hugh knows and respects that, but I've been so happy. And even though Hugh and I couldn't have a family of our own, we feel so privileged to have you in our lives, Grace. And we of all people know second chances are worth it.'

Grace hadn't known what to say. 'It might be a wild goose chase of course…'

'Fortune favours the brave, my dear, and you are many things, Grace, but above all of your tremendous qualities, you are the most courageous person I know, so be brave and go for it.'

So here she was, minutes away from…what? Her destiny? Or the most awfully embarrassing rejection of her life?

The bus pulled into the stop on Stephen's Green, and she alighted, her legs wobbly and her stomach twisting painfully. Every instinct in her said stay on the bus, get off at the next stop and catch another one back immediately. But she inhaled slowly and exhaled, forcing her breathing to steady.

The winter sunshine was warm on her face as she stood at the bus stop, the bus pulling out into the traffic once more. All around her, people were rushing. What was it about cities? Everyone was in such a hurry all the time. Nobody sauntered or stopped for a chat like they did in Knocknashee. Behind her, beyond the railings, mothers were in the park with their children, and across the road, the imposing façade of the Shelbourne loomed.

The hotel had once been three substantial townhouses overlooking Europe's largest garden square. It was elegant and graceful and oozed class and money. They'd met there once before, so it had seemed like the logical choice, but now it intimidated her.

She'd voiced her fears to Tilly last night, who said not to be ridiculous, why shouldn't she have tea at the Shelbourne. And her friend reminded her that Adolf Hitler's brother had worked there years ago, although Grace didn't know if that was meant to make her feel better or worse. She could use it if the conversation dried up, she supposed. It was easy to write to Richard, and the chat had flowed on the three occasions they'd met before, but what if things were different now?

The Irish Constitution had been drawn up inside that hotel in 1922, and that thought bizarrely gave her courage. If the founders of the fledgling Irish State could summon the guts to start a country from scratch, she could surely meet her old friend for a cup of tea.

She crossed the street and almost jumped out of her skin when a lady on a bicycle nearly collided with her, despite vigorous bell-ringing. By the time she got to the other side of the street, she was trembling. The gold statues of Egyptian women flanking either side of the front door shone in the sunshine, and she glimpsed the two ancient statues of Nubian women on the corners. All four wore gold anklets and were sculpted to look like some gossamer-thin fabric was draped over their curves. They each held aloft a torch with a glass shade. Normally she would try to remember the details to tell the children in school, but not today.

A liveried doorman, complete with top hat, raised his eyebrow as if to ask if she intended to enter.

She steeled herself with one more deep breath and climbed the marble steps up to the front door.

CHAPTER 27

The sweat prickled on Richard's back though it was cold outside. Snow had settled over the Irish countryside, and it all felt so silent and peaceful. He'd enjoyed the start of the journey, but now he was going to be late. The Belfast-to-Dublin train was supposed to have arrived at Kingsbridge station in Dublin at one o'clock, but now it was quarter to three and they still were stuck in a siding outside some rural station, miles from the city. Like in England, every other type of freight seemed to take precedence over people. He stood and paced, much to the undisguised annoyance of a pair of older ladies who had sat opposite him. All the way from Belfast, they'd discussed at length how inconsiderate someone called Gladys was for getting a cat, and especially a tabby, considering everything that had happened. They spoke in this kind of code, all nods and knowing eyebrow raises. He wished he could shout at them how he couldn't care less about Gladys or about the stupid damned cat, he just needed to get off this train.

His car was just shy of the platform, so he decided he would have to take matters into his own hands. He grabbed his leather bag and marched through the cars until he was in one that abutted the platform. He lowered the half window and reached down to open the door.

'Excuse me, sir, please get back on the train…' a uniformed railway man called from further along the platform, but Richard ignored him.

He strode up the platform. He was still a long way from the station; this area was clearly for freight only.

'Sir, please remain on the train, it will move shortly…' the man called as he approached.

'I'm incredibly late for a really important meeting, so I'm going to make my own way from here,' Richard said as he marched past him without stopping.

The guardsman must have decided he wasn't worth the bother and let him go. On and on

Richard walked, as fast as he could, until eventually there was a gate. He let himself out and found himself on a deserted road, green fields with a dusting of white snow in every direction. Fighting despair, he racked his brain as to what to do next. He was in the middle of nowhere, and he had no idea how far from Dublin he was.

He began walking in the direction the train should have been headed, when he heard hooves, the sound of horseshoes rattling over the concrete road. He turned and saw a boy of about thirteen standing and managing two slightly wayward-looking horses that were pulling a cart laden with coal.

'Can you take me into the city?' Richard called to him as soon as he was in earshot.

'Nah, mister, I've all this coal to deliver,' the boy replied. He was small and wiry, with a shock of brown hair and freckles. He wore a donkey jacket far too big for him and was covered head to foot in coaldust.

'How far from the city centre am I?' Richard asked.

'What? Dublin city? Is that what you are on about?' The boy, with a look of someone who'd seen more of life than a typical child of his age should have, was curious.

'Yes, Dublin city,' Richard said, wondering if he was a little bit slow. 'I need to get there really quickly, and I don't know how to get a cab here, so I'll give you money if you can get me to the Shelbourne hotel as fast as those horses can go.' Even as he spoke, it sounded like a ludicrous plan, but it was all he could think of. He needed to get there. What if Grace arrived and he was nowhere to be seen, so she just left? The thought spurred his urgency.

'Name your price,' he said to the boy, who had pulled the horses up to a stop.

'A fiver,' the boy said with a cheeky grin.

'Come on, I could buy the horses for that…' Richard objected.

'You're the one that needs to get to the Shelbourne, pal, not me.' He shrugged and flicked the reins as the animals pulled forward.

'Fine, but you have to swear you'll go as fast as you can.' Richard, disgruntled but silently acknowledging the kid was right, pulled a roll of Irish pound notes from his pocket, giving him five of them. This was literally highway robbery.

The boy tried unsuccessfully to hide his gleeful delight at the sight of that much money. He took it and shoved it down his trousers. 'Jump on.' As Richard settled on the narrow wooden bench beside him, the boy added, 'We'll have to drop the coal first, but if you help, it won't take long.'

Before Richard could object, the cart lurched forward and the horses trotted along the road.

The boy wasn't joking. They turned off after a few minutes and went down a snow- and slush-covered track, arriving a few moments later at a shed.

'Here we are, let's be having ya.' The boy jumped down and began unloading the cart. Stifling his frustration, Richard knew the only way to get going was to do as he asked, so with no regard for his clean white shirt and pressed trousers, he lugged the filthy hessian sacks off the cart with the boy. The shed was a three-sided lean-to with a corrugated tin roof. Several other sheds alongside it were being used as storage for other merchants. One held timber blocks, another gravel. Apart from him and the boy, there was no sign of life.

'What's your rush?' the boy asked as he heaved sacks as big as himself.

'I'm meeting a friend,' Richard said, panting under the weight.

Carrying the bags back and forth from the cart to the shed, Richard was soon soaked in sweat and coaldust. To his shame it was clearly taking more out of him than this kid.

'Won't the friend wait?' the boy asked as he dragged the last bag off.

'I don't know. Can we just get going please?' Richard panted as he climbed aboard the cart once more. The two horses, still tackled, were munching grass on the verge.

'Right-o. C'mon, John and Roy.' He clicked the reins, and the two animals reluctantly raised their heads.

'John and Roy?' Richard asked with a smile.

'John Wayne and Roy Rogers. I love the westerns – I usually go of a Saturday. *Stagecoach* is on today. I'd go once I've the coal delivered, but I won't make it today on account of you.'

'Sorry.' Richard felt he had to apologise.

'It's alrigh', I seen it before...' the boy replied magnanimously, as if he was delivering Richard out of the goodness of his heart and not for the extortionate fee of five pounds.

'Are ya nervous?' the kid asked as they trotted down the lane to the road once more.

'Of what?' Richard asked as the boy took the stub of a cigarette from behind his ear and lit it. He was too young to be smoking surely, but that wasn't something he was going to point out.

'Speed...' the boy said dramatically, eyes wide and, to Richard's mind, somewhat maniacal.

'Er...no...I need to get there fast...'

'Hold on then...' The kid turned the pair of horses onto the road and tapped them with the switch he held in one hand. The cart lurched and the horses broke into a gallop. Everything rattled, and Richard was bounced painfully on the bench. He clung to the wood of the cart with a white-knuckle grip as the boy stood and howled and the horses thundered on.

If he made it to Grace alive, it would be a miracle.

Eventually, battered and bruised, they reached the outskirts of the city, and occasionally when traffic forbade speed, they slowed down, only to pick up again the moment there was a gap.

'Here ya are,' the boy announced with a flourish as they thundered down a cobbled street full of pedestrians, bicycles and cars. Richard's teeth rattled in his head as the thin-wheeled cart banged over the cobbles.

'What, where is it?' he managed.

'There, that's the Shelbourne. Best of luck, mister. I hope she waited.'

Richard dismounted from the cart on wobbly legs and found he was indeed at the famous Shelbourne hotel. He checked his watch – it was twenty past four. He was an hour and twenty minutes late. She wasn't going to be there, he just knew it.

The doorman took one look at him, and his expression told Richard everything he needed to know. He walked up the steps regardless.

'I'm sorry, sir, I was due to meet a friend here at three o'clock, but I got waylaid and well' – he gestured at his general appearance – 'I don't look as I did this morning. I understand if you don't want me to enter in this condition, but could you check if a young lady named Grace Fitz…McKenna, Grace McKenna is inside, or if she's gone, maybe she left a message for me?'

Perhaps it was his accent, or just that the man took pity on him, but the doorman took a minute and then replied. 'Could you describe the lady, sir?'

'She's in her twenties, red hair, green eyes… she's not very tall…' He swallowed. 'Beautiful.'

The man sighed as if this was a necessary but irritating part of his daily life. 'If you hold on here, I'll go and ask if she's been here today.'

'Thank you, sir, I sure do appreciate that.'

As the doorman walked through the large glass doors, Richard caught a glimpse of his reflection. His blond hair, once oiled back, was now flopping over his forehead, and his shirt was filthy. To add to that, he had coal smudges on his face and his hands were grimy, and some of his knuckles were bleeding from when he'd had to grip tight to the cart as it wheeled around a tight bend – one of the planks had come loose and trapped his fingers.

Richard waited on the steps of the fancy hotel, enduring the looks of people coming and going, appalled that someone with such a loose grasp of personal grooming would deign to try to gain access to the Shelbourne. He didn't care what anyone else thought, but he had to see Grace.

Eventually the doorman reappeared. 'A young lady matching that description was in the Causerie lounge earlier. She was waiting for someone who failed to make the appointment, and she left about half an hour ago.'

Richard's heart sank. She'd waited for almost an hour. The thought of her sitting there, worried, then resigned and maybe furious, made him feel ill.

Dublin was a huge city. Had she gone back to Knocknashee? Should he try to go there? He had no time. He was due to present himself for basic training at the USAAF base at Bushy Park the day after tomorrow. There was no way he'd get back in time if he went to Kerry now. Jacob had nearly had a heart attack at him going to Ireland at all, and had made him swear he'd meet Grace, say 'whatever the hell you two numbskulls need to say to each other for once and for all' and return immediately.

Getting them into the training was a huge achievement for his friend. He'd had to beg and cajole, because this was for the top brass of press, not minnows like them, but he'd pulled it off. Richard knew he wouldn't even be in Europe if it wasn't for Jacob going out on a limb for him that first day. He owed it to his friend to keep his end of the bargain, and he wouldn't let him down no matter how much he longed to see Grace.

He had an idea. Trains to Cork, where she'd have to go first, were not that frequent; maybe she was at the station. He thanked the doorman and hailed a cab. The driver looked him up and down as if wondering whether to let him in. Eventually, hearing his accent, he did.

'Kingsbridge station please, as fast as you can.'

The cab drove through the Dublin traffic, and Richard shoved a handful of coins at the driver once they got to the ornate structure that was the station. It had a look of Renaissance palazzo about it, with architectural swags and fancies, but Richard hardly noticed. He ran in, stopping on the concourse to ask a guardsman where the train to Cork left from.

'One's just left, sir, about twenty minutes ago,' he replied. 'Next one not till' – he checked his watch – 'six o'clock this evening.'

He felt he could cry. That was it. He'd blown it.

Richard sat down on one of the benches, head in his hands. She was gone.

CHAPTER 28

Grace hated seeing their faces as she walked up the pathway to Marion's house. Tilly, Marion and Eloise all knew something was up. They weren't expecting her back for hours, and after all their work making this happen, she felt like she was letting them down.

'Grace,' Tilly said as she opened the door, 'is everything all right?'

She fought back tears but failed. 'He didn't turn up.'

Tilly enveloped her in an embrace and led her into the house. A look between her and Marion spoke volumes, and the older woman ushered the children, including Odile, to the kitchen for bread and jam, leaving Grace alone with Tilly and Eloise in the front parlour.

'I don't believe it,' Tilly said. 'There must be some reason…'

'If there was, he could have sent a message or telephoned the hotel or something. No, he probably knew what he was facing and decided against it, and I've made a total fool of myself for nothing.' Grace accepted the handkerchief Eloise offered.

'How long did you wait?' Tilly asked.

'Over an hour. I had to go because the staff were looking at me with such pity, I couldn't take it any more.'

'Something could have happened. He…was he coming directly from London? Or was he on an assignment somewhere else before?' Eloise was trying to make her feel better, she knew that, but it wasn't working.

'I don't know.' She sniffed, not bothering to try to stop the tears. 'I got one telegram saying he'd be there and nothing else. He didn't write or anything, so I have to be realistic. This was a stupid waste of time, and I'm just feeling so foolish. And I told Charlie and Hugh and Lizzie, and now everyone is going to be looking at poor crippled Grace, thinking she had a future with the big gorgeous American. What was going on in her stupid head – she must be daft as the crows to think that was a realistic possibility –'

'Stop this right now.' Tilly stood before her and gripped her shoulders hard. 'You have every right to believe that Richard Lewis and you could work out. For God's sake, anyone with eyes can see he's stone mad for you. Something happened to stop him getting there, Grace, I know it did. You'll just have to wait and see.'

'No, Tilly, that's enough now.'

Tilly's demeanour changed then. 'This is not like you, this poor Grace, of course nobody would want poor crippled Grace.' Her unusual grey eyes blazed. 'You're better than this, so stop with all this self-pity. Richard said he was coming and he didn't turn up, but Grace, there's a bloody war on in case you hadn't noticed. He could be stuck somewhere with no way to send a message. So stop jumping to the very worst conclusion.'

Grace was hurt. How could Tilly be so harsh? Eloise shot Tilly a glance and stepped in, taking one of Grace's hands.

'What Tilly means, I think, Grace, is that Richard loves you, and we all think he's in love with you, but even if he only sees you as a friend, which I don't think for one second he does, he wouldn't just stand up you...what is that phrase?' She turned to Tilly.

'Stand you up,' Tilly answered.

'Yes, that. I think Tilly means, though she can be a bit...well...less than diplomatic' – Eloise made an exasperated face – 'that there is going to be some perfectly logical explanation, and all you have to do is wait and he will contact you and explain.'

'Maybe.' Grace wasn't at all sure, but she just wanted this to stop. She wished with all her might that she was at home, in her own house, wearing her own clothes, and that she'd never embarked on this foolishness.

'So now, we are not wasting all of this' – Eloise waved a hand at Grace's hair, make-up and dress – 'so we are going out, all three of us, for a night on the town.'

Grace felt so weary. 'No, Eloise, thank you but –'

'I'm not taking no for an answer. We are going to Banba Hall. There's a *ceilí* tonight, and Tilly promised me we'd go, so let's all go.'

The wild Irish music of a *ceilí* was the very last thing Grace wanted, but she knew that resisting Eloise was difficult if not impossible, and they'd both gone to such trouble to have her look nice. A wave of guilt washed over her.

'Please?' Eloise begged theatrically. 'Take the tourist to hear the Irish jigs and reels?'

'Don't listen to her, Grace. She knows more about Ireland than the two of us, and she also knows absolutely everyone in the city as far as I can see, so if anyone here are tourists, it's us.' Tilly laughed. 'And I'm sorry. I shouldn't have been so blunt, but I just hate to see you run yourself down, and I thought you'd stopped doing it, so I just saw red. He'll have a good excuse, I know he will. So will we go dancing?'

Grace knew resistance was futile, and it probably was a shame to waste her fancy new look. Sitting in Marion's house moping wasn't a good way to spend her evening either, so she tried to summon some enthusiasm. 'Only if we can go to Burdocks?' Grace had been to the famous fish-and-chip shop once before and loved it.

'Cinderella, you shall go to the ball…' Eloise bowed low. 'Burdocks for a "wan and wan" it is.'

'You see, she's like a local. She had to explain to me what a wan and wan is,' Tilly whispered.

'And what is it?' Grace whispered back.

'One portion of chips, one portion of fish.'

The three girls trooped out, Grace feeling a bit

more optimistic. Maybe they were right and she should give Richard the benefit of the doubt. Even if he wasn't interested in her romantically, he wasn't the kind of man who would just leave a person hanging without a good reason.

In the hallway Colm was crawling on his hands and knees with Odile, three-year-old Donal and two-year-old Eoin on his back.

'*Níl*, Uncail Colm, *atá ann in aon chor*, Aintín Grace, *is capall é*!' Odile squealed with delight.

Grace laughed. 'Poor Uncle Colm. I know you think he's a horse, but maybe go easy on him, you three – he's after a long day at work.'

Marion grinned at her husband and her little niece, leaning against the door. Though they now had eight children between them, and Odile made nine, they took it in their stride. They had two full-time girls to help Marion, Colm had a very well-paid job, and the house was huge. They were as happy as it was possible to imagine anyone could be.

'I hope you're off out. Grace needs cheering up,' Marion said as she leant down to take baby Eoin up in her arms.

'If you don't mind?' Tilly was careful not to trespass on her sister's kind heart.

'Well, considering you minded our army

twice last week, I think we owe you...' Colm said, groaning as he slid Donal and Odile off his back and got to his feet. His little son clambered to be in his daddy's arms, and Odile reached for Tilly.

'Going to your aunt's removal and funeral is hardly a night out, though, is it?' Tilly replied. 'Tell you what, why don't you two plan a night at the pictures or something next week, and we'll look after the troops?'

Colm looked at Marion. Grace felt a pang of something. What was it like to have that kind of love? She and Declan had loved each other, but it was the new, first flush of romance before he was so cruelly taken from her. What was it like to be with someone for years, to share a family, a home, the mundane things of life that everyone took for granted but were, in fact, the most important?

'We never turn down an offer to get away from this lot.' Marion chuckled, tickling little Eoin, who buried his face in her neck. 'Now off with ye.' She held her hand out for Odile, who took it happily. 'Will we do a jigsaw, Odile?'

'The one of the bears,' Odile answered immediately.

'Burdocks and the Banba, a night fit for three

queens.' Eloise linked Grace and Tilly, and they left the house.

The three women got the bus into the city and walked up to Christ Church in the very working-class area known as the Liberties to get to Burdocks. The beauty of Dublin usually cheered Grace, and this part of the city, though poor, was fascinating to her, but tonight she struggled to find a smile. It was a cold winter's night, dark since four in the afternoon, and the stars and the moon shone brightly in the clear night sky. They passed St Patrick's Cathedral where Jonathan Swift, who wrote *Gulliver's Travels*, a favourite with her pupils, was once dean of the cathedral, and straight ahead was the beautiful Christ Church Cathedral. These buildings with their multitudes of histories normally fascinated her, but not now. Besides, they were in complete darkness; wasting electricity to light them was not an option, as rationing pulled the entire population thinner and thinner each week.

They pushed the steamed-up door of the fish-and-chip shop, and the salty smell, laced with malty vinegar, assaulted their nostrils. Behind the counter the couple that ran the place were shouting orders backwards and forwards and wrapping fish and golden crunchy chips in newspaper. She had not imagined she could be hungry, as her heart was broken, but Grace found her mouth watering.

As they took their place in the queue, the small shop filled with steam. There were several people ahead of them. A woman wrangled three small boys who were determined to climb on the counter, and behind her an elderly couple counted out coppers. First in the queue was a tall man with a broad back.

'One fish and chips please, and a cup of tea.'

She'd recognise that Southern drawl anywhere. Without saying a word to Tilly or Eloise, she skipped the queue, skirting around the small boys and apologising to the elderly couple. Then she tapped the white-shirted shoulder.

He spun around. She was right. There he was.

CHAPTER 29

'Grace…oh my Lord…Grace! I can't believe it's you. I went to the station, thinking I might catch you – I thought you'd gone back to Knocknashee…'

'Salt and vinegar?' the sweaty woman serving barked while glaring at the biggest of the three boys who had managed to finally scale the counter.

'Er…I'm sorry?' Richard looked at her in confusion.

'Salt and vinegar…do ya want 'em on your chips?' The woman spoke as if he were both deaf and stupid.

'Ah, yes…please, ma'am…' he replied, flustered.

'That's threepence.' She held the newspaper-wrapped bundle back with one hand as if Richard was going to snatch it without paying, her other palm outstretched. He reached into his trouser pocket and took out a shilling. She sighed as if getting him change was a huge imposition but handed over the food and the coins without another word to him.

'You're not next,' she barked at Grace.

'I know, I was just…' Grace began, but the woman had moved on to growl at the old man who was perusing the menu. She giggled.

'Come on, you can share mine.' Richard grinned as he took her hand and led her out of the shop, passing Tilly and Eloise who abandoned their chip order to follow them out. She felt such a surge of giddy excitement, she knew she must be grinning like a loon, but she didn't care. He was here; he hadn't stood her up. He was just late, and she knew he'd have a good reason. Maybe all wasn't lost after all.

'Well, you turned up, I see.' Tilly grinned.

As Tilly teased him, Grace snatched a glance up at him. He looked more dishevelled than she remembered him being, and his hand was bloody. His shirt, she noticed, was dirty, but his heavy well-cut overcoat covered it up. He was the most gorgeous man she'd ever seen and admitting it, even to herself, gave her a thrill.

'Hi, Tilly. I'm so sorry. Boy, have I been all around the houses today – I was sure I missed her. Can I take her away from you two?'

'I suppose so.' Tilly sighed theatrically. 'But he better have a good excuse, Grace. No listening to his auld *rawmeis* now.' She laughed.

'I'm Eloise by the way.' Eloise stuck her hand out to shake his.

'I've heard all about you. It's nice to finally meet you.'

'Likewise.' She leant over to Grace and whispered, 'I approve.'

Leaving Tilly and Eloise to get their chips, Richard offered Grace his arm. The bustle of traffic and pedestrians going home from work on the cold winter evening, heads bowed, scarves wound tight against the biting wind coming off the River Liffey, meant they couldn't begin to talk, but Richard saw a gateway to a little garden beside a church and led her inside. Coal smoke hung in the cold city air and she could see her breath. Within a few minutes they were in an oasis of calm, the noise of the city dulled by the walls and the bare trees. St Nicholas's church formed one boundary of the garden, and while it was overgrown and mossy, deep in its winter slumber, it was to Grace magical. A stone bench was set into the garden wall opposite the church.

'Here?' Richard asked, and she nodded, allowing him to lead her there. They sat, facing a small fountain with a lichen-covered cherub, the water frozen. Dotted here and there were bare cherry blossom trees, just like the one her mother had planted in their back garden that her father had teased her about. To his mind, the cherry blossom was a waste of a tree, the bud too delicate to withstand the wind so it flowered for only the briefest of time. Mammy said that was what made it so special.

An rud is annamh, is iontach. The rare thing is wonderous.

The garden was deserted apart from them; nobody in their right mind would be outside in this weather. She was glad of her wool coat and gloves, even if her hat flattened her lovely new hairstyle.

He opened the packet of chips and fish and spread it out on the stone seat between them, the steam and the aroma mingling.

'I forgot my tea,' he said with a smile, and she knew in that moment he was as nervous as she was.

'I can't believe you drink it willingly now. Didn't you used to hate it?' Grace asked, picking up a hot, salty chip and blowing on it. She marvelled at how easy it was to talk to him, as if no time had gone by and nothing seismic had happened.

'I did, but now I like it. Coffee in London is pretty disgusting, so I gave up trying. They do make a decent cup of tea, though, so when in Rome…' He used his hands to halve the long fish covered in golden batter, pushing one half towards her side of the paper.

'I borrowed this dress and I'm afraid I'll get grease on it,' Grace said, eyeing the delicious, but disastrous to silk, battered fish.

'You look so beautiful, and your hair, what I can see of it under your hat, that is, and…you're amazing.' Richard gazed right at her. Her heart was thumping – what was going to happen? Could she get the words out, the ones she promised Tilly and herself she would say? Or would her courage desert her?

'Thank you, I was supposed to meet someone earlier…'

He must have heard the faint hint of admonishment in her voice. 'I'm real sorry, Grace. I had to come in through Belfast, and so I had to take the train down to Dublin, but it kept stopping for no reason and eventually I just got off. I caught a ride with a kid delivering coal – that's why I'm filthy.' He held his hands up so she could see the black dust under his fingernails. 'And by the time I got to the Shelbourne, you were gone. I went to the station, like I said – I'm sure I looked flat-out crazy – but the guy said the train was gone and the next wasn't until six o'clock. I would have just gone to Knocknashee, but I have to get back to London – it's an urgent thing I can't get out of.'

'Well, fate intervened, so here we are,' Grace said as a small, fat robin rested on the fountain. They both looked at it and smiled. 'My mother always said the robin was one of your loved ones coming to say hello.'

They watched the little bird puff out its feathers before flying away.

'Declan?' Richard asked quietly.

'Maybe. I'd like to think so. He liked you a lot.'

'I liked him too. I sure was jealous of him, but I liked him.'

'Why?' Grace knew she was fishing now, but she couldn't help herself.

He fixed her with a blue-eyed stare, and it felt as though his soul was searching for hers. Her mouth was dry, and she couldn't have said a word even if her life depended on it. Long seconds passed before he spoke, and when he did, it was quietly.

'Grace, you know why. Because he married the girl I love more than any other person in the world.'

This was it. Just like that. He'd said it. She wasn't imagining it. There was no nuance or shade or room for misinterpretation. He loved her.

She swallowed. 'I got that letter you wrote, the one two years ago, after you came to Knocknashee the first time.'

'You did?' He looked confused. 'And you married Declan anyway?' She heard the hurt there, saw the shadow of doubt on his handsome face, fear that he'd got it wrong.

'I didn't get it until a few months ago, just after you left Knocknashee after the canon business. It must have got lost, but by then, everything was different. Declan was dead, you were with Pippa, you were going to marry her, so I just kept it and never replied,' – she swallowed again – 'I couldn't throw it away, so I kept it in the box where I keep all your letters.'

'Oh, Grace...' He ran his hands through his

thick blond hair. 'It's like we almost get there so often, and then something happens…'

'But we're here now,' she whispered.

'We are.' He reached over and took her hand in his. She saw him look down at the wedding and engagement rings Declan had given her. He turned her hand over, palm facing upwards, brought it to his lips and kissed it.

Then he released her, wrapped up the barely touched fish and chips in the paper and placed the bundle on the ground. Grace watched his powerful, athletic frame as he got down on one knee, facing her where she sat on the bench. Declan had proposed on a bench in a park too, in Tralee, and a robin had visited that day as well. But this man before her wasn't Declan McKenna; he was Richard Lewis.

He took her right hand, knowing Declan's rings were on her left, and extracted a small box from his pocket. 'I know there are a lot of things to figure out, and the world is sure messed up right now so making plans isn't easy or even advisable, but I want to do something I should have done years ago.'

Grace felt the blood thunder in her ears, her stomach twisting in anticipation.

'Grace, I loved you from that first letter. I just knew then, and I know now, that what we have is not usual. It's unique to you and me. Declan and Pippa – they were special people, and in another lifetime, they would have been perfect for us, but our fate was sealed when you threw that bottle in the ocean, and someone somewhere decided that you and me would have to be together. We sure had to go a circuitous route to get here, but I know, like I know my own name, that you are the person I want to share my life with, and whatever it takes for that to happen, I will do it, because I love you, Grace. With every beat of my heart, I love you. I've always loved you. And I always will. So will you marry me?'

He opened the box then, and she saw, nestled on black velvet, an exquisite claddagh ring with a green stone for a heart.

'I'll get you whatever kind you want, a diamond or whatever you like. This is just… Well, I remembered you telling me about them and… Look, maybe it's dumb and just for –'

'I love it,' Grace said quietly.

'You do?'

She nodded.

'So?'

She'd never felt more love for him than she did in that moment, kneeling on the freezing ground, the air smelling of fire smoke and chips. The robin was back, hopping on the fountain. 'I love you too,' she finally managed. 'I just never thought…but here we are.'

'So what do you say?'

Grace shut her eyes and inhaled. She felt them then, her parents, Declan, Agnes even, releasing her. She was allowed to be happy, and Richard Lewis was how. 'Yes, Richard. I would love to marry you.'

He exhaled then, a huge sigh of relief, and she realised he'd been holding his breath. He went to place the ring on her right hand, but she stopped him. For a moment he looked stricken. But she said nothing, just slipped Declan's rings from her left hand to her right. Then she offered him her left hand.

'You don't have to…' he said, his voice gravelly with emotion.

'I know. I want to.'

He smiled, and his eyes shone with unshed tears. As the robin flew away, he stood and gently pulled her up. His arms went around her, and he dipped his head to kiss her. Richard was bulky and tall, and she found herself fitting her small frame to his large one as his lips found hers. At last.

CHAPTER 30

He groaned as he pulled away from the kiss.

'What's wrong?' Grace asked, scared she'd done something wrong. After all, she wasn't as experienced at this sort of thing as he probably was.

'I hate to do this, but I have to go. I swore to Jacob I'd get back to London immediately. He nearly went nuts when I told him I was coming here.'

'Really?' Her heart sank. Why was it always like this? Could they never get some time alone?

'I know. If there was any way, any way on earth, I swear I'd do it, but this thing...I need to be back, it's really important. I've got to be on the mailboat from Dublin to Wales and an overnight train across Wales and England to get back to London. The boat leaves in an hour, and I might as well throw myself into the Irish Sea if I'm not on it.'

'It feels like this is always the way, doesn't it? Brief meetings and lots of goodbyes,' Grace said sadly.

'I know, but this time is different. Now you're my fiancée, the girl I'm going to marry, just the second I can. So even though I don't want to leave, I can go with a happy heart.'

'Can you tell me what the thing is that you have to go back for?' she asked.

Richard explained a plan for the USAAF to take journalists on a bombing mission over Germany, and why they wanted to go, and Grace fought the urge to beg him not to do it. He told her how Jacob was excited, and he was too, but that there was a chance they wouldn't come back. It all felt too close to the bone for her. What if she let him go now and never saw him again? It could happen, easily.

'I think you're very brave.' She tried to keep the terror out of her voice.

'No braver than other men like me who do it every day. I just have to survive it once.' He laughed. 'I'll be fine, I know I will. But if we miss the training, we're out, and they won't give us much notice. And they're only training us just in case they need us to be useful. It's probably just a precaution. I don't expect it would do the US any good to have to announce that their best foreign correspondents were all shot down.' He smiled. 'I didn't mean me, obviously, but Cronkite and Pyle and the rest of the big guys.'

'You are one of the best,' she said. 'Be careful, all right? I…I don't know what I'd do if anything happened to you.' Her voice cracked with the fear of it. 'Can I walk you to the boat?'

'Of course, if it's not too far?' He looked at her with such tenderness, she thought she might cry.

'I can do it, if I can take your arm.'

'Always,' he said, offering her his elbow.

They walked slowly, talking and enjoying the nearness of each other.

'Grace, can I ask you something?'

'Of course.' She looked up at him.

'What did you feel, honestly, when you got the letter I wrote telling you about Pippa and the baby?'

She composed herself before answering. If she was going to marry this man, she would need to be totally honest with him, and he with her. She might as well start now. 'I was shocked, and a bit horrified. And very jealous.'

He looked sad. 'I'm so sorry, putting you through that...'

'But I'm not the same person I was. I was a bit of a dreamer, I suppose, believing in fairy tales, neat, perfect love stories. But the more I see of life, Charlie, Tilly, Eleanor, Eloise, my brother, the Warringtons, I've come to realise that things are not always what they seem.'

With a smile, he helped her skirt around a couple in a passionate embrace, and she continued. 'Life isn't some neat thing, tied up in a bow. It's messy and complicated, and sometimes the path is bumpy and crooked. We all have to make decisions, and I realise now successful relationships are based not on some stupid childish idea of love but on two imperfect people trying their best to be kind and support each other in good times and in bad.'

A blast of icy wind down the Liffey cut through the cashmere coat, and she shivered. Richard took off his heavy overcoat and put it around her.

'You're only in a pullover, you'll freeze,' she gasped, while relishing his body heat from the coat.

He shook his head. 'I'm fine. Carry on.'

'That's all I have to say really, just that what we have is special, but we, like everyone else in the world, will have to work hard. I'm willing to do that if you are?'

'I am. I swear to you, Grace, I'll do whatever it takes to make you happy. You know, this war has changed so many things for us all. It's allowed our generation to throw off some of the rules, but I'm not sure Knocknashee is moving at the same pace.'

Grace laughed. 'Oh, I can guarantee it isn't. But we can navigate that, if we're honest.'

He turned to her, placing his hands on her shoulders. 'I'll always be honest with you. We've had so much mixed-up communication because of the postal service but also fear of telling the truth, but let's make a deal now – no more wondering, no more veiled references. We say it like it is.'

'You've got yourself a deal, Mr Lewis.' She snuggled up to him, wrapping her arms around his waist 'Now, you need to promise you'll come back to me.'

'I'll take great care, I swear to you, Grace, and I'll be back before you know it.' He pulled her gently into a nearby doorway and kissed her again. 'Once I come back, we can make a plan, but if you'd like, we could set the wheels in motion before then?'

She opened the buttons of his coat she was wearing, and held him close, savouring his body warmth, as he kissed her head and hugged her tightly. Then he kissed her again, longer this time, deeper, and though she knew she should release him, that it wasn't proper to exchange such passionate kisses in a doorway, her body wouldn't let her pull away.

Two matronly ladies passed and saw the two lovers. 'The devil finds work for idle hands,' one of them said archly, which reduced both Grace and Richard to giggles.

They walked on.

'Well, I wouldn't really know how to arrange… Everyone I know gets married in the Church and…' She was embarrassed to bring it up, especially as the obvious obstacle hadn't seemed to have occurred to him.

'Won't we get married in a church?' He seemed perplexed. 'I'll marry you right here, on this street, but I thought you'd like a church wedding?'

'Well, I would, but…since you're not Catholic and Catholics aren't supposed to marry outside of… And they don't allow non-Catholics to…' She was mortified. It sounded like she was being sanctimonious or pious, but it was just the truth.

They stopped again, but this time he placed his hands on her shoulders. 'I'll convert if you want me to. I'll go to a priest, I'll do whatever they need me to do. I want to make you happy, Grace. I want you to be completely comfortable with it, and I know your faith means a lot to you, so…'

'I couldn't ask you to do that.' She gasped, 'I don't think I could do that for anyone, so I wouldn't expect…'

He smiled. 'Sweetheart…' He chuckled, a sound that made her feel like she had butterflies in her stomach. 'Grace, my precious Grace, my darling girl, my future wife, I would do anything for you, anything. And if me becoming a Catholic is something that would make this better for you, then I will do it with an open heart and full enthusiasm.' He kissed her again, softly this time. 'I know there's stuff we have to work out, where we'll live, what we'll do. But know this – I will do whatever it takes to be your husband. I'll live on the moon if you want to, I will do whatever you want me to, to make you happy. All I want is to be with you. I care about it more than my family, more than my job, more than my religion, more than anything.'

It was her turn to smile now. 'Well, that gives me a licence for all kinds of tyranny, doesn't it?'

He threw his arm around her shoulder then, pulling her close. 'Yes, ma'am, I'm putty in your tiny hands.'

They strolled on down the docks towards the late boat. It was pitch dark now, with just a few dimmed street lights.

'And your family, you're sure they won't mind?'

'That I'm fixin' to marry you?' He did a jokey version of his own accent, and she chuckled. 'Or the religion thing?'

'Either? Both?'

He shrugged. 'We just don't take church as seriously as you do, Grace, so no. My mother probably won't like you, but she doesn't like me much either, or Sarah, and she can't stand Jacob despite her words to the contrary, so don't worry about her. And my father is... Well, when he meets you, he'll know why I want to marry you, and he'll support me. I wrote to him, told him all about you, and he wrote back, said I should go for it and tell you the truth. I thought I had in that last letter, but maybe not, huh?'

'Definitely not, it was clear as mud.' She laughed. 'But Tilly said I was too cold in my reply to the awful news of Pippa and the baby. I'm so sorry, Richard, I just didn't know what to say.'

'Were you shocked?' he asked her as they reached the quays. The sharp wind up the Liffey stung their faces.

'Well, I'm very sheltered, Richard, and our Church is fairly unequivocal on such matters, so I suppose I would be lying if I said I wasn't.' She blushed at her gaucheness, but she had to be honest.

'So you and Declan never…before you were married?' he asked gingerly.

This man was going to be her husband; he had a right to ask. 'No. Never. We wanted to, of course, but…' She sighed, hating how provincial and old-fashioned she sounded. 'It's just not allowed, so…'

'Grace, I know it sounded bad, but I just want you to know I'm not the kind of man…that, you know…' He was so earnest she believed him

'Only wants to get a woman into bed?' she asked primly.

'Well, I just mean…' He was flustered now, not knowing the right thing to say, and Grace felt bad for playing with him.

'Because, Mr Lewis, I very much hope that you are,' she whispered in his ear. 'Just because I won't let you until we're married, doesn't mean I don't want you to try.' She put her arms around him again, this time allowing her hands to roam over the muscles of his back. He sighed and held her close, and as he kissed her again, she could feel his body respond to hers. She kissed him even more hungrily. Eventually they broke apart, needing air.

'Miss Fitz, I'm shocked,' he teased. 'I thought you were a good girl.'

'Oh, I said I was a Catholic, not a nun.' She winked and patted his face.

'Well, I better get to learning my prayers and whatnot as soon as possible, because I can't wait to have you in my bed.'

They reached the gangplank. Richard had paid for a ticket from Dublin back to Wales when he sailed over to Belfast so all he had to do was show his papers before boarding.

'You coming, mate?' a Cockney voice called out of the gloom.

'Yeah, be right there,' Richard responded.

'So it's goodbye again then,' Grace said, blinking back tears.

'*A la prochaine*, as they say in France.' Richard

smiled, his hands on her shoulders. 'Until the next time.'

'*Slán leat, agus Beannacht Dé ort,*' she said as he gathered her to his chest.

'What does that mean?' he whispered.

'It means may you be safe, and may God bless you.'

'Say it again, and I'll try to copy it. I guess I need to learn the language, right?' He grinned, and her heart melted.

She repeated the phrase, and he mimicked her, making a good enough job of it.

He chuckled. 'How long till I'm fluent?'

'Well, at the rate of one phrase a year, I would think you should be able to hold a basic conversation by the time we're in our eighties?' she replied, feeling the fear of letting him go dissipate a little. He was right, this was destiny, written in the stars. She and Richard would be together.

Across the street, someone got out of a taxi and Richard hailed it. The car made a U-turn, pulled up beside then and Richard leaned in and handed the driver a roll of banknotes, asking him to wait for a few moments, then to drive Grace to Marion's house.

'I don't want you wandering around here at night on your own.' He murmured to her.

He held her tight then, and to their amusement, a sailor sitting on a bollard used for winding rope took out a mouth organ and began to play 'We'll Meet Again', the Vera Lynn hit.

Slowly, as the music filled the cold night air, they began to dance. Richard crooned in her ear, in a surprisingly sweet tenor, and she joined in.

'We'll meet again, don't know where, don't know when, but I know we'll meet again, some sunny day. Keep shining through, just like you always do, till the blue skies drive those dark clouds far away.'

CHAPTER 31

KNOCKNASHEE

FEBRUARY 1943

Grace had had a letter from Richard that morning, saying he'd been called for and completed the training. He couldn't go into detail and wrote kind of cryptically in case the letter was intercepted, but he'd found he'd enjoyed it and was looking forward to using the skills he'd learnt. He was very busy with all that was happening. He was becoming ever more circumspect in his letters on the subject of his work.

According to most people, Britain and even Ireland were a nest of spies, so it was increasingly important not to commit anything to paper that might help the Germans. So instead he spoke of their future, wondered where they would live, what he would do when the war was over. He was at pains to say he had no big plan, and so long as he was with her, he didn't care where in the world he ended up. For all that, though, she tried and failed to picture him in Knocknashee. Every time she thought about them together, it was in some nameless place, she couldn't imagine where. It wasn't here, but it wasn't Georgia either. London? Dublin? Paris?

His letter was lovely, so full of joy and love and passion that she'd blushed as she read it. In all their correspondence, he'd never been anything but friendly and proper in how he spoke to her, but this letter was full of how much he loved her and how gorgeous she was and how he couldn't stop thinking about her.

She could recall one piece by heart, she'd read it so often.

I was sitting in a freezing-cold classroom with some god-awful boring flight lieutenant droning on about enemy plane insignia when I heard my name being called. I started and realized I was daydreaming.

He came down and slammed a book on my desk and barked, "You better take your mind off her, son, and bring it back to being able to distinguish a Messerschmitt from a Fokker, because if you don't, she'll be a widow before she becomes a bride."

All the other guys laughed of course, and Jacob told them all about you and what I had to do to get you. Now they all call me Romeo, but I don't care. I love you, Grace, and I don't care who knows it. I want to shout it from the rooftops.

I wrote to my parents, and as expected, my father replied, full of congratulations and with instructions to bring you to Savannah as soon as I can. My mother tacked on a message asking if you were related to the F. Scott Fitzgerald who wrote The Great Gatsby? *I laughed so hard at that, and I had to read it to Sarah, who just rolled her eyes. Typical of my mother. To her, pedigree is everything, so she was looking for something to say at her bridge club.*

Don't worry, though. She might rate your bloodline, but nobody else in my family thinks like that. Everyone is going to love you. Nathan sent a telegram congratulating us and saying how much he was looking forward to meeting you and welcoming you to the family, and Miranda sent a bottle of Bollinger, which is typical for her, with a card saying "It takes a big woman to congratulate the winner when you're the loser, but the best woman won."

He'd included a card from Sarah and Jacob, offering congratulations on her engagement, and she put it on the mantel.

Everyone was so happy for her. It was wonderful. It had taken her a full twenty minutes to walk up the street, with her neighbours coming to congratulate her. Even Pádraig O Sé said he thought the Yank was all right and she could do worse. Margaret O'Connor even managed to say something nice about Declan and how he'd be happy to see her with someone good who'd look after her.

Margaret had taken over the undertaker's business run by her late husband, and what she lacked in Seán O'Connor's gentle charm, she made up for in ingenuity. Charlie had told Grace that while she was in Dublin, old Mrs O'Dea, who lived up the side of the mountain out at the end of the peninsula, died. Getting the funeral carriage up to collect the body was going to be impossible; it was all scree and loose gravel. So under cover of darkness, Margaret borrowed Dr Ryan's car, drove up the steep track and put the late Mrs O'Dea into the passenger seat before rigor mortis set in. She then drove her down and popped her in the coffin at the base of the mountain. A Knocknashee solution to a Knocknashee problem. Grace thought she must remember to tell Richard about it when she wrote.

It was a bright sunny day, so welcome after the weeks of rain and cold, so she arranged to meet Tilly for a picnic. Odile had been inside since they came back from Dublin, and she needed a run around outside. It was still cold, but wrapped up in coats and warm hats, they'd be fine. They arranged to meet on the beach, where Odile could run and gallop, and if she fell, she wouldn't hurt herself.

She and Tilly had a special spot a bit further up the beach than where everyone else normally congregated. It was stonier and had a big flat rock where they could lay out their picnic. They'd been doing it for years. Tilly picked her up at the post office with the trap pulled by Rua the horse. They made their way along the coast road and stopped at a gap where they could get down fairly easily to the flat rock, leaving Rua happily munching the long acre at the side of the road above them. Ned, Tilly's ancient pony, was enjoying a lovely retirement in the field behind the school, where he was doted on by the pupils and spent his days being petted and chomping buttercups.

'*Is tusa cosuil le maighdean mara*, Aintín Grace!' Odile said as Grace took off her hat and allowed her copper curls to fall down her back. Even though it was cold, the exertion of getting down the rocks had warmed her up.

'And in English?' Grace asked the little girl gently.

She frowned. 'You're like a…' She paused.

Grace helped her. 'Mermaid. That's a new word for you now, isn't it? Can you try it?'

'You are like a mermaid,' Odile repeated happily. She loved using her three languages, as every time she did, she garnered huge praise.

'*Maith thú a storín…*' Tilly laid out their picnic and handed her a buttered slice of white soda bread with a few precious raisins in it.

'What do we say?' Grace prompted her.

'*Merci, go raibh maith agat,* thank you,' Odile said with a laugh. It was her new party piece, using all three languages at once. She was such a bright little thing, so funny and full of joy. You couldn't be grumpy around Odile.

'Can I try your ring on?' the little girl asked.

Odile was fascinated by Grace's engagement ring, the claddagh with the emerald heart, and though Tilly warned her not to let the child have it and said she wasn't taking responsibility if it went missing, Grace let the youngster try it every time they met.

'Be very careful of that, Odile, it's very precious,' Tilly warned as the ring dangled on the child's little index finger.

'Like me,' Odile said.

Tilly kissed the top of her silky head. 'Yes, very precious, just like you.'

As the little girl ate her snack on a blanket on the sand, Grace and Tilly sat on the flat rock. It was a perfect height for Grace, because sitting on the ground was hard for her – not the sitting part, but the getting back up.

'Will we play "who loves me"?' Odile asked. It was her favourite game, naming off all the people she thought loved her. She would start with the obvious, Tilly, Mamó, Grace, Eloise, Charlie and Dymphna, but it went quickly to people they hardly knew but who Odile was sure loved her nonetheless.

'We will...' And Tilly started naming the usual suspects.

'And my daddy, and my mammy...' Odile said innocently.

Tilly looked at Grace, her face a question. This had never come up before. Grace shrugged.

'Yes, your mammy and daddy definitely love you,' Tilly said.

Odile seemed to drop the subject then and went on to sing one of her many nonsense word songs.

'How did she come up with that?' Tilly whispered to Grace. 'I never said. I intended to obviously, but she was so small…'

'She must have heard us talking. She's so bright.'

'I don't suppose Richard has had any word from Didier recently, has he?' Tilly asked quietly. 'We were so delighted to get that note from the Spanish man, Nico, but now it feels like ages ago, and Mam says she'd know if he was dead, but it's been so long…'

Grace shook her head sadly. 'I asked him in the last letter, and we talked about it in Dublin, but he hasn't seen him. He could well be gone back to France, and news out of any of the occupied countries is almost nonexistent.'

'I'm sure he'd tell us if he found anything out.' Tilly sighed. 'Sometimes I'm sure Alfie's going to be fine – he's like a cat, that fella, with nine lives –

but then other times...' She swallowed. 'And when I hear Odile speaking French, or singing... Eloise taught her a song, something about an elephant swinging on a spider's web. It's an old folk song she'd learnt when she was a little girl. Anyway, I just get a pang of sadness, wondering if Odile will ever speak in French to her own family. And then I feel so guilty, Grace, because even though I pray every night for her mother and Alfie and Constance to come back in one piece, a part of me dreads her return, because she'll take Odile...'

Grace gave her friend a one-armed squeeze. 'That's completely understandable. You've been her mother since she was a tiny tot, and now look at her, a happy little girl. Of course you'd hate to lose her. But even if Bernadette survives, and we pray she does, there's no guarantee she'll take her away. We'll always be in Odile's life, Tilly, how could we not be?'

'She might turn up and take her back to France?'

Grace sighed. 'Things are turning for the Allies, and it seems like Hitler might be on the back foot a bit. It's looking a bit more optimistic anyway, though that wouldn't be hard. But there's a long road to go yet, Til. I'd say let's try not to worry or look too far into the future. Easier said than done, I know.'

Tilly shrugged. 'There's nothing we can do anyway. So tell me, how's Richard?'

Grace smiled. 'He's fine. Busy, and...' She paused. Surely it would be no harm to tell Tilly?

'And what?' Tilly's head was to one side as she poured tea from a flask and then handed Grace a slice of soda bread.

'Well, he's not supposed to tell anyone, but he told me. He's going on a bombing raid with the American Air Force – Jacob is too and a group of other correspondents from various papers – to see what it's like first-hand. He's had training in operating a gun and how to parachute out if things go bad. I hate thinking about it, and I know other men are doing that kind of thing every day and why shouldn't he, but it scares me half to death honestly, Til...'

'Wow. That's amazing. Scary absolutely, but to be up in a plane, and to drop bombs on Germany... It would be satisfying considering all the damage they inflicted on England. Men get all the best jobs,' she grumbled.

Grace laughed. 'Trust you to think like that. I'd hate to go, but you'd probably jump at it if they let you.'

'A chance to give them a taste of their own medicine? You bet your life I would, and to fly in a plane, like a bird…I'd give anything to do that.'

Grace fell silent then. A noisy gull squawked overhead, and she gazed out over the water. A seal popped its nose out, and it reminded her of the day she threw the bottle in the sea, the bottle containing the letter in which she poured her heart out about how awful Agnes was. The seals were there that day too. How much life had changed in the four years since then.

'Try not to worry, Grace…' Tilly said gently, reading her thoughts.

'I think sometimes that God would never be that cruel to take Richard from me as well as everyone else…' She turned to Tilly then. 'He wouldn't, would he?'

'No. He wouldn't. Richard is going to be fine,' Tilly replied, but they both knew they were just empty words. They didn't know that, just like they didn't know about Alfie or Constance or Bernadette or Maurice and his family. Nobody knew what the future held, and reassurances that everything was going to be all right were hollow.

'Sarah and Jacob sent a nice card, saying I was welcome to the family and that they were delighted for us. Sarah was funny – she said she's been looking at her brother's mopey face long enough and she was relieved he was finally happy. It was really nice of her, because she and Pippa are good friends still. And everyone's been so nice, I'm almost afraid to let myself be happy.'

'That was nice of her. She sounds like an interesting girl. Remember she sent me that book years back, *The Well of Loneliness*. It's a book about two women who love each other. She must have figured out that I was…well, like I am, before even you knew.'

'I know. Isn't that amazing? I must have said something about you to Richard – well, I always talk about you, but you know what I mean – and he told her, and she deduced from that what you might like to read.'

'It was the first thing I ever read that made me feel like I might not be totally unnatural,' Tilly admitted quietly.

'Oh, Tilly… I know we don't talk about it much, but it was so nice to see you and Eloise in Dublin, meeting your friends, just being yourselves. I'm so glad you have that. And I was a bit jealous of Eloise, that's the truth. I hated the idea of her taking you away from me. But did she tell you we had a chat, and she was fearful that she could never win you if it was a choice between her and all of us here, so we just agreed to share you.' Grace laughed at the idea.

'She told me.' Tilly sighed. 'Imagine you two fighting over me like a tug-of-war.'

'Well, now we're friends and we might gang up on you, so that might be worse.'

'I'm glad you two get along better.' Tilly moved a stone with her foot, keeping her gaze down. 'I love her, Grace.'

'I'm happy for you, Til, truly I am. And she's wonderful. No wonder you love her. I feel like a dishrag beside her most of the time – she's like something from a magazine or the pictures.'

'Who are you telling? I don't know what she sees in me, I swear. Someday I think I'm going to wake up and she'll be shaking her head, asking herself what was she thinking.'

'Don't be daft. You're gorgeous too. Sure isn't every farmer and fisherman on the peninsula driven half cracked trying to get your attention?'

'Trying to get my farm more like.' Tilly smiled ruefully.

Grace chuckled. 'Well, they're barking up the wrong tree there.'

'Do you think people know, Grace? About me, I mean?' Tilly looked unusually vulnerable.

'They don't. And they won't if you don't tell

them. I think most people might have some idea there are men like you, as in men who like men, I mean, but I don't think that the idea of women being like that enters their heads. It never entered mine till you told me, and I'm your best friend.'

'Ah, but sure you're blind as a bat.' Tilly nudged her playfully.

Grace glanced to the right. 'There's someone coming.' She nodded to the rocks. A figure was climbing over the fingers of old red sandstone that stretched from the cliff to the sea. At low tide it was just possible to walk around them, but the tide was coming in now, so climbing over the uneven terrain was the only way to get to where they were sitting.

Whoever it was was making most ungainly progress as the two girls watched in curiosity. As the figure managed to get over the biggest rock, using both hands and feet, they stood up, and Grace couldn't believe her eyes. It couldn't be.

She laughed at the sight, as the person's clothing was most certainly not conducive to rock climbing.

CHAPTER 32

'Father Iggy!' she called in delight.

He waved and beamed as he walked towards them. Grace got up and went to meet him. It wasn't the done thing to hug a priest, but she didn't care. She threw her arms around him, and he hugged her back.

'I can't believe you're here!' Grace cried. 'This is great – we really missed you.'

'Oh, I missed Knocknashee, I can promise you that. Though I'm about as nimble as a billiard table. I thought I could hop over those rocks to save myself the long walk around, but I overestimated my jumping skill.' He grinned. 'Hello, Tilly, and oh my goodness, that's not Odile? She's after growing up so much.'

Odile was happily munching a piece of apple Tilly had cut up and peeled for her.

'Hello, Father, it's lovely to see you. Sit down there till I give you a cup of tea. Will you have a bit of soda bread?' Tilly rinsed out her own cup and poured tea for the priest into it, cutting another slice of the home-made loaf.

'Not at all, Tilly. I don't want to be taking a bite from your mouths, sure you only have enough for yourselves.'

'Ah you're grand Father…' Tilly handed him the mug and slice of bread buttered with a scrape of precious jam. 'Mam packed too much as usual. We've loads. Now, tell us, what has you here?'

The priest, who had always been on the chubby side, was much slimmer now. The buttons of his long black soutane no longer strained at his belly, and his dark hair was going grey at the temples. He still wore his thick spectacles that made his eyes look enormous.

'Well…' He paused dramatically. 'I'm the new parish priest.'

'Of where?' Tilly asked.

'Of here. I've been sent back to Knocknashee.' He couldn't keep the glee from his voice.

Grace could hardly believe it. Father Iggy was back. This was the best news, and her first thought was how much easier Maurice's arrival would be if Father Iggy was there, setting the tone for the parish. She just knew he would be welcoming and kind, and she felt a lot of her anxiety dissipate.

'I'm over the moon, Father, really over the moon. We have so much to tell you, but it can all wait. Sit down and tell us all your news.' Grace made some room on the rock, and the little priest climbed up beside her and Tilly.

'Oh, Father Iggy, everyone will be so delighted.' Tilly beamed. 'Father Iggy is back, Odile...' The little girl looked up at the black-clad priest with suspicion. Of course she didn't know him; she was only a baby when he was sent to Cork.

'How did that happen?' Grace asked, incredulous that her friend was being restored to the parish. She blinked back a tear as the priest met her gaze.

'Well now, Grace, that's a bit of a mystery. I got into a bit of hot water above in Cork. I know the Warringtons mentioned it to you, and the jungle drums being what they are...'

'I never said it to anyone...' Grace interjected, dismayed. She hated the idea that he thought she was gossiping about him.

'Oh, I know you didn't, Grace. I didn't mean

that, just that it was fairly public.' He turned to Tilly. 'My superior wasn't being very… Well, he and I saw things differently, I suppose, and I went against him and that's not allowed in the clergy, so the bishop of Cork was none too pleased with me. I ministered to the congregation as best I could, but it wasn't an easy time. I was tested and found wanting often, I'm afraid.' He sounded so sad, Grace wished she could comfort him.

'Well, I don't know about that, Father Iggy,' Grace said defiantly. 'The way I heard it, you did a kind, decent thing, and that girl's family needed your mercy and compassion. And I know you can't say it, but the parish priest was wrong then. I don't think it's what Jesus would have done.'

'Well, either way I promised to obey and I didn't, so I broke my vow.'

'Priests are also to follow the teachings of Christ, and nowhere in the Bible does he treat people with callous cruelty the way that priest did…' Grace was getting angry now.

'Ah, Grace, you know how it is. Anyway, I got a summons to the bishop's palace three weeks ago, and I was sure I was going to be in big trouble. The Reverend Mother who runs the home for girls in Cork, girls who have babies out of wedlock, wasn't too pleased with me either. She and I had a bit of a set-to. I was too friendly with the girls apparently. The poor *craythurs* are so lost and alone and fearful, all I was doing was having a friendly chat and a bit of a laugh, but that's not allowed, it seems. God knows there's nothing much to laugh about if you're in there, and they're treated like they did something desperate altogether. And if you'll pardon me being indelicate, they didn't get pregnant on their own. I might have pointed that fact out to the Reverend Mother, and so that didn't go down well at all. So I thought, here we go again, God only knows where I'm to be sent now, somewhere even more difficult, that's why he's called me in.' He tried to look contrite, but Grace knew that deep down he wasn't.

'And what did he say?' Tilly asked. Both girls were hanging on every word. Odile was getting tired, so she was snuggled up in Tilly's arms.

'He didn't say much, to be honest.' Father Iggy's face was open and truthful as always. 'Just that as a favour to the bishop of Kerry, I was being transferred back to this diocese, but he didn't know where. He never said a blessed bit about my being like a square peg in a round hole above in Cork, which I was, of course.'

'And you didn't argue.' Tilly grinned.

'Indeed and I did not, only out the door to pack my bag before you could say Jack Robinson for fear they'd change their minds.' He chuckled.

'So you were able to come directly here?' Grace asked, surprised at the speed of it all.

'Well, no. I was sent to a retreat in Galway, and I needed it. I needed to reflect on my time in Cork and what I could have done better. And then when I was there, one of the days, Bishop Buckley came to see me. And we had a big, long talk about everything, about Canon Rafferty and my experience in Cork and lots of other things. He's a very nice man and a good bishop. I know people think he's a bit haughty, but he's not really – he's decent, a good man.'

'And what did he say that brought you here?' Grace sipped her tea.

'Well, that's the puzzling thing. He asked how I felt about coming back here, to Knocknashee. As you might know, this very rarely happens. They move us around and almost never send us back to a place you were before. And I said I was the happiest I ever was in my whole life here, and that I think of my time in this parish with such fondness.' He took off his glasses and wiped them with the sleeve of his soutane. 'I told him the truth, that I never had much in the way of friends growing up. We were farming, and it was just work and more work, and there wasn't enough land for us all, so being the second boy in the family, it was the seminary or the emigrant boat. I liked the idea of being a priest, though I'm not sure I was holy enough, to be honest with you, but they took me anyway.' He smiled, and Grace felt such a wave of affection for him. His was a common story: The eldest got the farm, and the girls could be married off, but for the second and subsequent sons, there was nothing.

'Did you like it? The seminary?' Grace asked.

'Ah, 'twas grand. I loved reading and studying and that kind of thing, and I wasn't up milking cows at the dawn or thinning turnips or footing turf, so I was delighted with myself. I got along fine, but I didn't form any deep bonds or anything like that. I didn't really know how to, I suppose. All the other fellows were much better than me at that class of thing. I was a loner.' There was no trace of self-pity; it was just how he was.

'But when I came here, I made real friends for the first time in my life, and I missed you all something wicked when I left. Us priests aren't really supposed to form attachments, even friendships really. It's sort of frowned upon in case it clouds your judgement or makes you show favouritism or something…'

Odile sighed heavily in her sleep, and they all smiled at the sleeping child.

Tilly rolled her eyes. 'It's like they forget you are human beings too.'

'And then Bishop Buckley said a strange thing…' Father Iggy went on. 'He said, "I think a good friend, a loyal friend, is a treasure beyond measure, and if you have that, Iggy, and I know for sure that you do, you're a lucky man."'

Grace didn't give anything away. The last thing she wanted was anyone thinking she'd pulled strings, or speculation as to how she could, so she remained passive. Tilly shot her a glance but said nothing.

'Well, whatever the reason, it's wonderful news,' Grace said. 'Everyone is going to be so happy, and we could use some good news, we really could. Poor Father Lehane is gone down to the size of a rasher from all the tearing around, burying the dead, baptising the babies, tending the sick, saying all the Masses, hearing confessions – the poor man is run ragged.'

'I know, the poor divil. I told him next week he's to go home and see his family – he hasn't seen them in over a year. He needs feeding up and a good rest.'

The tide was lapping very close to them now.

'We'd better get away before we're soaked,' Tilly said as Grace started to gather the cups. 'Come up the roadway and I'll drop you back, Father. I'm bringing Grace home anyway.'

'Your poor horse doesn't need to be dragging me as well, Tilly,' he said, folding the blanket. 'I'll walk away. I'll be grand.'

'Sure there's nothing left of you at all, Father. Yourself and Father Lehane are wasting away. You're like a pull-through for a rifle these days,' she teased.

'Era, the grub in Cork isn't a patch on here… and I wasn't being offered cakes and buns at every stop either, I can assure you.' He winked.

Tilly laughed. 'No wonder you wanted to come back to us. 'Twasnt us at all that drew him, Grace, 'twas the cakes and sweets.'

'Well, you'll find Herr Hitler has put a stop to our gallop in the cakes department, but we'll manage to cobble something together, I'm sure.' Grace assured him as she allowed Father Iggy to help her up the rocks to the trap.

Tilly carried the still sleeping Odile, and Grace and Father Iggy followed, Grace leaning on his arm while he carried the picnic basket. As soon as Tilly was far enough ahead and out of earshot, he murmured, 'What did you say to him?'

Grace turned and looked fondly at her old friend, so happy to see him again. 'I don't know what you mean?'

'Don't you know 'tis a sin to lie to a priest?' He raised his eyebrows, a smile playing on his lips. 'I know you went to see him.'

'I was invited to tea in the palace, and we had a nice chat, just about how the best way to serve God and a community is to try to smooth down things that might be upsetting and to encourage things that help people. It was all very general. I never mentioned your name and neither did he.'

He nodded. 'Well, there is no doubt in my mind that you're the reason I'm here. Thank you, Grace.' He swallowed, and she heard the catch in his throat. 'I'm very happy to be back, and I wouldn't be only for you, so thank you.'

'That's what friends are for, Father.' She smiled as he helped her up the last rocky outcrop to the road where Tilly waited with Rua and Odile.

CHAPTER 33

LONDON

MARCH 1943

Richard sat in the bar of the hotel and listened to the newspapermen talking. He was in awe of Andy Rooney and Walter Cronkite and felt humbled to be in their presence. They showed him nothing but friendly collegiality, and he was grateful and listened to as much as he could to improve his skills as a journalist.

They were discussing the way coverage of the

war had never really been balanced but how now it was unashamedly on the side of the Allies. It was as if the press were another wing of the armed forces and doing their bit to boost morale and explain to American readers back home why continued effort, men and resources had to keep coming.

Cronkite spoke. 'I've no intention of being impartial. We're all on the same side. I'm reporting on the heroism of our boys in the face of Nazi bestiality, and I make no apology for it.'

Andy Rooney agreed. 'We're no propagandists, but I suppose the truth is we write about the British civilians killed, the hospitals bombed by the Germans, but we never refer to the German hospitals we bomb, killing their sick and injured. According to our reporting, we never do that, but the truth is we do.'

'Well, we'll see first-hand soon,' a newspaperman from Iowa named Bill Tyson said.

'At least it's B-17s we're going up in, not B-24s,' Art Carlson from Florida said. 'One of the gunners said he was always happy to see B-24s on a mission because the Germans went after them first. They're much less agile than the B-17s, so if we get chased, we stand a chance.' He winced as he took a sip of the British beer.

'Though I don't mind admitting it, I'm scared to death.'

'We'll be in close formation,' Cronkite explained. 'Wingtip to wingtip is the way to take on the Luftwaffe. They're on the lookout for lone aircraft – they won't draw fire from several planes in tight formation.'

'Libs are more stable, though, right?' asked a cub reporter from the *New York Times* who Richard didn't know and who wasn't going up. 'Libs' was a nickname for the Liberators, B-24 bombers. The B-17s were called Forts, short for Flying Fortress.

Harrison Salisbury from the United Press answered. 'Yeah, certainly, but not as quick or as easy to manoeuvre out of a tight spot, so it's a toss-up. Truth is, if you fly with the Eighth these days, you hold a ticket to a funeral, your own. Casualties are running at twenty percent.'

Richard was sitting beside Warren King, an Australian correspondent. 'Bet this chat is cheering you right up, eh, mate?' he whispered as he nudged Richard and signalled for another beer.

Richard was scared, no point in denying it. But he saw the value in what he was doing in a way he hadn't before. He would do anything, everything he could to encourage American enthusiasm for this war.

The conversation went on, and Warren turned to Richard again. 'What was the training like?'

Richard liked the cheery Australian and was happy to share information. He sighed. 'Three days. We were sent to the air gunnery in Bovington. The first thing was we were put, six at a time, wearing oxygen masks, into a truck-mounted pressure chamber to check if we could handle the change in pressure and altitude. If you passed that, you learned how to assemble and disassemble a fifty-calibre machine gun, and then we learned some first aid.'

'Strewth, mate, that sounds intense.'

'That was just the first day.' Richard smiled.

'So what came next?'

'Aircraft recognition. You have to decide within one thousand yards if an airplane is friend or foe before opening fire – you have to be sure. Then we went up, hit the highest altitude of twenty-five thousand feet, in masks of course, but it was something.'

'Tough?' Walter asked.

'Yeah, it sure feels claustrophobic. You have to fight the panic.'

'And there's nobody shooting at you yet.' Warren exhaled and lit a cigarette. 'Y'know, I was envious of you blokes when I heard you were going up, but the more I hear about it, the happier I am to stay right down here on terra firma.'

Richard knew Warren was going to write a piece on it, but he didn't mind. Australian mothers were sending their sons too, and they deserved to know why just as much as American mothers did.

'And what was the rest of the training about?'

'Firing weapons, how to solve a jam, more identifying aircraft. We won't be put in a gunnery position, of course. It's just in case the gunner is put out of action, then we might be called on.' Richard knew he sounded blasé, but he felt anything but.

He glanced at the lobby and saw Sarah and Jacob enter, so he excused himself and went to join them.

'We got our clearance,' Jacob said excitedly. 'We're going up Thursday.'

Richard's heart thumped loudly in his chest. He was surprised Sarah couldn't hear it. Jacob had taken the training in stride – the altitude and pressure seemed to take no toll on him whatsoever – and Richard envied him his nonchalance.

He nodded. 'All right.' It was all he could manage.

Jacob spotted a CBS newsreel cameraman he knew and went to speak to him, leaving Richard and Sarah alone.

'You doing OK, little brother?' she asked kindly.

He nodded. He wasn't, but there was no point in saying that.

'Wanna get a decent cup of coffee?' She winked.

'Where?' He raised a suspicious eyebrow. There was good coffee to be had but only on the black market, and he didn't agree with it; it was wrong and unfair.

'At home.' She was bursting with excitement. 'Wait till you see.'

He followed her out. They jumped in the car he'd inherited from a Californian reporter who'd gone home and drove back to the flat.

On the table was a large box, opened and heavy looking.

'What is it?' Richard asked.

'Look inside and see,' Sarah said, hardly containing her glee.

He extracted a smaller box, beside which were three bags of what he knew by the delicious aroma were coffee beans. He read the side of the box. 'A La Pavoni espresso machine with new piston pump.'

'And a grinder. I love my daddy.' She extracted another 'contraption', as Pippa would call it, with a handle on the side. 'Richard, we can make proper coffee…' She sighed contentedly.

'Isn't it rationed at home too?'

'Please, darling Richard, just this one time, please don't ask too many questions and just enjoy it, pleeeeeease.' She theatrically clawed the front of his shirt. 'Just make coffee, proper, delicious, American coffee, made with actual coffee beans, not roots or sticks or puddles or whatever garbage they use here, and for five minutes, let's be on the porch at the cottage, the salty ocean breeze cooling our skin after the heat of the day, Esme putting hamburgers on the grill, hot dogs with mustard and ketchup, and her sugar cream pie with ice cream for dessert.'

Richard indulged her and allowed himself to be there, at a time when life seemed so complicated to him, when he was on St Simons and he'd received that first letter from Grace. Well, Doodle, their old dog, had found it. And that put him on a path to here, and despite everything, he wouldn't change a thing.

'I assume Father and Esme took Doodle with them when Esme came to Savannah?' Richard asked, thinking of the old dog he'd loved since he was a boy. A shadow crossed Sarah's face.

'What?' he asked, dreading the answer.

'It was around the time Pippa lost the baby. Esme wrote to us both, but I got the letter first. Doodle died in his sleep, curled up in his basket after a big feed of leftover brisket. I thought you were sad enough, so I didn't tell you.'

Richard felt tears prick his eyes.

'Oh, honey, it's OK to be sad. We all loved that dumb dog. But he had a great life and he died with no pain.' She wrapped her arms around him.

Embarrassed to be crying over a dog when so many people were being slaughtered daily, he wiped his eyes. 'I'm fine, I... It's just a lot right now...'

'You don't want to go on this bombing mission, do you?' She was always so astute.

'Not much, no, but I will. It's the right thing to do, and if I can better explain how important it is, and people at home give another big push, then we might just win the damned thing and we can all get on with our lives, what's left of them.'

'Are you scared? I know I'd be petrified,' she

said as she started to assemble the coffee machine.

'Yes, but more than that, I don't want to die. I feel like I finally got it right with Grace. I don't want to leave her.'

'Well, we can just pray you don't.' Sarah examined the parts as she extracted them from the box.

He laughed. 'You sound like her now, with the praying for things.'

'I don't know, Richard. We didn't have much of that when we were growing up.' She spoke slowly, pensively. 'But when we meet the refugees, Jews especially, so many have lost their faith. They agonise over how God could do this to them. They're good people, they did nothing to deserve it. But I think maybe God isn't doing this, Hitler is. We have free will, and he's using his for evil and chaos, but look at all the good people all over the world who are risking everything to stop him. Could that not be the influence of God?'

'Who knows?' He sighed. 'The longer this goes on, the less sense it makes.'

'I know. Will it only be over when everyone is dead?' She shook her head.

'Sarah, if I die, will you go over and tell Grace yourself? Jacob and I have both listed you as our next of kin, so if there's news, you'll be the one to get it, and I'm sorry, but would you do that for me?'

Sarah's brown eyes filled with tears; she wiped them away with the sleeve of her raggedy sweater. Her hair was in need of a cut and she dressed like a hobo, and he realised in that moment how much he loved her.

'I promise,' she said, her voice choked.

'And go home, OK? If we're gone, go home. Don't stay here. They'll need you. And you'll need them.' He opened his arms, and she walked into them; he rested his chin on her head.

'OK. But just don't die. Either of you. Deal?' she said into his shirt.

'I'll do my very best. I love you, Sarah. And tell the folks at home I love them too, in case…'

'Write and tell them yourself.' She grinned, playfully punching him in the chest. 'I'm not your messenger boy.'

'I will.' He released her. 'Call me when the coffee's ready.' He ducked with a chortle to avoid the slap she aimed at him for his misogyny.

He would do exactly that, write to everyone, so if the worst happened, at least they'd know. He placed his hand on the door handle of his bedroom when he heard her say from the kitchen door.

'Esme would say "don't y'all go a-borrowing trouble now." So let's try to hope for the best, OK?'

'You bet.' He winked at her. 'And she'd say that sweater fits you like socks on a rooster.'

They both laughed. Esme was as Southern as it was possible to be.

'And Richard?'

He turned back.

'I love you too.'

CHAPTER 34

Dear Grace,
 I feel like I should have some other way of starting a letter now that you are my Grace and not just Grace. Darling Grace, love of my life Grace, amazing Grace?

I got the word I'm going on Thursday, so this is the only chance I'll have to write. I'll put it in the mail as soon as I seal it, so hopefully by the time you read this, I'll be back in one piece. I'll telegram when I get back like you asked. Boy, it sure feels nice to have you worry about me. I know you always did, but in this special way, as your soon-to-be husband, well, it's nice.

Nice. I can see you rolling your eyes. For all that I'm a writer, I don't have the huge vocabulary to write flowery love letters. But I do love you, Grace, so *much that sometimes it scares me, because the thought of losing you again, or anything happening to keep us apart, just makes me... Well, I just can't bear it.*

But Sarah reminded me of something Esme says. I told you about her—she takes care of us. Well, she used to. She's a real Southerner, and her phrases would make you laugh. I'll tell you some when we next meet so you'll know what she is saying when you meet her.

But she always used to tell us when we were little and worrying about something, "Don't y'all go a-borrowing no trouble, y'hear?"

That means worrying is pointless, and she's right. Thinking about bad things that might happen sure is dumb, so I'm trying not to do it.

I've got a few other letters to write, so I'll keep this short, and I'll telegram you before you even get this. But just so you know, Grace, you're the best thing that has ever happened to me, and I can't wait to be by your side and in your bed (I know that's not gentlemanly, but it's true) for the rest of my life.

Take care, my precious girl.
Love you always and forever,
R OXOXOXOXO

He folded it and addressed the envelope before drawing another sheet towards him.

Dear Mother,

Today I am going on a special assignment, and I just wanted to write and tell you...

He paused. Tell her what?

...tell you that I wish you well. I hope you will try to understand that Daddy was only supporting Sarah and me. He didn't make us go to war; we were going either way. I would have been a terrible banker, and Miranda and I were not a good match. I have told you already about Grace. She's a very special person, and I'm very lucky to have her.

I would urge you to accept Sarah and Jacob. He's a good man, and they love each other. And if anything happens to him, she will need love and support. And if this war has taught me anything, it's that love is important. In fact, it might be the only important thing. Daddy still loves you, and making him choose between you and us was a stupid thing to do, you know it was, but I'm glad you were able to find a way back. Well done on going to the wedding—it's a hard thing to admit you were wrong. Forgive, move on, and be happy. We all deserve a bit of happiness.

All the best.

Your son,

Richard

It might not be the warmest, but at least it was something.

Next, he wrote to Esme.

Dearest Esme,

I'm going off on a bit of an adventure on Thursday, and I wanted to write to you just to say hello and to thank you for all the care you took of us all, and especially of me all my life. We all know I was your favorite! I only just found out about Doodle—you must have been so sad. None of us believed you when you complained about him. We know you loved him, and he knew it too. Sarah said he died full of brisket.

What I wouldn't give for a big serving of your brisket now. The food here is so bad, but I guess that's the war. I don't know if that's really true, though. I think the food before the war might have been pretty bad too, but you didn't hear that from me!

I'm engaged to a girl—the girl who wrote the letter that Doodle found. She's wonderful, Esme. I can't wait for you to meet her, and I've told her all about you and how important you are to us.

So thank you again, and God bless you, Esme. I love you a bushel and a peck and a hug around the neck.

Always,
Richard

He felt a pang as he wrote the words of the nursery rhyme she used to croon to him when he was little. If he hurt his knee or had a stomachache, she would give him a cookie or a hug, say 'I love you a bushel and a peck and a hug around the neck' and tickle him. Never in front of his parents, though; they wouldn't have approved of the help being so familiar with the children. It was as if all those coloured women were good enough to raise white children but not good enough to love them. Yet every one of his friends loved their maid more than their mama; it was just how it was.

He put the letter in an envelope, sad at how easy it was for him to write to Esme when the note to his own mother was stilted and halting. It was because they all knew Esme was more of a mother to him than Caroline Lewis ever was. If he died, Esme would cry for him, not Caroline.

He drew another sheet towards him.

Dear Daddy,

I used to call you that when I was little, so here we go. Firstly, thank you for the coffee machine. I won't ask how you got your hands on three big bags of Brazilian coffee beans, but we are very grateful. You've been so kind, and it really made us feel so much better and not so far from home when your boxes of treats arrived. I know it was Lynette who did the shopping and mailing, but on your instructions, so thank her from us too.

I'm going on a special operation on Thursday. I

can't say more, but I wanted to write to you just in case something bad happens. I don't anticipate it, but just in case. I'll send a telegram when I'm back, so you'll probably get that before you get this letter.

I feel sad about how much time we wasted, and how much I wish we'd had the relationship we have now when I was young. I didn't really know you and I guess you didn't know me, but I feel like over the last few years, we've become close, and I'm grateful for that.

I wrote to Mother as well. I hope you and she can continue to patch things up if that's what you want. But I will say this again—if it's not, and someone else could make you happier, then I wish you would. We don't get long on this earth, and nothing is guaranteed.

I can't wait to introduce you to Grace when I take her to Savannah to meet you all. You told me to find someone kind—well, there's nobody kinder than her. She's funny and smart and compassionate and beautiful. She's my dream come true.

I've written to Esme too. I don't need to tell you, but she raised Nathan, Sarah, and me, and we love her. So please take care of her.

I've told Sarah to go home if anything happens, and I know you'll support her.

I hope this isn't goodbye, I really do, but if it is, thank you for everything.

Your loving son,
Richard

He wrote one more to his brother, Nathan, thanking him for being a great big brother, for always sticking up for him if other kids picked on him and for trying to manage their mother on their behalf. He sent his love to him, Rebecca and the girls.

Five letters in hand, he went downstairs and along the sidewalk to the mailbox and popped them in. As they dropped, he offered a silent prayer. *Please, please, let this please not be the last my family and Grace hear from me.*

CHAPTER 35

KNOCKNASHEE

MARCH 1943

Father Iggy was back a few weeks by now and everyone was so happy and relieved it had lifted the spirits of the whole village. As he said mass, Grace reminisced on that first Sunday when he returned.

The collective delight was palpable as Father Iggy appeared on the altar. Some people had seen him, of course, but after finding Grace and Tilly on the beach, he withdrew to the parochial house to take the baton from Father Lehane, who was at the point of collapse.

F<small>R</small> I<small>GGY</small> <small>INSISTED</small> the poor curate take a holiday and Dr Ryan had offered to drive him to Tralee to catch a bus home to see his family for a much-needed break.

The congregation waited for the homily, the part of the Mass they'd dreaded when Canon Rafferty was there, as it was always full of admonishment and fearmongering, telling them how their minds and souls were in the gutter and if they didn't mend their ways, nothing but the fiery pits of hell awaited them, but as usual Father Iggy was warm and kind. How the canon was privy to the secrets of people's souls and minds was never explained.

There had been no updates on the canon since he left, though much speculation went on. Some people said he was in prison, others thought he'd been sent on the missions, others thought he was in an enclosed order of monks in County Donegal. There had not been a whisper about the discovery of all that money and the letters from his Nazi taskmasters in his desk, or anything about his association with the Germans.

Sergeant Keane was tight-lipped. He said he had no idea; he was a local guard in a rural community and wasn't kept informed about anything as high up as that. Grace wasn't sure he was being totally honest, but it wasn't anyone's business, she supposed. That said, people were hurt and angry, and the idea that anyone in their community would aid Hitler in his evil work was abhorrent to them.

Ireland may well have had her issues with her nearest neighbour over the years, and with good reason, and the Irish would not move from their position of neutrality, but they were never going to be in favour of what Hitler was doing. Allied airmen who were downed in Ireland were, according to Richard, who had it from a source in the British army, being returned over the border, no questions asked, while any Germans found were incarcerated. Likewise the food, the fuel, the resources that Britain so badly needed were coming from here. So while Ireland was neutral, it was definitely neutral on the side of the Allies. Many Irish people had family or friends working in the war effort in some capacity, so Grace had mentioned to Father Iggy that people were still very upset and fearful that the canon had got away with it, or that he wasn't working alone.

'Well, isn't this a wonderful treat for me,' Father Iggy began, 'to be back among you all. To be here in Knocknashee in the springtime, seeing all of your familiar faces.' He beamed around the little church.

'As you all know, poor Father Lehane did Trojan work running the parish alone for the last while, and he's gone to visit his family for a much-needed rest, so you are stuck with me, I'm afraid. Once Father Lehane returns, we'll manage this lovely parish between the two of us, so I would beg your forgiveness and patience just a little while longer since I'm flying solo as it were.' He smiled, and a ripple of relieved laughter spread along the pews.

'Now before we get onto cheerier matters, I did want to say something. I know there has been much talk about the events that unfolded in our lovely peaceful village, and all I can say on that matter is that every aspect of that situation is being dealt with by the authorities, and if any wrongdoing is uncovered in the course of the ongoing thorough investigation, it will be dealt with. The investigation is – and you have my word on this – being taken very seriously, and there is no question of anything being swept under the carpet. And I give you my solemn word that any perpetrators, regardless of their position, will be brought to justice.'

Grace could feel the electric energy in the church change slightly. They loved Father Iggy and trusted him not to lie to them, so if he said in not so many words that the canon wasn't getting off scot-free, then he wasn't. Grace marvelled at her friend's ability to manage people; it was a rare gift. He was intuitive and decent, and people could see it. It felt like the village could finally exhale.

'Now moving on from that, could I ask all of the children to come up to the railing there in front please?' He gazed around, a smile on his face, his eyes huge behind his thick glasses.

One by one, unsure at first, Grace watched her pupils approach the railing where people knelt to receive Holy Communion. Once all of the children were gathered, the priest walked off the altar and came down among them, bearing a brown paper bag.

'Now I normally am here to celebrate the birthday of Jesus with you all at Christmas, but this year I was in a different parish. And as you all know, because of the Emergency, treats and sweets and the like are in very short supply.'

The children hung on his every word, and Grace smiled; she knew what was coming.

'But as you also know, I have a personal connection to Daidi na Nollag.' He chuckled. 'I'm fierce old, you see, so he was in my class at school. He had no long white beard or red suit in those days, but he could jump like I never saw. Clean up in the sky, he could jump, so I suppose that's why he got picked. Anyway...'

The adults laughed. It was March and the weak springtime sun shone outside, so the mention of Santa Claus was incongruous, but they were happy to see the priest indulge their children, who missed having an odd sweet treat.

'And he gave me this little bag of lollipops, and I think I have enough for everyone to have one.'

The children's eyes lit up with delight at the prospect. How he'd managed to get his hands on so many treats, Grace had no idea. He'd done someone a good turn, she was sure of it. He grinned, seeing their faces, as he handed out lollipops.

'He said he'd sent the robins to watch all of the children in Knocknashee, and you know the robins work for Santa, don't you?'

They all nodded enthusiastically, holding their

precious loot in their hands, waiting to unwrap them until they were outside.

'So when the robins see you helping Mammy and Daddy at home, or being kind to someone, or sharing, or being good for your teachers in school, they report back to Santa Claus and tell him what good boys and girls you are. And everyone in Knocknashee was so good, and the robins were so full of praise, Daidi na Nollag said, "Come here to me, Father Iggy. I know 'tis March, but will you give them these from me so they know I'm delighted altogether with them."'

Beaming, clutching their rare treats, the children returned to their seats. Once they were all settled, the priest went on. 'Now I know we're not supposed to eat in the house of God, but on this one occasion, I think it would be all right, because it's a kind of delayed birthday party anyway. So let you suck away there while I'm chatting to the mammies and daddies and everyone else.'

They didn't need to be told twice. Soon every child in Knocknashee was sucking on their lollipop.

'Now that the important work is done, I just wanted to say, I'm available for anything you might need. Call to the parochial house any time.

You'll notice I've slimmed down a bit' – he patted his belly – 'because the baking in Cork...while lovely of course' – he lowered his voice to a whisper – 'isn't a patch on Knocknashee.'

Another ripple of laughter. Mass was normally a sacred, sombre occasion, but Grace was so glad he'd hit the right note.

'And so finally I don't have anything else to say but for you all to keep doing what you do so beautifully. Pull together as a community. Now, as never before, we need to feel the support of those around us. Nobody has much, but what we have, we share, and nobody has to carry any burden alone. If you need help, ask and it will be provided. True, there are bad things happening in the world, and a lot of pain is being caused as a result, but for every one person intent on hurting another, there are five, ten maybe, who are fighting back. For some, unfortunately that has to be with bombs and bullets, but for most of us, the way to fight evil is with love.'

He moved away from the pulpit then and continued with the liturgy. Grace could feel the tension that had permeated the village since the Canon Rafferty incident dissipate under the soothing balm of Father Iggy's words.

After Mass she stood outside talking to Nancy

O'Flaherty and Peggy Donnelly about an Easter pageant. The women thought it might be a nice idea to cheer everyone up. A night of music and dancing, and maybe the children could perform some of the songs they'd learnt in school. Grace was happy to help and get involved. Sometimes she found the long school holidays too empty, and she missed Richard terribly. Tilly was up in Dublin a lot, Charlie and Dymphna were busy with work and the children, and without someone of her own to fill her days and nights, it could be lonely.

Arrangements were made for a meeting in the parish hall behind the church the following Tuesday, and everyone dispersed, feeling more optimistic than they'd had for months.

She had boiled some bacon, and was going to cook some cabbage and potatoes, and Mary O'Hare had dropped in a loaf of her soda bread, so Grace planned a simple lunch and after that she'd write to Richard. She'd not heard anything for a while, and she knew he'd write if he got word that he was going on that bombing mission, the thought of which terrified her so much, she tried not to think about it.

She let herself in and turned on the wireless – it made the house seem less empty – and was listening to an orchestra performing light classical pieces when the sound of someone knocking caused her to look up from peeling the spuds. She wondered at how much worse the food situation would be for her if she hadn't a constant top-up from her friend's farm.

Wiping her hands on a tea towel, she went to the door. Almost nobody in Knocknashee would knock and wait; they usually knocked and then pushed the door that was always on the latch, calling her name. Also on a Sunday, it was strange to have a visitor; everyone was at home having lunch after Mass.

She opened the door, and was stunned into silence. There stood a man who looked exactly like her father, a small woman with dark straight hair and dark eyes and two girls who looked just like the woman.

'Hello, Grace. I'm Maurice.' The man spoke in a deep rumbling voice, just as her daddy had done.

'Oh…you made it…' Her hand flew to her mouth. Even though she knew it was a possibility, she had put it to the back of her mind. 'Please, come in, come in…' she said, flustered.

They had one small brown leather bag, nothing more, and they looked exhausted. As a precaution in case they showed up unexpectedly, Dymphna had suggested they wash and freshen up the beds upstairs so at least rooms were ready for them.

She led them into the sitting room, and they stood there, the four of them in a cluster, the two little girls burrowed behind their mother.

'I'm so happy to see you, and so relieved you made it in one piece...' Grace was trying not to babble, nerves and excitement combined to make her self-conscious.

'Thank you so much for offering us sanctuary. We are very grateful.' Patricia sounded as though she'd left Cork last week, not years ago.

'This is your home, Maurice's home. You are so welcome.' Grace took a step forward. 'And you must be Kathleen?' She spoke gently and kindly to the taller of the two girls.

'Kathleen, answer your Auntie Grace.' Maurice nudged his daughter.

The little girl nodded. Her dark hair was pulled into a ponytail, and she was wearing a dress that might once have been white but now was grubby and grey and fraying. She had no stockings, her feet in shoes on which the sole was coming away from the leather. Beside her stood a girl with lighter brown hair. She was wearing a pair of boy's short trousers and a ragged sweater, but at least she had shoes and socks.

'And this must be Mary?' Grace asked with a kind smile.

'Yes,' the little girl said meekly. 'But everyone calls me Molly.'

'Well, you are very welcome to Knocknashee, Kathleen and Molly. Now would you like to see your room?'

'Can we stay here, Mama?' Molly looked up at her mother.

'I think so, for now anyway,' Patricia answered, looking uncertain.

'Did you get my telegram or letter?' Grace asked, and her brother and his wife shook their heads.

'We got the telegram, thank you, but we got the chance to go very soon afterwards, so we took it,' Maurice replied. 'We might not have got another one, so we were gone before the letter arrived.'

'Well, I just wrote to say of course you must come, that this is your home as much as mine and you are all so welcome here.' She stepped forward and gave him a hug. 'Welcome home, Maurice. Mammy and Daddy would be glad to see you, and your family.'

He wrapped his arms around her. 'I'm so sorry, Grace. I should have told you the truth a long time ago, but I just didn't want to make trouble for you. But we had no choice…'

'It's no trouble, and we'll face the twitching curtains together,' she said with a grin. 'Now, which is most pressing, some food or a rest?'

'We are very hungry,' Molly said, her little voice cutting through the indecision.

'Well then, how about you come into the kitchen and we'll see what we can find, and once you've eaten, you can all go upstairs and have a sleep?'

'Could we wash up first, do you think? We've not had access to washing facilities for several days, and I'm afraid we smell like it,' Patricia said apologetically.

'Of course. The bathroom is on…' She stopped herself. 'You know where the bathroom is, Maurice. I've put you and Patricia in your old room and the girls in my old room. There's just one bed, I'm afraid, but they should both fit. I'm in Agnes's old room.'

'Thanks, Grace, that's wonderful. I can't…' He choked up. 'It's so strange being here without Mammy and Daddy or Agnes – I keep expecting them to come through the door. You're used to them not being here by now, I suppose – and again, I'm sorry I was no use to you – but it's a strange feeling to be back.'

'You'll get used to it, I'm sure, but yes, it must be an odd, lonely feeling,' Grace said kindly.

'We'll never be able to thank you for taking us in, Grace…but we'll do anything we can to help. We'll work, we won't get in your way…' Patricia promised.

'Don't be silly. I'm so happy to have you here. Come on let me show you to your rooms,' she led them upstairs. 'It's very lonely here on my own sometimes, so having company will be lovely. Now, I'll let you get organised. My friend Dymphna, she's Charlie McKenna's wife – do you remember him, Maurice?'

Her brother smiled. 'I do, I remember Charlie well. Him and Daddy were great pals.'

'Well, he remarried. Maggie died, God love her. Dymphna has two children. Her little girl, Kate, is around your age, Kathleen, so you'll have someone to play with, and she left a bag of clothes on the bed that might be useful, and I have some things you can have if you like, Patricia. But as for you, Maurice, I'm afraid I don't have anything…'

'Oh, don't worry about me, I'm fine. But the

girls only have what they're standing up in. We had a suitcase, but it...well, I don't know, it got lost along the way.' Maurice looked bone-weary.

'Not to worry. Someone in the village will have something to fit you. Bacon, cabbage, spuds, soda bread and tea suit everyone?'

'That would be delicious, thank you, Grace,' Patricia answered.

Grace went downstairs and put some potatoes on to boil. The war had rationed all the treats, but there was nothing like a spud, boiled in its jacket, the skin bursting open when it was cooked, a few slivers of creamy butter into the crease formed where the skin was opened. A sprinkle of salt, it was the nicest thing in the whole wide world. She took the bacon from the salt water and boiled the cabbage leaves in it to give them more flavour, and cut several more rounds of soda bread. She set the table for the five of them and prepared the simple meal, marvelling at her new reality. Only half an hour ago she was thinking how lonely it was, and now here she was with a full house of her very own family.

She fought down the feelings of anger at her brother for abandoning her. There would be time enough for that.

She wished she had a bit of ham or chicken or

something to bulk up the meal, but she didn't; she'd used her ration for the week. It was going to be tight while Maurice and his family applied for ration books, but Tilly would help them out, she knew. It might mean not much meat, sugar or tea, but there were plenty of potatoes and vegetables and brown bread. And they had a few pots of blackberry jam left in the larder since last autumn. They wouldn't starve.

The people of Knocknashee would help out, just like Father Iggy had said at Mass, or at least they would once they got over the shock of Father Maurice Fitzgerald returning as the husband of Patricia and father of Kathleen and Molly.

The primary thought she had as she prepared lunch and wondered if the tiny cube of butter she had left would stretch to five people was relief that Father Iggy was back. The idea of Maurice landing up with an unexpected family and in his newly laicised state and the canon being the one to sit as Pontius Pilate over them all was one that made her blood run cold. Father Iggy would understand and offer the hand of friendship to his former brother priest, she was sure of it.

CHAPTER 36

LONDON

MARCH 1943

Sarah sat in the flat, refusing to open the door. If she opened it, then the news would come, whatever it was, and she would have to deal with it. If she just stayed here, doing nothing, just barely breathing, then everything remained as it was. Nothing changed.

She was at the kitchen table of the garden mews, the new coffee machine their father had sent on the small table beside the Bakelite cooker that worked intermittently. They had to keep feeding the gas meter with pennies, and even then it didn't always work. The gas mains in the city were in a horrible state after all the bombing, and there wasn't the time, the money or the men to fix them. The gas pipes were like so many other facets of life here that were far from ideal: the bus journey that should take fifteen minutes that took an hour; the lines for food, when more often than not, the thing you wanted was sold out; the lack of absolutely everything. People just 'kept calm and carried on', as the posters glued to every surface told them to do.

She could put up with deprivation, she could manage on short rations, she could survive eating disgusting things like spam and liver and tripe. Jellied eels were all she could get for their supper two weeks ago – revolting, but she could do it. But answering the door, facing what they had to say, that she could not do.

They knocked again and pressed the doorbell, the shrill sound breaking the still silence. It was warmish outside. She could hear the voices of the kids from upstairs playing in the garden. Then another voice, an older person, and the girl – what was her name, Fran? Flossie? – answering.

Then the back window rattled with the sound of knuckles on glass.

Go away go away go away go away go away. Sarah refused to look around, refused to turn and see whoever it was trying to find her.

'Mrs Nunez?' The knocker was not going to leave. 'Mrs Nunez, please open the door. I have to deliver this, and it's my third attempt…'

The voice was young, a teenager maybe. East Coast accent. Massachusetts possibly. It was no good. She couldn't avoid this. Robotically, without turning to see whoever had come around into the garden, she went to the front door, opened it and waited. The USAAF-uniformed man was older than she'd thought. He was in his late twenties, she guessed, but his voice was younger. He looked fresh-faced and innocent. Probably just arrived, got the running-around-delivering-messages duty. She pictured a mom and dad back in Boston, his photograph proudly displayed on the sideboard, his mom worrying every day for her precious boy, the dad reassuring her based on no information. Someone should tell them he was no more likely to die over here than if he was walking down any street around their house. It might save her sleepless nights. *He's not doing anything dangerous, Mrs...*

whatever your name is. Your son will come home to you in one piece, and you'll get to brag to your friends in the sewing circle or at the bridge night or whatever you go to. You get all the bragging rights and none of the fear.

'Are you Mrs Sarah Nunez?' His voice cut through her reverie.

She nodded. It felt a little bit like she was underwater.

'I got this for you. I need to...' He stopped. 'This is for you.'

His accent was definitely Boston; she knew by the long 'ah' sounds.

He held out a buff envelope, and she took it, turned and went back in, closing the door behind her. She couldn't speak to him. She had shut the door in his face. That was rude, she knew, but she couldn't conform to social niceties, not now.

She returned to the seat she'd recently vacated, propped the envelope on a coffee mug and stared at it. It was typed, her name and address. The 'N' in Nunez was smudged a bit, like whoever typed it whipped it out too soon and the ink was dragged. It was an innocent-looking envelope, not fat. Thin. It only contained one sheet, she knew, with a typed name and address. But really, it was a bomb. A tiny innocuous-looking bomb that was about to detonate, and nothing, absolutely nothing, would ever be the same again.

She didn't know how long she sat there. She heard the mother from upstairs call the children in for their tea. She heard the bells in the local Catholic church ring. They did that at 6 p.m. for some reason, she didn't know why. Richard had gone there once or twice. He was planning to convert to Catholicism to marry Grace, he'd said. It seemed a lot of trouble to go to, but then if Jacob wanted her to convert to Judaism, she probably would. But he would never want that. He had no evangelical tendencies. He saw his religion as an intrinsic part of him, but he had no need to convert anyone. Richard had been quick to point out that Grace was not a demanding person either, but that her faith meant a lot to her and they had some rule about Catholics not marrying non-Catholics. A Southern Episcopalian, kind of lapsed, wouldn't do at all, it would seem.

Would he and Grace have married in Ireland?

She recalled her and Jacob's wedding day. The happiest of her life. She had never pictured herself as a traditional bride, but when it came to it, it was exactly what she did, the white dress, bridesmaids, flowers, the whole thing. The virginal white gown seemed a little hypocritical seeing as they'd been living and sleeping together for years, but it didn't matter. But when she brought her wedding day to mind, the city hall, the reception afterwards at the yacht club, she smiled. They had decorated the ballroom in white with pink flowers, bougainvillea and roses. Champagne flowed, and the food was delicious, and everyone watched as she danced with her husband for the first time. Her parents were there, and Richard. And then she danced with her daddy, and Jacob danced with her mother, which had been a bone of contention but he did it for her. Her memories jumped all over the day. She thought about the morning, getting ready, fixing her hair, putting on make-up, taking a glass of champagne from Esme in a delicate crystal glass. Her father walking her down the aisle, flowers in her hands, Jacob in a suit waiting for her...

She wondered what the sound was, then realised it was laughter. Her own laughter, but it was like it was coming from outside of her. The memory of Jacob Nunez, whose idea of dressed up was a shirt with a collar, wearing a suit and tie in city hall in Savannah. He never complained once. He did it all for her. He looked so funny, his hair combed, dazzling white shirt, suit immaculate, shoes polished. She almost didn't recognise him.

He would have done anything for her, anything at all. Jacob, her Jacob, who hated all pomp and ceremony, would have preferred no fuss at all, not even a ceremony in the synagogue for some reason, with fish and chips wrapped in newspaper for the wedding banquet. The memory of her scruffy fiancé wearing a suit for their fancy wedding day made her laugh till she cried.

CHAPTER 37

KNOCKNASHEE

MARCH 1943

Patricia and the children were still sleeping. The strain of the arduous, terrifying and uncomfortable journey had taken its toll, and they'd fallen into bed early last night. Grace had given Nellie, the rag doll her mother made, to the girls, and they put her between them in the bed. At seven in the morning, Grace had risen – it was a schoolday – and tried to creep downstairs without disturbing them, but as she was making a cup of tea, she heard Maurice.

'Good morning.'

She spun around. The sun from the kitchen window silhouetted him in gold. 'I'm sorry, I tried not to wake you…'

'Not at all. I'm a bad sleeper, where my wife could sleep for Ireland.' He had the same lopsided smile she remembered her father giving her, and a pang of loss washed over her. His hair was thick like Daddy's, reddish brown and kind of wavy. He had gold hair on his arms; she could see because he'd rolled up the sleeves of his frayed blue shirt. He was tall, maybe six feet, and broad. His dark trousers had a hole in the knee, and his shoes were scuffed and badly in need of soles and heels. He was a similar build to Richard, she realised, and handsome in an understated way. There was something serene about him, like he was unflappable, a quiet confidence that she found soothing.

'Would you like some tea?' she offered, feeling a little awkward now it was just her and her long-lost brother. Her fury had subsided, but she was still angry. How could he just have abandoned her?

She scalded the earthenware pot, there since their parents' time, and once it was warm, added a spoon of precious tea leaves from a paper bag. Her mother would always make it with two, but such extravagance was not an option these days.

'If I'm not keeping you?' he asked.

'Not at all. These mornings we're not too strict on time – they like to play in the yard before lessons start. It's a long winter here when they can't really play outside, so they need it.'

She took the glass jug of creamy milk that Tilly had delivered earlier, adding it to two mugs of tea.

'Mammy and Daddy used to do the same thing…' Maurice remembered with a sad frown.

'Is it all very different here or much as you remember it?' Grace asked, setting the two mugs on the table. She sat down and he sat opposite.

'Both, I think. I knew in my head you'd grown up of course, but whenever I pictured you, it was as a child, so meeting you as an adult…that's new.' He smiled.

'Am I like you thought I'd be?'

'You remind me of Mammy so much, though you have Daddy's colouring, but in temperament you're like her. So tell me all about you, and what your life is like.'

Grace thought for a moment. Then she told him everything. He was a good listener, attentive and not judgemental. It all poured out of her like a torrent, from the time their parents drowned, to her getting polio, to the death of Agnes. She left out the deathbed confession and all the business with the canon and Declan's baby sister – time enough for that when he'd settled in – but she told him about Declan, and then about Richard.

'I remember Declan McKenna as a small boy. He was a clever little chap, I remember that. I'm so sorry, Grace. That is a lot of loss for a person as young as you to bear.' His voice was kind, and he reminded her of a gentle bear. His accent had changed, she noticed. His English was perfect, and he had a slight American intonation. Not Southern like Richard, but definitely a touch of it.

'It was. But I'm all right now. I wasn't for a while, but I am now. I'll never forget Declan, and a part of me will always love him, but Richard and I...' She coloured.

'Go on. I'm in no position to judge anyone, as you know.' He smiled ruefully.

'Well, I met Richard – well, I didn't meet him, but I came in contact with him when I wrote a letter to St Jude, complaining bitterly about Agnes. She wasn't the easiest...'

Maurice chuckled. 'You don't need to tell me. She never liked me and told me that often.'

'Well, so you know how she was.'

The whole story of the letters to Richard and their connection came out then, and how Agnes had always told her she would never have someone of her own on account of the polio. They drank their tea and chatted in such an easy way, she felt relief flood her body. Maurice was restful to be around.

'It looks like you manage away fine, though, despite her dire predictions,' he said, and she heard a note of pride in his voice.

'I do. I followed the treatment devised by an Australian nurse called Nurse Kenny, and I really got a lot of mobility back. My doctor, Hugh Warrington, he and his wife kind of became surrogate parents to me over the years, really helped, and Declan made me a bath house out the back there, with a hot water heater and everything. Declan was a bit of a genius when it came to building things.' She nodded towards the back yard. 'So I use that when we can get gas to run the heater and do my exercises, so I do all right. I wear a calliper most of the time, but Pádraig O Sé made me a built-up shoe…'

'Is he as charming as ever?' Maurice grinned.

'He told me once that I'd be a terrible priest, I was wrong entirely and I wasn't only codding my parents saying I had a vocation, I was codding myself too. Though he wasn't wrong, I suppose, in hindsight.'

'I'm sure you weren't a terrible priest, you just fell in love. That's not a crime.'

'Will we lay low, or should we go out and about, do you think? What would be easiest for you?' he asked, getting up to rinse the cups.

'Don't hide away on my account. Charlie McKenna knows you're coming and the whole story, so do Dymphna and Nancy O'Flaherty – you remember the postmistress?'

He nodded. 'I do, a lovely lady. I remember her and Ned were the best dancers on the peninsula.'

Grace smiled. 'Ned's with God now, but Nancy is still here. She'd love to see you. She was always fond of you.'

'I'll look in this morning then, get the ball rolling, I suppose. And is Canon Rafferty still here?' he asked, wincing.

'Well now, the short answer is no, and the long answer will take more time than I have, but the parish priest now is called Father Ignatius O'Riordan – everyone calls him Father Iggy –

and he's a really good friend of mine. I'd go and introduce myself to him if I was you. You won't find a nicer man.'

'It's a relief to know the canon is gone. Did he die?'

'No, but he won't be back. I'll tell you everything later, but now I have to go to school.'

She went to leave, and he took her hand. 'Thanks, Grace, for everything, for making us feel welcome, for accepting…well, for welcoming my family. I had no idea how it would go, but you made it feel like we were coming home. Patricia is normally so stoic – she does what's needed and never complains – but last night she cried tears of pure relief. It's been… Well, as you say, we have plenty of time and there's a lot to tell, but it's been awful. So thanks.'

'As I said, Maurice, this is your home. You are as entitled to be here as me.'

'Well not really, the parish owns it and you're the headmistress, so I don't have any right to it, but I'm more grateful than you know that you let us stay. You're cross with me, despite the welcome,' he said quietly. 'And I don't blame you.'

There it was again, that kind of uncanny way of knowing.

'I was very angry, to be frank. I've had to deal

with a lot, all on my own. I could have used the help of my big brother.' She marvelled at how forthright she'd become over the years.

'I bet you could, and I was nowhere to be found. I'm very sorry, Grace. I'll try to make it up to you, that's all I can say. I thought you'd be like Agnes, and to be honest, I was angry at Mammy and Daddy for a long time too, for forcing me into a life I said I didn't want. Patricia and I just decided to start again on our own, leave it all behind us. But you're right, it wasn't fair.'

She nodded. There would be plenty of time. And she found her overarching emotion was relief, not bitterness.

He smiled and gave her a brief one-armed hug, a brotherly hug. It felt like everything was finally working out.

'Of course you'll have to brush up on your Irish, otherwise nobody here will talk to you,' she said in their mother tongue, and he laughed.

'I was thinking that,' he said, switching to flawless Irish, 'and I've taught the girls too – I've spoken to them in Irish since they were babies. Patricia's is a bit rusty, but it will come back. I never imagined I'd ever speak it again in my home place, but life is strange and I'm really glad I kept it up now.'

'Well, that's going to make everything much easier. We'll bring the girls over to the school when they feel ready. There'll be no shortage of friends once word gets out. Not much ever happens here, so you and your family will be great excitement.'

'Right, I won't hold you up. Is there anything needs doing around here? Any odd jobs? I'm determined to earn our keep until I can find some work.'

'Not at all, you just relax. It's been a horrible time for you all. Maybe take the girls to the beach.' She paused. 'You'll need to apply for ration books and all of that, but in the meantime, we'll manage. Tilly O'Hare, do you remember her?'

'Your little friend from the farm up the hill, always up to mischief?' Maurice grinned.

'The very one. Well, she's a grown woman like myself now, and she farms the land since her father died. She gives me as much veg and bread and eggs as I need, so we'll have to count on her generosity as well. She ploughs her own land, and she has a few milk cows and sheep and even pigs. She was shaving one of the pigs the other day for slaughter and he got away from her, but his freedom was short-lived. Tilly is an expert farmer,' she said with pride.

'That's great, and if she wants some work done on the farm, I'd be happy to do it in exchange for the extra food.'

'That's a great idea, but look, let's take it one step at a time. Rest today anyway. No doubt we'll be inundated with visitors once word gets out. Everyone will want to have a look at you.' She laughed.

'Like creatures in a zoo?' he replied ruefully.

'Something like that.' Grace grinned and left for school.

CHAPTER 38

All eyes were divided between Father Iggy and the new members of the Fitzgerald family, who were sitting in the third row of Sunday Mass.

'I know I'm speaking for the parish when I welcome home Maurice and Patricia Fitzgerald, and their two little girls, Kathleen and Molly. They were very lucky to get out of the Philippines, which has sadly fallen to the Japanese, but they knew where to come for sanctuary. Back to their own place. Many of you will remember Maurice as Father Fitzgerald, but he made the very brave decision many years ago to be laicised when he realised that God had called him to a different ministry, that of family life.'

Grace could sense the tension but knew Father Iggy would strike the right note. He and Maurice had become friends over the last few days and had made it known too. Since they arrived last Sunday, Maurice had climbed up and fixed the leaking slate on the church roof, he'd painted the blistering church porch and mended the kneelers on several of the pews that had been broken for years. There could be no doubt in anyone's mind that Maurice was not at odds with the Church.

'To be a father and a husband, or a wife and mother, is as noble a calling as God asks of us, and like the saints and prophets we read about in the Bible every week, sometimes God calls on us to be brave, to do the right thing, which often is not the easy thing. So I speak for everyone I know when I say welcome home and we're happy to have you here.'

It was as if there was a collective exhale. Grace noticed the village was like a classroom – once you got a few ringleaders on your side, then everyone else tended to follow suit. Father Iggy, Nancy O'Flaherty, Charlie and Mary O'Hare had all welcomed Maurice and his family warmly and said repeatedly that it was the hand of God that got them out of the Philippines and across the world safely in times of such strife.

Kathleen and Molly began school three days after they arrived and were in Grace's class. As Maurice promised, their Irish was very good, albeit accented, which made the other children snigger a bit, but a look from Grace was enough to put a stop to that. She had developed a look that spoke volumes when someone wasn't on their best behaviour. Her mother had had one too, and every time Agnes looked at a child, it was with that look. Grace used it sparingly but to great effect.

Bags of clothes were donated for the family, and while one or two sniffy remarks were overheard about spoiled priests, overall the arrival of the four new Fitzgeralds was met with kindness.

Grace had popped into the cobbler's to collect the four pairs of shoes she'd left in for repair.

'That small pair there are gone beyond help,' Pádraig said gruffly, nodding in the direction of Kathleen's T-bar shoes on the counter. 'I soled and heeled these and they're grand again.' He picked the other three pairs from the little nooks behind the counter and dumped them beside Kathleen's. Maurice's looked good, as did Patricia's, and Molly's were not too bad to begin with. Kathleen's were the ones that were unfixable.

Grace gathered them and put them in her basket. 'Thanks.' She took out her purse. 'What do I owe you?'

'A shilling,' he responded gruffly.

She handed over the money and went to take Kathleen's as well. She had no idea how to fix them, but she wouldn't leave them to him.

'When my mother,' Pádraig began, his back to her, 'may the Lord have mercy on her, died, she gave a bequest to your brother for the missions. Where did that go, I wonder?'

'To the Church,' Grace answered firmly. This was exactly the kind of talk that caused problems. Nobody else had dared ask, but it was important the message was delivered, so she answered him rather than shutting him down, which she normally did. The word would spread soon enough if she told him. 'Every farthing that was donated to my brother for his missionary work was handed over to the order after he was laicised. There's no way to prove that now, but he told me that and I believe him.'

'And he's with the fancy woman how long?' he'd asked, his eyes hard.

'Her name is Patricia Fitzgerald, and she is his

wife and my sister-in-law, and they married after he was released from his vows. He did nothing wrong. He acted morally and honestly all the way through, he never took a penny that was intended for the Church, and he didn't begin the relationship with his wife until he was free to do so.'

'All right, calm down, will you. You're very touchy this morning, Miss Fitz.' He laughed in that infuriating way of his. He would be so insulting, so rude, and if you got indignant or upset, he laughed at you for being too sensitive. He loved getting a rise out of people; it was his reason for living, to get under people's skin. If you reacted at all, that was a victory for him, so everyone tried not to, but this was more important than Pádraig O Sé's mind games.

'I just want everyone to know the truth, that way there's no speculating behind anyone's back.' She knew she sounded prim and proper, but she didn't care.

'Well, aren't you the fine international bunch now? Maurice with his foreign wife –'

'Patricia is Irish.' He knew perfectly well Patricia wasn't foreign, and she saw him suppress a smirk.

'If you say so,' he said, with a face that implied *I believe you but thousands wouldn't*. 'And sure you're hitching up with that big, tall Yank. 'Tis like a local wouldn't be good enough for one of the Fitzgeralds at all.'

Grace wouldn't react, he'd congratulated her earlier and she knew he liked Richard, he was just trying to get a rise out of her . 'Oh, we're very exotic, Pádraig, right enough.' She smiled, though she wanted to slap his smug face. Honestly the man made her blood boil.

She turned to go, wondering what she would do about a pair of shoes for Kathleen. Everyone in Knocknashee wore their shoes down to the uppers at the best of times, not to mind now, when everything was in short supply, and everything was passed on to younger siblings or cousins. Kathleen and Dymphna's Kate were the same size, but Kate only had one pair, so that was not an option. Maybe they could scrape enough coupons together to buy her a new pair, but Maurice would not allow it probably. He had offered his services to everyone in the village as a labourer in return for anything they were given and refused to allow Grace to spend her money on them. He was up at Tilly's the last four days painting the new milking parlour because Tilly had bought three more cows. He wouldn't take any payment, knowing that Tilly was feeding them all from the farm for free. They would be better once they had ration cards, but there were a lot of forms to fill out before that.

Maybe Lizzie would be able to put her hands on a pair? People donated things to the hospital all the time. She'd write and ask.

As she pulled the door, the familiar ding rang around the small cobbler's shop.

'Hold on a minute...' he said, and she turned.

To her astonishment he held up a pair of girls' shoes. Not new, and not in perfect shape, but they were in one piece and freshly heeled and soled.

'These might fit her,' he said gruffly.

'How much are they?' she asked.

'Era, take them away. The *gobdaw* that dropped them in never came back for them, someone on holidays down here from Dublin, must have forgotten. Anyway, they won't come back now so...'

Grace took the two steps back to the counter. 'Thank you, Pádraig, that's very kind of you.' She took the shoes and fixed him with a look. 'You're a lot nicer than you let on.'

'Keep that to yourself,' he answered with a growl. 'Now get out. I'm busy and I've no time to be gassing here all day like an auld woman.'

He'd coloured slightly at the compliment, and

Grace wondered at human nature not for the first time.

She crossed the street and went into O'Donoghue's with her ration book. She'd get all she could, and hopefully if Biddy was feeling generous, a rare enough eventuality, she might give her a bit more knowing the house was full.

The conversation stopped as she entered the shop, and she knew the women gathered were gossiping about Maurice.

'Hello, Miss Fitz,' Biddy announced with a broad beam, a sure sign that she'd been the ringleader of the gossip. 'Beautiful day, isn't it?'

'Indeed it is.' Grace smiled back, not wanting to give them the satisfaction of knowing she felt uncomfortable. She took out her list – butter, ham, tea, sugar, raisins, flour and soap. Everything was rationed, so she handed over her ration book and Biddy glanced at the coupons.

'Your brother has no ration book got yet, I suppose?' she asked, filling the order from behind the counter. She was notoriously stingy, weighing everything to the fraction of an ounce for fear she'd give you even a tiny bit more than you paid for.

'No, not yet. He's applied but –'

'I suppose his wife and children will need to be verified…as…'

Grace was sick of this. 'Verified as what, Mrs O'Donoghue?'

'Well, you know…entitled to a ration book,' the woman said baldly. The other three women, who Grace recognised but didn't acknowledge, found the basket of cabbages and bunches of carrots in a box fascinating, their ears flapping, as Charlie might say.

'Patricia is married to Maurice, and anyway she's an Irish citizen in her own right, and Kathleen and Molly were born abroad but are his daughters, and they get citizenship from their parents, so I don't know why you think that might be in doubt.' Grace gave her a steely glare. At least the woman had the decency to look embarrassed.

'And do they eat…well, what we eat? Maybe growing up over there, they…' She pressed on, obviously not shamed enough.

'Oh no, mostly they love cats and dogs, frog spawn and live spiders, but they're having to make do with porridge and eggs here.'

Margaret Goggin, one of the mothers of a pair of boys in the older classroom, stifled a giggle. She was nice and had obviously fallen in with the gossip, but she wasn't like that. The other two, Hannah Keohane, married to one of the Keohane brothers, and Mary O'Reilly, the district nurse who worked with Dr Ryan, were right scandalmongers.

Biddy bristled. 'There's no need to be sarcastic, Miss Fitz. It was a civil question.'

'I wasn't being sarcastic, but anyway, why would what my family eats be any of your concern? I have ration stamps enough for the things I asked for, so that will do us fine. Now what do I owe you?' Grace suppressed a smile. She was turning into a right tyrant in her old age.

Biddy had gathered everything and placed the items on the counter. ''Tis quick you claim them as your family then, when only five minutes ago, we were all sure your brother was an ordained priest doing God's work out foreign, bringing the gospel to the heathens.' Her hackles were up now, and she wouldn't take being admonished in public by Grace well at all.

'It's not a question of claiming them – they are my family. Now, what do I owe you?' Grace was cut glass.

She totted it up. 'Will I put it on your account or will you pay now?' she asked acidly.

Knowing how much the woman liked getting cash, and despite having the cash in her purse, she said, 'Put it on our account please.'

Biddy looked po-faced but did it, adding the sum in the ledger that Pádraig O Sé called the Domesday Book behind her back. He might be cutting, but he could be very funny.

She placed the items in her basket – as usual she got not one halfpenny extra, despite the full house – and left, her head held high.

She would not allow small-minded people to drag her down or make Maurice feel like he'd done something wrong.

She crossed the street. She'd worn her steel today knowing she had to walk around the town, but her leg was aching. She'd not been as religious with her exercises as she should have been since Maurice and the family arrived. It had been four days now since she did them, and she could feel it. She'd go back and fill her bath, Charlie had managed to get her a barrel of gas for the water heater, and do her stretches. She was determined to walk up the aisle to marry Richard without a limp, and if that was her plan, then she knew what she needed to do.

Two weddings to wonderful men. It felt so

much more than her share, but she would take it with gratitude. She had been thinking about asking Charlie to give her away, but now she thought she would like Maurice to do it. He was her brother, and it felt right.

She was lost in thought when she crossed the road and didn't notice the woman at her door until she was almost at the gate. The door opened. Patricia was there, and she realized Maurice must be home as well because the bike Charlie had lent him was resting against the gable.

She didn't recognise the woman. Maybe it was someone to ask about the ration books or something like that.

She opened the gate, and the woman spun around. Something about her looked so familiar, but Grace was sure she'd never met her before. She was tall and willowy, with dark hair in waves that hung to her shoulders. Her dark eyes fell on Grace.

'Grace?' she said.

'Yes…I –'

'I'm Sarah.' The woman's eyes filled with tears before she could say another word, and Grace didn't need her to. Ice sloshed around in her stomach, and a film of cold sweat formed on her skin. She wouldn't hear this. She felt as if she were falling, rapidly, from a great height. It was happening again.

CHAPTER 39

The next few minutes were a blur. Maurice stood beside her, and Patricia and Sarah, and they led her inside. Someone was crying – her? She didn't think so. Maybe.

Sarah was sobbing, and with Patricia trying to comfort her. Grace saw Kathleen and Molly standing stock-still in the doorway, faces expressionless. Just out of her peripheral vision, someone ushered the little girls away.

Maurice sat her down and went on his hunkers beside her, holding her hands. His voice was deep and sonorous, but she didn't know what he was saying. It was like he was underwater. The sounds were soothing, and Grace found herself fixing her eyes on his face, allowing the noise to wash over her.

This was better. Better than the awful message Sarah had brought. She didn't need details; there would be time for that. All she needed to know was that Richard was gone. He went on that dangerous mission and now he was gone. Richard was dead.

Her thoughts became abstract. She must be like the ill-fated red-haired woman. Local fishermen would never take a red-haired woman on a boat, for it was sure to sink if they did; red-haired women brought bad luck. She was that; she was bad luck. Her parents had been cursed by her birth, and they drowned making a sea crossing they'd made many times before, and not even in winter; it was a sudden freak squall. Agnes was cursed to be her sister. She was the reason Agnes was so miserable, having to care for Grace, no way to make her own life, so all she had was Grace and the horrible canon. Then, dying of a stroke in her thirties, so unusual, and Agnes was healthy. Then Declan, blown up by a marine mine. The chances of it happening must have been miniscule. He was a teacher, for God's sake, not even a fisherman, and anyway Ireland was neutral, and yet he was killed by a weapon of war? It was uncanny. There was no other explanation – it was being close to her that did it. Why had she never seen this before? She was the common denominator; she was the link. Everyone she loved was destined to die.

More voices, Sarah still crying, tea being brought in, Maurice sitting beside her now, his arm around her as Patricia led Sarah to the fireside chair. Time expanded and contracted. Charlie was there, and Dymphna. Soon it would be Tilly and Mary and Odile, and maybe Nancy, everyone arriving to see what they could do. This was a well-choreographed piece; everyone knew the part they had to play.

Someone belonging to Grace was dead – places, everyone.

The Warringtons would arrive tomorrow – Nancy would make sure they knew – and the house would be full, and people would keep offering her food and tea and she would keep refusing it, and eventually they'd all leave and she'd be all alone. Each time before this, she was sure it was just terrible misfortune, but now she knew the truth. It was her.

She might have slept. She was taken to her bedroom and then downstairs again.

'Grace? Grace?' Another voice. Father Iggy

was here, sitting on one side of her, Maurice on the other.

Richard is dead. Richard is dead. Richard is dead. Richard is dead.

She was dry-eyed…numb. This feeling was so familiar. She knew exactly how it went.

First it was shock, feeling like you might faint, or be sick, like the bottom was falling out of your world. Then nothing. Numb to everything. That passed too, she knew. The numbness faded, and when it did, the pain became unbearable, the raw, aching reality of it. And facing it – and you had to face it – was all that was in front of you. You couldn't go back; you had to go forward with this new reality. Memories were no comfort in this phase, nothing was. That peace, the ability to smile at a recollection, was a long way off yet.

She should pull herself together. All over Europe people were feeling this exact thing. In England, in Germany, in France, in North Africa, in Hawaii, in Japan, in the Philippines, in Australia – no corner of the globe was safe. Someone – thousands of someones – at this exact moment, was sitting in a kitchen, in a sitting room, in a bedroom, getting this exact news about someone they loved. And she felt united with them. She didn't know them and never would, but this profound loss, it was universal. She was just one more. Her pain was no better or worse than anyone else's. She wasn't special. She was just an ordinary bereaved person. Again.

'Grace.' The voice was louder now, and she turned.

'Listen to Sarah, Grace,' Maurice said. Sarah sat beside Grace, in the space vacated by Father Iggy. Maurice didn't move.

She turned to Richard's sister, looking at her for the first time. She'd seen a photo, but they'd never met, which was strange considering she felt like she knew her. Did Richard talk about her to Sarah? Maybe not. Maybe she knew Sarah – all the travails with Jacob and her mother and her father's change of heart and Algernon Smythe and her rejection of the life laid out for her – but Sarah didn't know her from Adam. His sister was like him. She could see his eyes, his mouth. She was dark where he was blond, but they were both tall.

'Grace, I'm so sorry. I didn't mean to fall apart like that. You must think I'm crazy…' She had the same accent as Richard, that beautiful drawling accent, the only other person she'd ever heard speak like that.

'No…I'm sorry too. Please, tell me what happened.'

Sarah seemed to steel herself to retell it. Her hands were clasped together on her lap, and Grace noticed she was much less glamorous than she'd imagined her. In the photo taken years ago at a yacht club in America, she looked very chic, but now she was dressed in a plain wine dress that had been washed so many times, the vibrancy of the colour was well faded, and a blue sweater on top that may have been a man's. On her feet she wore boots, not dainty ladies' shoes. She didn't look a bit like an heiress to an American banking fortune.

'I got a message, hand-delivered, and afterward I spoke to someone at the Air Force. The plane Richard and Jacob were in was shot down. I know he told you about the bombing raid he was going on? Well, somewhere over the border between France and Germany, they were flying in tight formation with other planes – it's safer that way, they say, but…' She sighed, a ragged breath. 'They were attacked. The witnesses, guys in the other planes, couldn't see. It was dark and they were under heavy fire, so the few who managed to get back couldn't tell them much. All but two of the planes were lost.'

Grace felt a glimmer of hope. 'So he might have parachuted and –'

'I don't think so, Grace. Their plane burst into flames, and the four or so who got back saw no parachutes – they could see nothing. They were trying to fight off enemy fire and get out of there, I guess.'

'So what did the people you spoke to afterwards say?'

Sarah exhaled heavily. 'They said it would be foolish to get my hopes up. Even if by a slim chance they did get out of the burning plane, they were inexperienced at parachuting, and even if they managed to land in one piece, they were deep in enemy territory. The officer I spoke to told me to accept they were gone, that it was easier in the long run.'

Grace didn't reply. The silence hung between them. Maurice sat beside her; Patricia and Father Iggy stood by the fireplace, which was full of tory tops now that it was spring. Their mother always painted the pine cones nice colours and placed them in the hearth, and Grace had continued the tradition when Agnes died. Agnes would have stood for no such nonsense.

Grace stood. She wanted to be able to look

Sarah in the eye, even though the other woman was a good six inches taller.

'Is Jacob dead, do you think?' she asked. Her eyes raked Richard's sister's face for a clue.

Sarah shrugged. 'I honestly don't know. I think I'd feel it if he was gone, but...' She swallowed. 'I don't know. I think he probably is, Richard too.'

Grace nodded. Would she feel it if Richard was dead? She didn't feel it when Declan died. She'd dreaded it the way everyone did, then worried after the explosion, but did she know it? Feel it somehow? She didn't think that she had. Maybe that was just a load of old claptrap.

'Have you told your father?' Grace asked.

Sarah nodded, swallowing back tears. 'I leave to go home from here, my father arranged it. I promised Richard that I'd go back to the States if...well, if this happened, and he asked that I come and tell you in person first, so...'

'I appreciate that, so much.' This heartbroken woman had taken the arduous trip across the sea to come and deliver this news face to face. That was so kind.

'I'll get going now. The bus driver is coming back this way, and I'll get to Cork to catch a boat...'

'Are you sure you can't stay for a while?' Maurice asked. 'You'd be very welcome, and you look exhausted.'

Sarah gave him a weak smile. 'Thank you, but no. I need to get home. And it was hard to get a crossing, so I need to make it.'

'What will you do?' Grace asked, realising how stupid the question sounded.

Sarah paused. 'The same as you, I guess, try to figure out how to live without them.'

'You'll be all right,' Grace heard herself say. 'Not today or next week or even next year, but the terrible pain like you can't breathe does pass. I know from personal experience.'

'He loved you so much, Grace, since those first letters when we were back in the States. Once you were in his life, nobody else stood a chance.'

Maurice, Patricia and Father Iggy withdrew silently then, leaving them alone.

'I think I felt the same, but…it was like he was a character in a film or a novel, too beautiful and exotic to be real…' she said softly.

'He said that about you. He often wondered if he'd dreamed you up, or at least attributed gifts to you that were more imagination than reality. But every letter and the few times he met you –'

'Four times.'

Sarah answered, 'Oh I didn't know exactly…'

'I met him four times. When he came here with Odile in the summer of 1940, then when he found out something to save my life last year, we met in Dublin and then he came down here, and then earlier this year in Dublin again, when we almost missed each other.' She smiled at the memory. 'But I've so many letters, so many…'

Sarah went to the rough-looking ex-army-issue haversack she carried and extracted a bundle of letters, rolled up and held together with an elastic band. 'He kept every single one,' she said, handing them over.

Grace could see her familiar handwriting, small and neat, in lilac ink, on every page. She took them, and it felt so very final. Now she had them all. Every letter he wrote her and every one she'd written to him. 'We joked about making a book, for our children maybe, of our letters…' Grace said, unable to finish the sentence.

'If you do, I'd love to see it sometime,' Sarah replied.

'What will happen in America? Will you assume he's dead and say prayers or whatever the thing is in your religion, or…'

'I don't know. I think my father will want to

have a memorial service. I guess he wasn't US military as such, though it happened on an Air Force mission...but he'll want him remembered somehow. As for Jacob, I don't know. I've never met anyone in his family...'

'I'll ask Father Iggy to say a Mass for them both.'

Sarah looked touched. 'He was going to convert to Catholicism for you, did you know that? He'd started attending the service in the church near our place in London and he even spoke to the priest about how to do it.'

'He never told me that.' Grace choked up again.

'I think he wanted to do it and just tell you when it was done.'

The clock ticked on the mantelpiece.

'He was very fond of Jacob,' Grace said. 'And he loved you so much. He told me often how having you with them in London made him feel less homesick.'

'For me too. We were kind of close growing up, but we became something different over here, friends as well as brother and sister, I guess. And he and Jacob were opposites, but they complemented each other and were a formidable team.'

'Have you told Kirky?'

Sarah nodded. 'He's very gruff, but he gave them a break when they had no experience, and he loved their work. He helped get me home, and I could tell he was upset.'

The use of the past tense struck her. In Sarah's mind they were dead. Best to think that way, best believe it rather than spend a lifetime waiting. There was no miracle coming, there was no one-in-a-million chance that he survived. He hadn't. Best get on with grieving.

'I'd better go. The bus driver said he'd pass back through in forty minutes.' Sarah looked out at the street.

'I'll walk you to the bus,' Grace said, and took Sarah's arm. Richard's sister looked a little surprised. 'I find it easier to walk when I can balance on someone, is that all right?'

'Sure, of course.'

They walked across the road as Bobby the Bus drove around the corner, having done the loop of the peninsula.

'Keep in touch, Grace, let me know how you're doing?'

'I will, and you do the same. I'm so sorry for you, Sarah.'

'We get it.' She kissed Grace's cheek. 'Like nobody else, we get it.'

EPILOGUE

His head was pounding, and he couldn't bear to open his eyes. A strange odour of cordite, and something else, musty, earthy, assailed his nostrils. He was cold – was he wet? He didn't know. A wave of nausea overtook him, and as he managed to lean over a bit and retch, every part of his body screamed in protest.

'*Monsieur, rester immobile, et silence,*' a man hissed. He felt a strong hand on his chest, shoving him back. He could smell the man's breath; it stank of cigarettes. His eyes felt like they were gummed shut. Light dappled his face – he could sense it.

'*Il y'a une autre...*' Another voice, a woman's maybe. He could hear something else too. Engines? Voices? He struggled to focus, the pain forcing every other thought from his mind. What were they saying? Something about another? How did he know this language?

'*Mort?*' The man again. Dead. *Mort* definitely meant dead.

'*Peut etre,*' was the whispered reply. '*Je ne sais pas.*'

'*Ils le verront lorsqu'ils atteindront le sommet de la colline,*' the man hissed again.

Something about the top of a hill. Someone would see? He knew bits of this language somehow.

'*Est-ce qu'on risquera de le trainer?*'

The pain was overwhelming. He didn't know what part of him hurt. All of him.

The owners of the voices left; he sensed their absence rather than saw it. He tried to open his eyes, but the blinding light seared his eyeballs and he shut them again. Panic. Where were they going? He didn't know why, but he needed them. He tried to sit up, but his body would not obey. He could do nothing but lie here.

Shouting then, men's voices. Vehicle engines

roaring to life. Gunshots. He thought he might pass out with the pain. Maybe that was better. Succumb to it, drift into it. Anything was better than this agony.

THE END

GLOSSARY OF IRISH WORDS AND PHRASES

Mamó – granny/nana

Daidó – grandad

Oiche Chúin – Silent Night

Seanchaí – storyteller (pron: shan-ack-eee)

Piseóg – a superstition (pron: Pish-owg)

Ráiméis – nonsense talk (pron: Raw-maysh)

Shook – an Irishism for unsettled

GLOSSARY OF IRISH WORDS AND PHRASES

Eejit – idiot

Lá Fhéile Pádraig – St Patrick's Day (Prom: Law Fay-lah Pawd-rig)

Céad Míle Fáilte – a hundred thousand welcomes (Pron: Kayed meelah fail-tah)

Leanbh - a child (pron: lan-uve)

Alanah – an endearment, my child.

Naomhóg – a small fishing boat unique to Western seaboard of Ireland (pron: nay-vowg)

'Dia dhaoibh a mhúinteoirí – Hello teachers – literal translation God be with you teachers.

'Dia is Muire agat a Charlie. – response to hello – literal – God and Mary be with you Charlie

Currach – an Irish canoe (Pron: kur-okk)

A chuisle mo chroí – pulse of my heart – a term of endearment (Pron: ah kooshlah muh cree)

GLOSSARY OF IRISH WORDS AND PHRASES

Óinseach – an affectionate admonishment (Pron: own-shock)

Go n-eirí an t-ádh leat.- The best of luck

Is mar banphrionsa thú a Grace, tá do ghúna go h-álainn – you're like a princess Grace, and your dress is beautiful.

ABOUT THE AUTHOR

Jean Grainger is a USA Today bestselling Irish author. She writes historical and contemporary Irish fiction and her work has very flatteringly been compared to the late great Maeve Binchy.

She lives in a stone cottage in Cork with her lovely husband Diarmuid and the youngest two of her four children. The older two come home for a break when adulting gets too exhausting. There are a variety of animals there too, all led by two cute but clueless micro-dogs called Scrappy and Scoobi.

ALSO BY JEAN GRAINGER

The Tour Series

The Tour
Safe at the Edge of the World
The Story of Grenville King
The Homecoming of Bubbles O'Leary
Finding Billie Romano
Kayla's Trick

The Carmel Sheehan Story

Letters of Freedom
The Future's Not Ours To See
What Will Be

The Robinswood Story

What Once Was True
Return To Robinswood
Trials and Tribulations

The Star and the Shamrock Series

The Star and the Shamrock
The Emerald Horizon
The Hard Way Home
The World Starts Anew

The Queenstown Series

Last Port of Call
The West's Awake
The Harp and the Rose
Roaring Liberty

Standalone Books

So Much Owed
Shadow of a Century
Under Heaven's Shining Stars
Catriona's War
Sisters of the Southern Cross

The Kilteegan Bridge Series

The Trouble with Secrets

What Divides Us
More Harm Than Good
When Irish Eyes Are Lying
A Silent Understanding

The Mags Munroe Story

The Existential Worries of Mags Munroe
Growing Wild in the Shade
Each to their Own
Closer Than You Think
Chance your Arm

The Aisling Series

For All The World
A Beautiful Ferocity
Rivers of Wrath
The Gem of Ireland's Crown

The Knocknashee Series

Lilac Ink
Yesterday's Paper

History's Pages
Sincerely, Grace
Folded Corners
Allied Flames

Made in United States
Orlando, FL
08 July 2025

62745906R00259